ƒP

The Gin Closet

A NOVEL

Leslie Jamison

Free Press
New York London Toronto Sydney

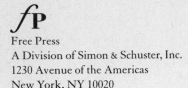

Free Press
A Division of Simon & Schuster, Inc.
1230 Avenue of the Americas
New York, NY 10020

First Free Press hardcover edition February 2010

FREE PRESS and colophon are trademarks of Simon & Schuster, Inc.

For information about special discounts for bulk purchases, please contact
Simon & Schuster Special Sales at 1-866-506-1949 or
business@simonandschuster.com.

The Simon & Schuster Speakers Bureau can bring authors to your live event.
For more information or to book an event contact the Simon & Schuster
Speakers Bureau at 866-248-3049 or visit our website at
www.simonspeakers.com.

Manufactured in the United States of America

10   9   8   7   6   5   4   3   2   1

Library of Congress Cataloging-in-Publication Data
Jamison, Leslie.
The gin closet / Leslie Jamison.—1st Free Press hardcover ed.
1. Adult children—Family relationships—Fiction.
2. Domestic fiction. I. Title.
PS 3610.A485G86 2010
813'.6—dc22   2009020264

ISBN 978-1-4391-5321-5
ISBN 978-1-4391-5787-9 (ebook)

For my grandmothers

Patricia Cumming Leslie

and

Mary Dell Temple Jamison

O love, how did you get here?
O embryo

Remembering, even in sleep,
Your crossed position.
The blood blooms clean

In you, ruby,
The pain
You wake to is not yours . . .

(FROM SYLVIA PLATH, "NICK AND THE
CANDLESTICK")

The Gin Closet

STELLA

On Christmas I found Grandma Lucy lying on linoleum. She'd fallen. The refrigerator hummed behind her naked body like a death rattle. There were bloody tissues balled in her fists, but she was alive and speaking. "I just wanted a little yogurt," she said. "I got a nosebleed."

Her arms fluttered in the air, clutching for handholds, human fingers, anything. It was the first time I'd seen her whole body— her baggy ghost-skin and all the blue veins underneath.

I'd ridden a train through the brittle Connecticut winter with a wedge of gingerbread and a ham sandwich full of fatty cuts, her favorite kind. I had a bag of presents. From the floor she asked: "Are those for me?"

She was shivering. I'd never seen her this way, so fluent at this grasping. Her face twitched as though she were trying to hold her features steady while something happened underneath. She took my hand. Her fingers were greasy with lotion. "I need Matilda," she said. Her voice was calm and sure, as if this request was entirely reasonable. I'd never heard of anyone named Matilda.

I gripped her wrist and slid one hand under the hunch of her

back. Her skin was loose between the bony marbles of her spine. "Don't pull," she said. "It hurts."

I called my brother. Tom said, "You need to ask her: 'Lucy, did you hit your head?'" I cupped my palm over the phone and waited for her reply. He waited for me.

"It was only yogurt," she said. "Just a little bit I wanted."

I knelt down next to her. My boots squeaked on the linoleum. "But did you hit your head? Can you tell me that?"

"If I had," she said. "I'm not sure I would remember."

I reported back to Tom. He said I should keep her awake for at least two hours. This was the rule he remembered about concussions, in case she had one. He was with our mother, Dora, on the other side of the country, probably sipping seltzer at a Pacific restaurant where everyone was thinking cheerfully unconcussed thoughts about their sushi. It was a first-generation place, he told me, mercifully open on holidays. It was the first day my mother had taken off work in months.

"Tom?" I asked. "Do you know anyone named Matilda?"

"One sec," he said. "I'm putting Mom on the phone."

Her voice was loud and sudden: "You need to do what Stella says! You need to let her take care of you!"

"Are you trying to talk to Grandma?" I asked. "Should I give her the phone?"

"Oh," she said. "Of course."

Grandma Lucy gripped the cell phone with her quaking fingers. My mother spoke so loudly that her voice sounded like it was coming from the floor under Grandma Lucy's ear. She rolled onto her side and handed me the phone. Tom said, "Two hours, yeah?" I heard noise in the background, the rustling of glass and gossip. I hung up.

Grandma Lucy didn't want any gingerbread or tea. She didn't want presents. She just wanted to go to sleep. It wasn't dark yet,

not even close. The day had been ruined, she insisted. She wanted to wake up and have Christmas tomorrow.

I checked my watch. I took a breath. Two hours: I would do this. We found a holiday special on television. Animated clay reindeer scampered across the glittering snow. I had to keep shaking Grandma Lucy to make sure she was awake. "Hey," I said. "You're missing the part with the reindeer. With the snow."

"This show is terrible," she said finally. The opinion itself, saying it out loud, seemed to give her a second wind, and she suggested we open presents after all. Her thick curtains made the sunlight feel oozy, as if it were coming through gauze bandages. She lived on the third floor of a block of condos with stucco walls the color of blanched almonds. Most of her neighbors were bankers who commuted into the city.

My grandmother loved Connecticut. It was where she'd fallen in love with my grandfather and where they'd gotten married. He came from old New England stock, but he'd been the one to insist they move west, to get away from his family. Then he took off to roam the world and never came back. He left her with a little girl to raise all by herself. His family promised her as much money as she needed for the rest of her life.

Grandma Lucy had fallen in love with that whole family—their old blood, their traditions—and she'd wanted to give my mother a sense of where she came from, so they spent summers on Cape Cod in a family property that my mother recalled with disdain. "It was nothing but a dirty bribe," she told me. "Giving us that beach house for a couple lousy months. Money was like a bastard child out there—everyone knew about it, but you never heard it mentioned." My mother didn't have any memories of her father, but her anger toward him seemed vast enough to cover years of open wounds. It extended to his people with a ferocity that made up for my grandmother's forgiveness.

Lucy had always understood, without needing to be told, that she wasn't welcome at the year-round family haunts. That perhaps it was better if she stayed out west. But after she'd finished raising her daughter in Los Angeles, she'd come back to this sacred desolation, the eastern cold and money of Greenwich. She could buy anything she wanted, but she didn't want much these days, and her sparse rooms seemed mournful in their neatness.

"She never blamed him for leaving her," my mother said. "I never got that."

Lucy was like a well-behaved child with her Christmas gifts, orderly and attentive. I'd gotten her a variety pack of bubble bath and a pair of pot holders that said in stitched letters: I'M HOLDING NEW YORK'S FINEST CASSEROLE. I'd always known Grandma Lucy as a maker of casseroles full of cream soups and canned corn, fridge biscuits torn into chunks. They were ocean-salty and smooth as silk. She cooked our dinners whenever she came out west to help take care of us, whenever my mother's work got especially intense, but my mother usually hated what she made. "These stews have been processed up the wazoo," she said. "It will take me years to shit them out." She actually said this once at dinner. Grandma Lucy frowned and started clearing dishes from the table.

My mother had always criticized her mother's cooking—how hard she tried and how she still wasn't much good. She gladly took recipes from the family who had disowned her. *Like she didn't have a speck of pride,* my mom said. *And they always tasted terrible.* There was a blueberry pie whose flakes of crust peeled away like dead skin. *Finally, she just gave up and threw those recipes out,* my mom said, her voice proud. *She said: "I've had a lot of pies in my life. Never had a pie like this."*

So these NEW YORK'S FINEST CASSEROLE pot holders were a kind of wink, delayed by years, and a bit of a victory stamp. We weren't on my mother's side of the country anymore, and Grandma Lucy could make her casseroles in peace. She squinted at their diamond-quilted squares. "I can't make New York's finest anything," she said. "I live in Connecticut." She laid the pot holders neatly on her coffee table. "Six kinds of bubble bath," she said. "How about that?"

When she pulled her wool skirt over the sticks of her legs, her panty hose were thin enough to show the damage of her age—plum-colored bruises across her shins and thighs. "It's like a cage in here," she said, meaning her body. "Every part of me aches, or else it itches." She insisted that the itching was a deeper discomfort than I could know. "It's not *on* the skin," she told me. "It's happening underneath."

Then she paused as if trying to recall something. "I got you a present, too," she said finally. "But I can't remember what it was."

I told her we wouldn't worry about that for now. What if I ran a bath instead? Maybe it would feel good against her skin?

"We'll use the bubbles!" she said. She was so lonely, so ready to please me. How was I only seeing it now? Her eagerness came loose like unspooled thread. You couldn't yearn like this unless you'd been lonely for years, practicing. Now her body was weak enough to yearn along with her.

I ran a bath with honey vanilla, her choice, and sat on the toilet seat while she folded herself—thin legs, white belly, arms like baggy insect wings and glimmering with soap—under the steaming surface of the water. I brought a book and kept my eyes tightly locked on it, line to line, so she wouldn't feel me staring. I glanced up once. She curled her finger to beckon me closer. I leaned in.

"She filled a bath," she told me. "To bring them back to life."

"What?" I said. "Who did?"

She closed her eyes and shook her head. Very slowly, she inched herself farther under the water. I could see the red flush of heat marking her skin where she'd gone under. Who had filled a bath? Who'd died? It could be from a movie. I knew she watched a lot of them. What else could you do, alone all day, with every body part giving up separate ghosts—eyes and legs, lobes of the mind?

"Who did what?" I asked again. "What came back to life?"

"She was gentler than your mother, no matter what she did. She gave me a bruise here once, but she was always gentle underneath." Lucy ran two fingers across her cheek, leaving a film.

I said, "I don't know who you mean."

"No," she said. "We never told you." She hugged herself. She could have been speaking from the middle of a dream.

"Never told me about what?"

"About Matilda," she said. "Your mother's sister."

"You have a—" I stopped myself. "Where is she?"

She spoke so softly I could barely hear: "I don't know."

In her croaking voice, Grandma Lucy told me about her younger daughter in reverent bursts, as if Matilda were a dream that would be lost if she weren't told fast enough. It had taken all these years just to say her name out loud.

Grandma Lucy said she'd taken Matilda—only Matilda, not my mother—to the tide pools every summer. This was in Chatham, near the big salty mouth of the Atlantic. "I showed her sea urchins," she said. "Little bundles of purple pencils."

She'd explained—to her and now to me—about starfish. How they ate with their stomachs outside their bodies. Their color was like orange juice concentrate, she said, so unbelievably bright. Maybe she had shades of freezer foods in mind for every animal. I remembered all the times my mother had said, *She's just a housewife, through and through.*

"Matilda loved those pools," Lucy said. "She really did."

She'd loved feeling the urchins' points and watching the crabs for hours, as they fought for homes in rock caves, but she'd flinched from the starfish when they sucked on her arm. "She said it felt like someone taking a breath right next to her skin," Grandma Lucy said. "I told her it had a mouth on its belly."

"It thought Matilda was food?"

"No." Grandma Lucy laughed. "It thought she was home."

She described the shoreline—meadows that stretched all the way to the water, full of a particular prickly weed. Matilda called it Grandma Grass, because the wind made it sound like an old woman sighing. "Grandma Grass." Lucy paused. "I guess that's me now."

It was only when she started shivering again that I thought of how the water must have cooled around her skin. She couldn't lift herself from the tub. I had to dunk my arms to hoist her up. Her wet body dripped all over my jeans and my cashmere sweater. She sat on the toilet seat, shaking.

That's when she got to the part about the dead things. One time my mother had filled a bathtub with bits and pieces of the ocean: a collage of ash-gray barnacles lined up like toy soldiers, a small flock of ghost crabs that hoisted themselves across the tub with weary ticktock steps, old men in their shells. They tapped the porcelain with their pincers.

"Your mother left them for days," Grandma Lucy said. "She was like that. Always curious."

"And Matilda tried to save them?"

Grandma Lucy held the towel around her narrow shoulders while her white hair dripped bathwater. She told me about this younger daughter—new to me, gone to everyone—the one who found a tiny ocean dying and thought she could run enough bathwater to bring it back to life. What happened? The barnacles washed away like scabs. The crabs weren't the kind of crabs that needed water all around them. They drowned.

* * *

On the train home, I called my mother. I told her Grandma Lucy needed help. No problem, she said. We'd hire a nurse for visits.

"She doesn't need help sometimes," I said. "She needs it all the time."

My mother was an immigration lawyer and a fearsome pixie beauty. She negotiated her daily schedule as a creature separate from herself, uncompromising, a force to be obeyed: client meetings, spinning classes, therapy sessions. "I call Mother all the time," she said, hurt.

I knew if she'd been in the room, she would have pulled out her daily calendar to show me where she'd penciled these calls: little X's tucked between names and telephone numbers, between appointments crossed through once, twice, three times, until the final hour perched uneasily in a hasty box of pen strokes. My eyes got lost when I looked at that book. It was a maze. I knew my mother was in there somewhere.

None of it made sense, I said, why Grandma Lucy was naked and fetching yogurt, and what about this bleeding? All this shivering? Maybe it was loose firing, her explanations—*I had a nosebleed*—just words that came into her head and seemed right.

Had she been lucid or not? my mother asked.

I didn't know, I confessed. She veered.

I could hear background fuzz. This meant I was on speakerphone. It was still Christmas, even in the West, but I could tell my mother had returned to her office. I knew she liked to pace the length of her long windows, their panels stuck with skyscrapers like splinters.

"She's probably not getting enough exercise," she said. "She barely leaves the house."

I thought of Grandma Lucy sprawled on the floor, hands flapping like birds. A mustache of blood had pooled in worm trails from her nostrils.

"I don't think exercise is the issue, so much," I said. "She's just . . ."

"She's what?"

"She needs help." I paused. "Like I said."

I knew grown children did this all the time—put their lives on hold to care for the failing bodies of their parents, to help them eat and smile and shit without making a mess. My mom wanted to look into live-in care options. It was no problem, she said. She had the money. "But Mother isn't going to like it," she said. "Not one bit."

Strangers being nice never make anything better, Lucy had told me. *They just make me feel alone.* She'd rather wither away completely than make this final submission to a stranger's care.

I suggested another plan. I could come up four nights a week. I'd cook and keep her company.

My mom said, "You'll make me look like a terrible daughter."

"Oh?"

"There's always *somebody* falling, isn't there? And you catch them."

"She fell," I said. "I didn't make her fall."

She stayed silent. So did I.

I said, "She told me about Matilda."

Nothing.

"Mom?"

Finally: "I wanted to be the one to tell you."

"You had years."

"I always meant to," she said. "I just didn't."

I waited.

"I knew you'd think I was terrible."

"For what?" I said. "I don't even know what happened."

"You want to know what happened?" she said. "Matilda left *us*. She left first. She came back, but she never really came back. She never tried."

"She ran away?"

"It was complicated."

"It's been so many years . . . I mean, Christ, my whole life. You never wanted me to know?"

"We agreed we wouldn't talk about it," she said. "It was easier for Lucy."

"It was. It's different now."

"What did she say?" my mom asked. "About Matilda? How did she sound?"

"What do you mean?"

"Was she angry?"

"Not angry, so much. Just sad."

"How did she bring it up?"

"I don't know, Mom. She was lying in the tub and rambling. She fell and maybe hit her head, and she was hurting and being honest. She missed her daughter." I paused again. "That's how she brought it up."

My mother was quiet.

"I wish you could explain it," I said. "How it got—"

"It happens, okay? When something happens like this in a family," she said, "it doesn't do any good to try to figure it out."

Her voice sounded like a bronze bell, hard-struck and twanging across the miles, so sharp it was difficult to believe it wouldn't leave a humming aftertone. *Happens*. Like earthquakes or cancer. Like the steady clock-ticking of an old woman falling apart. My mother wouldn't understand what was happening to her mother's body until she saw it for herself.

"You don't know anything about her?" I said. "Nothing at all?"

"We know she lives in the desert," she said. "God knows where in Nevada. Or maybe she doesn't anymore. It's been years since we've heard."

A moment earlier, there had been some part of my mother open—some part I'd never heard. Now she was blistered and brittle in a way I recognized, ready to take offense. It was the way she talked about her father when she spoke about him at all.

My mother claimed to have disavowed his clan—*nothing but a big nest of WASPs*, she said—but her voice betrayed stray notes of pride. They'd been the movers and shakers behind our nation's early history. I imagined skeletal, bespectacled men who levied sugar taxes and traded fur pelts, paid the boys who cleaned up tea from the harbor. As a child I'd loved thinking about the Boston Tea Party. What if someone had founded an entire city on soil made from hard-packed tea, Darjeeling or English breakfast? Would the heat of summer make the air smell like it was steeping?

"It's history," I told my mom. "And our family was part of it."

"It stopped being your family when he left," she snapped. "It stopped being your family before you were even born."

So there I was, a child of the West, where history was marked in decades, where the history of a woman, her very name, could dissolve like heat off the freeway, an ugly shimmering, the inscrutable residue of what was already gone.

I moved to Manhattan when I was twenty-two years old. I'd had big plans for New York in the beginning. Everyone does, I guess. The first time I ever saw Manhattan, I was visiting Tom at Columbia. He'd left home an angry teenager with blue-streaked hair and a band called the Hangovers. But in his new life, in this new city, he had become very proper: an economics major with a girlfriend named Susannah Fern Howe. Her parents lived in Newton. "As in Fig?" I'd asked, but he didn't seem amused. They had another house off the Cape. "Like where Mom went when she was little?"

"*Off* the Cape," Tom corrected. "Martha's Vineyard. An island. It's different."

He'd grown different, too. In high school he'd been hard as nails and full of mockery, teasing me about the ways I hardly knew the world, making vague reference to his friends and the confusion of their sex-having. Now he'd grown distant, polite in my company, as though both of us were already adults. I was ten, and he was already telling me New York was a "peerless city," whatever that meant, the opposite of Los Angeles. All I knew was I wanted to go shopping in the Village.

"Shopping, yeah," he said, winking. "We've got a little bit of that."

Already: *we*. He and the city owned things, held them.

I'd been picturing vintage stores full of gauzy dresses and leather sandals. He took me to Fifth Avenue, where the money in my pink plastic purse wasn't going to buy me anything. "What about the bohemian stuff?" I asked. "Bohemian" was a word I'd learned especially for my trip. We ended up on a street full of discount denim outlets, the kind with clattering metal shutters. Yellow jeans were going for ninety-nine cents a pop. "Here's the Village," he said. "Happy now?"

I moved there ten years later, to prove I could be. My mother had been asking me for years—*What were my plans? My goals?*—but I couldn't think of any answer that was my own, that wouldn't have been, beneath it all, a reply to her questions.

The problem wasn't realizing that New York was different from the place I'd dreamed it would be, but rather, knowing that it *was* that place, somewhere I hadn't yet discovered. I knew there were vintage stores like the ones I'd imagined, where elegant women ran their long fingers over lace skirts and tucked their feet into weathered ballet slippers to strut along hard sidewalks full of flakes that glittered in the sunlight. It was out there, that block. I kept trying to find it.

Living in New York seemed like a career in itself: just being there, opening my gills to the grit and heartbeat of the city. The coffee shops were thick with everyone I'd known in college, where I'd understood myself most sharply, my edges contoured by the constant presence of other people: our long chats in empty dining halls, our dinner parties of bland shrimp and burnt rice. We'd spoken without reservation, in arguments and monologues, and there was always someone listening. Drunk, maybe, but listening. What were we going to do next? We spread ourselves like a glaze across hundreds of blocks, across brownstones.

I slept in a room that had been a closet. You could still see the painted hooks where the wardrobe bar had been attached. I came home late, buzzed, and curled into my twin bed with a book of Lorca's poems about the city: *They are the ones. / The ones who drink silver whiskey near the volcanoes / and swallow pieces of heart by the bear's frozen mountains*. I spent my nights wondering: Who were the ones? Where were they drinking?

"You're like your father," my mom told me. "You make a career out of all the little things." She didn't mean this as a compliment.

My father, no longer her husband, had worked for many years as a personal assistant for an artist named Enrico. Enrico was the unofficial leader of a group of artists known as the Border School. "Rothko at the Dump," he was called, because he took big heaps of trash and painted them a single color or a wash of two. His pieces were called *Dump 1, Dump 2, Dump 3*. It was a startling effect—the color so regular and vast, the rustling texture of the rubbish beneath. They made me feel a bit seasick, gave me that heave-ho of wanting to move closer and farther away at once. Afterward I always wondered: What was its purpose, that vertigo? It changed a moment of your life and went away again.

As it turned out, my mother knew me better than I knew myself, because I became a personal assistant as well. I got a job working for a journalist on the Upper West Side whom I called Ms. Z. She had a real name with more letters, but she never quite seemed like a real person, not quite, so I used the Z by itself. Much of New York seemed composed of these types: ideas about people that had become actual people, walking around with scripted lives curled in their guts, ticker tapes of ridiculous words waiting to get spoken.

Every morning I went to Ms. Z's apartment on Seventy-first, just off the park, and worked in a loft above her living room. Her furniture was ugly and expensive: heavy fabrics with thick tassels and brocade cushions, couches for looking at rather than sitting on. But she did have floor-to-ceiling windows with views of the dark green Ramble. You could see people having small adventures, dropping Popsicles and fighting with lovers.

Ms. Z wrote books about things like women having sex and women getting old and old women having sex. She worked a hefty lecture circuit and I wrote her speeches. I interviewed inspirational single women and inspirational married women and inspirational anorexic women and inspirational suicidal women—or rather, women who had considered suicide and turned away. I also booked her Jitney tickets and took out cash from ATMs so she could pay her several cleaning women, none of whom were legal.

One day she had a pre-interview over the phone for a television appearance. It was a talk show about aging. *Aging!* The show came with punctuation.

I listened to her voice piping aphorisms like song lyrics into the phone downstairs: "It's not about staying young. It's about loving old."

She called me down afterward. "Book my Botox," she said. "I'm not going on TV without it."

I heard her say this, and then, almost immediately, I heard the echo of how I'd repeat it to other people. And I *did* repeat it, on that night and other ones. I put on high heels and walked a mile through rainy streets to a cocktail party underneath the Brooklyn Bridge. I arrived and opened my mouth to drink and speak. "Guess what my boss said?"

I told friends, acquaintances, strangers, anyone who would listen. It didn't matter if you knew me or not. The anecdote worked either way. This was New York. Telling stories wasn't about talking to anyone in particular, it was just about talking. Something had happened to you that might capture another person's attention. It was lonely, this kind of speaking. The truth of being young felt like an ugly secret everyone had agreed to keep.

Every night I said things like: Today my boss and I got drunk at lunch. Today my boss was on *Oprah*! Today I spent a thousand dollars on gift baskets. Today I used the word "autumnal" twice, and both times I was speaking to tulip salesmen.

The places where I said these things mattered as much as saying them. The facts and feelings of my life were only as important as the places where they caught in my throat. The Pegu Club, the SKINnY, Milk and Honey, Marlow & Sons and the Slaughtered Lamb and Kettle of Fish and the Dove and Freemans and the arepas place off First and a coffee shop called Think, and a restaurant called Snack, and a restaurant called Home.

We all stayed out late because we knew we were supposed to, spinning the furious and elegant yarns of cowards. We stretched our lives like taffy on racks. We found the grave and humorous correlations between our lives and the lives of celebrities, the course of unjust wars, the third world and its charlatan leaders, the globe and its various Achilles heels—the oceans, the atmosphere. We made fun and then we stopped making fun, quite abruptly, to show we knew how to take things seriously. We ate well. We talked about the food; we talked about the food we weren't eating—in other restaurants, other boroughs. We talked about sadness, how we'd never really known it. We talked about genocides that people had forgotten because they only talked about the holocaust. We talked about ourselves, mainly, and who we were fucking.

I talked about Louis, a married professor who hosted me, his phrase, from time to time. Stupidly, I had fallen in love with him. He'd written a book about the early female mystics, the ones who starved and hurt themselves, called: *How Did Julian Find His* [Sic] *God?* He asked me questions about my two years of anorexia. Three if you counted another year I didn't get my period. "It was my sick God," I told him. I was like that—up for it, sporting.

"You're young," he said, putting his hand on my knee. "But you should take yourself more seriously."

I told my friends what he'd said, and we laughed. They'd always told me I should try the opposite.

There were things I didn't tell anyone. Today I got on my hands and knees in Ms. Z's bathroom and scrubbed away urine stains left by her dying dog. Today I watched Ms. Z make her housekeeper cry. Unsaid, rephrased: Today I got paid to watch a grown woman cry.

I compressed my days neatly into appetizer courses. I worked as a personal assistant for a woman with a reputation for treating people like shit, and she treated me like shit. I couldn't spin witty versions of the rest. In the darkness I began caring for my collapsing grandmother. She wasn't being inspirational or having sex or treating anyone like shit. She was just getting old.

I went to Grand Central after work, on alternating days, and took the train to Greenwich. The cars were crowded with suited commuters riding to the suburbs, heading into their twelve-hour furloughs, loosening their ties. Beside them, I lurched into the hardest hours of my day: helping Grandma Lucy walk around the block, fixing Coronas with cuts of lime, her single indulgence, spreading creams and potions across the crinkled paper of her rosacea-blooming cheeks.

Outside the train windows, Connecticut unfurled into an endless spread of lumberyards and fenced-off freight ghettos, graveyards for retired buses and port-o-potties, all the wreckage hushed under sudden dusk. Sometimes I rode in the bar car, where men tucked away plastic cups of watery gin to brace themselves for the trials of their wives and children. *You'd rather be alone?* I thought. *You sure?* I imagined Grandma Lucy watching the door for my entry, perched like a bird in her silent apartment full of colors: yellow walls, blue carpet, purple couch, these cloying shades her only company.

All these hues had come with age—a concession, perhaps, to the quiet desire for cheer in solitary circumstances. Her old living room in Los Angeles had had white walls and a white couch, invisibly matted with the white fur of her white cat, Boo. He'd had a brother named Radley, a tabby who'd gone to live with new owners a few months after Grandma Lucy got him. I always wondered if he was sent away because of that couch. Boo died when I was sixteen. Grandma Lucy kept his ashes in a silver box behind her best china.

We spent our evenings watching movies about spies and bank robbers. We put on big boots and walked around her parking lot. She took pleasure in the way I dressed, so I chose my outfits carefully: wide skirts with big blooming scarves, blouses edged with sequins or delicate stitching. "You're your own person, Stella," she said. "I like that." The truth was, I shopped at stores that other people liked first or that trusted bloggers recommended. But it felt worthwhile to bring a smile to her face.

Though Lucy worked hard to keep the scraps of her life in

order, it was getting harder. She took a lot of pills but didn't know their names, only what they did: *This one is for my heartbeat when it gets too fast,* she said. *There's another one for when it's skipping.* I arranged them in small cubbyholes marked with the days of the week. I learned her body through the steaming bathwater: blood bruises darkening her thighs, sagging breasts draped like plastic bags over the bulb of her stomach. She had a long nose that was smooth and sweeping, its profile assertive. She wore frosty pink liner around the edges of her thin lips, but she couldn't apply it right. The color always faded farther in, as if she'd sucked it all inside. She'd loved makeup for as long as I'd known her.

"Your mother's always been a looker," she told me once. "But she never seemed to notice."

Lucy had always believed that if she could make her daughter different from her, different enough, she'd turn out satisfied. Now she was eighty years old and still asking herself: Had she?

Grandma Lucy had a body that looked sturdy and practical. It was hard to believe she'd been the source of my mother's traits: a fierce and petite frame, a set of features that seemed stone-carved. Every part of my mother was thin, down to her fingers. She looked like she was about to split along a thousand secret fissures.

I looked more like Lucy than I looked like my mother. I had a certain beauty, but it wasn't delicate. You didn't want to protect me; you wanted to see if I would break. I was taller than most men by the time I got my period, over six feet, and my build was solid and demanding. My only fragile parts were my eyes—light blue and often teary, generally leaking. My father called them "windy." My limbs looked heavy and felt that way, too: the straight stalks of my legs, my veiny palms and blunt fingers like weapons. "You've got a strong presence," my mother said. "You should be proud of it."

My mother dismissed beauty in the way that only beautiful women can. One time she told me, "Looks matter, I guess, but you can't do much about them." Then added, "And they never get you what you really want."

She'd been angry when I asked for a bridal magazine for my tenth birthday. I loved looking at those porcelain women, silk dresses cinched tight around their doll waists. They had limbs so thin it seemed as if you could fold them into a box like twisted puppets. I imagined their interior lives as neatly appointed rooms, their emotions like furniture draped with sleek fabric and cut in smooth lines—the calm of self-possession, the tranquillity of being fully desired. I'd seen a picture of my mother in her wedding dress, and it took my breath away—*I came from her,* I thought, *I couldn't have*—but knew I could never give her my admiration, or even a piece of it, because it wasn't the kind of admiration she wanted.

Grandma Lucy had always been reserved about her body, never used words like "pee" or "snot." Now she couldn't hide anything. She had attacks of diarrhea on the couch and on the carpet. She was eating prunes because her pain medication made her constipated. "Maybe the prunes aren't such a good idea," I said. She was too frail to get to the bathroom quickly. She walked by balancing one hand against the walls or tables. Her nerves cried wolf; the itching had not abated. She was convinced ginger could help.

"Ginger?" I said. "Why ginger?"

She pulled a folded sheet of yellow paper from her pantry, where it had been tucked behind tins of salt and flour. It showed a map of the human body, covered with Chinese characters and bright red arcs connecting limbs, like an airline poster showing flights between cities. It had been Matilda's. Grandma Lucy explained as best she could: "She thought everything was all linked up. She thought you could make your stomach feel better if you massaged your toes the right way." Matilda also had particular ideas about which colors should be the last ones you saw before falling asleep: pale blue and gold. "She painted her ceiling," Grandma Lucy told me. "Made her bedroom stink like turpentine for days."

It was Matilda who'd had this crazy notion about ginger, that you should hold it under your tongue until it burned. It would distract you from your other aches. "It's worth a try," Grandma Lucy said now. "I haven't got much to lose."

Every Tuesday a woman named Juana came to the condo. She'd been working for Grandma Lucy for years. She cleaned and fixed pots of soup that we stored in the fridge all week: turkey chili that looked like dog food, soups thick as paint, chicken noodle with strands of thready meat. Lucy had grown to like baby textures. She had gums that bled like inky pens. Already she'd lost most of her appetite and a lot of weight, too. I had the most luck getting her through a bowl of split pea or bisque, the smooth ones, cream of this or that. When she clutched her spoon, her knobby fingers showed ghostly margins where the larger flesh had been.

One time she fell asleep eating chowder. Later, I found kernels of corn stuccoed all over her couch. Juana took me on a tour of their cleaning products. She showed me how to use carpet cleaner on the diarrhea stains and explained the difference between brands: This one you can use on the couch, this one not.

"Too harsh?" I asked.

She pinched her nose. I understood. Too smelly.

Juana was very emotional about my grandmother's condition. One afternoon I found her crying in the kitchen. "No more," she said. "I hate it."

I hated it, too, but I'd never cried about it. I'd often wanted to, but I wasn't sure I was able. I patted Juana's arm. My fingers felt wooden and inhuman.

"You're very—how do you say?—strong," she said. "Very strong."

I shook my head. I wasn't strong. I was just organized into little sections inside. The sections didn't touch each other, necessarily. I hadn't seen some of them for a long time.

I returned to the city after midnight and called the friends I knew would be awake: the ones who didn't have jobs, the trust-fund artists and the downright poor, the ambiguously depressed, with diagnoses and without, the ones who lived so far into Brooklyn they essentially lived in Jersey. We talked with beer on our breath, leavening our words with wisdom. They talked about how they'd seen rats as large as dogs in their stairways, how they'd unlearned the aesthetic rules of prior centuries. I talked about how I'd faced mortality in Connecticut. We stayed awake until dawn because we wanted to feel reduced by fatigue—in just that way, sharpened into spokes—or else we were afraid of dreaming.

One night I didn't call anyone. I wanted to find a man, any man, who could offer his face as a label for my loneliness. I already felt alone. I needed this stranger, wherever he was, whoever he was, as proof. I found him at an Irish bar in midtown, a bald man sitting by himself near the bathroom. I liked his voice when he offered me a whiskey. I told him I wanted it neat.

When he repeated my request to the bargirl, he was forceful and assured, as if he understood exactly why I needed it like that. He'd make sure they got it right. If I squinted, his head looked like it was glowing. It was as blurry as a lightbulb seen through tears.

We drank. We talked about the perils of age and the delusions of youth. Sometimes he tapped his skull like a good-luck charm: *Knock on wood*. He asked me why I was staring at his head. I said, "I like how it gleams."

I drank a little more. He drank a little more. He said he was a doctor who specialized in brain lesions. "Seek and destroy," he said fondly, tapping the wood of his scalp once more. I wondered if he'd even gone to med school.

I asked the bargirl for a maraschino cherry so I could chew the stem. How did people tie these with their tongues? It seemed like a testimony to something about the human body, something the mind could not control. *Seek and destroy*. You could damage any part of the brain you wanted, and some people would still be able to tie those stems into knots. I wouldn't, but others would.

"I'm only trying to help her," I said. "But I don't think it's enough."

"Sweet girl." He smiled. "It's enough."

He put his arm around my back, and I felt his hand moving underneath my skirt, grabbing my ass. I slapped his arm. "I'm saying something true about my life."

"And?"

"And you don't even give a fuck."

He squeezed me harder and laughed. "Of course I don't."

I beckoned him closer with one bent finger, made like I was going to tell him a secret. Then I leaned into his ear and spat.

"You little bitch!" he said. "What was that?"

I looked from side to side—for another person's face, for the door. Whiskey blurred the lights. I didn't leave any money. I barely stumbled as I left.

One day my friend Alice invited me to a launch party for a film. Not a movie, she said, but a film. Alice was attractive enough to have a good time anywhere. She was half German, half Japanese—"Axis-bred," she said—and gorgeous, her smooth skin eerie like a doll's. The certain knowledge of her own allure lay beneath her beauty, its seed as well as its product. She knew how to abuse substances in a serious way without becoming unseemly.

She told me it was going to be absurd, this party, full of people from Los Angeles. "I'm from Los Angeles," I said.

She paused to consider this. "You are," she said. "But not like they are."

She wanted to go early, elevenish. It still meant I would have to skip my trip to Grandma Lucy's. I called Juana and asked if she would mind bringing some soup that night. Could she stay while Lucy ate it? She could. Sometimes Grandma Lucy spilled on herself without realizing. A streak of tipped-over oatmeal had once left a red flush across her thigh, grains stuck as if they'd been pasted on her skin.

The party was in a dirty Bushwick warehouse. The film, which almost no one had seen, was about schoolyard bullies. The gimmick was the bullies had superpowers, but the good kids had even better ones. There was comic violence but not upsetting violence, for reasons that had to do with ratings. There were possible political implications. A woman at the party was speaking loudly, maybe drunk, maybe sober, about valences. It was an allegory for the war on terror, she said, official torture policy and so on. "So what's the takeaway?" she said. "All's fair as long as only the bad guys get hurt?"

Alice had spent the commute telling me about her current lover, his distancing mechanisms and terrible cologne. I could nod in earnest. Louis never wore cologne, but he had plenty of distancing mechanisms, like his wife. He made our silences—our failure to understand each other, his failure to try—seem like inevitable symptoms of the human condition.

Now the party was so loud I could barely hear Alice when she spoke, though I could tell from her face—lips pursed or cracked wry, circling an O toward her frosted martini—whether she was expecting me to laugh or frown. Occasionally, she wanted me to reply. She wanted to know, for example, if Louis's approach was very theoretical. His approach to what? This was one of the questions I hadn't heard, or paid attention to, very well. I kept coming back to an image of Grandma Lucy eating dinner: a seersucker robe plastered against her knees, damp with chicken broth, folded over the nest of cracker crumbs and blue pills caught between her cushions. Every so often Alice touched my arm and said something like: "Isn't that just the *intensest*?"

Alice and I had eating disorders at the same time in college and shared them like an extracurricular, the way some people share cocaine or volleyball. She taught me her tricks, like drinking hot water to keep warm. She could go through fifteen cups at a meal, wrapping her fingers around each glass to absorb the heat. She told me that green-tea farmers did this during Shizuoka winters in their drafty wooden shacks. She trained herself to believe she had the yearning built into her bones. I thought about her bones more than I thought about other people's bones. They were like tree branches under her skin. I remembered this old version of Alice like a legend, a collection of surreal details, but really she was just starving, we both were: sick in the heart and showing it.

We recovered together, or said we did, touring a circuit of therapy panels and discussion groups. We made fun of their clichéd slogans and the girls who didn't look skinny enough to need them. We got a little bigger ourselves. We said we hurt, and this was the truth. We *did* hurt. We felt something, but we used it, too, and this was the worst part. When we finally saw our pain, dredged it up and spoke it, we found it mangled by our manipulations, the ways we'd twisted it around to get what we wanted. We could barely recognize it. It was barely ours. Then Alice got bad again, worse than I'd ever been, and we kind of drifted apart.

Now we frowned together at our past selves. "That was so fucked up," Alice said. "How we were back then." Alice wasn't plump, but you could see the weight in her breasts. She was a B cup now for sure. She had a strange way of talking about her disease: "It was the worst thing that ever happened to me," she said. "And the best."

She was on Prozac now. "It's a hard drug," she said. "It takes something."

It didn't take everything. She was still an animated storyteller, full of tales about the people who commissioned her art pieces for their lofts and condos. She had a keen interest in other people and a sharp sense of humor whose edges, rising without warning, showed me how I must seem to other people, refracted and grinning like a clown. Once in a while she'd pause in the middle of an anecdote and stare off into the distance, as if scanning the horizon. Maybe she was waiting for the return of her disease or else another kind of trouble. There was this hope in her eyes, just a flicker.

The room around us was full of characters, local and foreign, like smudges brought to life from cartoon strips: hipsters with mullets, in suspenders; girls in leggings, their narrow wrists moving like flying fish through glittering glass bangles. A woman sat with two ferrets curled over her shoulders like parentheses. A man wedged a photograph of David Bowie into the V of his sweatervest, where his chest hair grew thick and tangled, and asked me to take his picture. "Use my cell phone," he said. "It has a camera."

People spoke loudly because they wanted to be heard and overheard by strangers. One woman had gotten another knife commercial but she was worried this meant her hands were too butch. A man was DPing for a documentary about Monopoly buffs in Tennessee. A guy knew a friend of a friend who was making a feature-length about rabies. There were also a lot of people dancing. I liked that.

Alice liked to talk about my second life, up north. "Everyone I know is getting degrees or working," she said. "But you're really *experiencing* something."

Alice complained about her lover, the one who smelled like European lovemaking, and his vanity complex about her art. "It's like every canvas is a mirror," she said. "He just sees himself."

I saw: broth, robe, pills.

"Lame," I said.

She said, "It's not like every piece of art is about him."

Most of her art probably was about him, or at least the idea of him. I said, "Really lame."

"Don't take this the wrong way," she said. "But you use smaller words than you used to."

Grandma Lucy had a small balcony, tucked between the balconies of finance bachelors, where she liked to sit at twilight, even during winter. Around dusk she got peaceful and confused. Doctors had a name for this. They called it sundowning.

"Dora ran an orphanage in Africa," she said. "She helped build it. She broke her finger."

"My mother helps African *people*, you mean," I said. "With her law firm."

A home-care nurse who'd started coming once a week explained about the twilight thing. "It happens with older folks," she said. "They get confused. It's like clockwork. Who knows why?"

Sundowning was like shape-shifting. Grandma Lucy's real self—rambling and delirious, eager to believe in histories that never happened—waited until nightfall and then emerged into the shadows. Lucy would start talking to me like a blind person, her gaze slanted away from my face, as she remembered her lost daughter's favorite sandwiches and how much trouble Matilda had falling asleep at night.

Between the hard clarity of her days and the medicated speech of her nights, there were these twilights, when it was impossible to tell which parts were real and which might have been imagined.

Matilda could be an actress by now, or a poet or a waitress or a bank teller or simply a suburban mother, quietly stupendous. Lucy said that Matilda was the kind of woman who might have died young. At first it shocked me to hear her imagine the death of her own daughter this way—calmly, a bit wistfully—but I realized death did not make her feel the way it made me feel. It was so near she could almost hear it, a distant hum, and who knew what it held? Maybe it held her daughter, waiting. Maybe it would bring them closer than they'd been.

My mom called me every day. She wanted reports over the phone. "I'm not getting the full story from Mother." She paused. "She's always been too damn proud." She couldn't see what was happening to her mother's pride. "Is she eating enough?" she asked. "What is she eating?" I told her about the meals but could not explain the long hours between them—hours of mess and boredom, embarrassments of the body. Nobody can tell you that a person is dying, or what her dying looks like, until you see it for yourself.

Grandma Lucy often spoke about Matilda, though she didn't talk about why she'd left, or been left, or broken ties, or been broken. She talked only about what her daughter had been like when she was young.

"It never should have happened," she said once. "It was a terrible thing."

"What thing?"

I thought this would be it, perhaps—a story that had never been told, a story about the break.

"Matilda was just a girl," she said. "But after him . . ." Her voice was sharp and singing, as if an old nerve had rubbed raw against the wind.

I got a sick feeling in my stomach. She'd been raped or gotten pregnant.

"She was gone after him. I don't think I ever found her again."

One night Alice took me to a play about AIDS in rural Africa. It was performed by a mime troupe, meant to echo those who didn't have a name for why their families died. They clawed at their skin to mime lesions, and traced bony fingers down their torsos to show the slender sticks that human bodies could become.

Afterward we drank. We drank Jack and Diets and told strangers in a strange bar about this sadness that we'd seen.

A phone call woke me up before dawn. It was four in the morning, and Grandma Lucy had fallen. "I'm alright," she said. "But I've been lying here for hours."

She'd needed to use the bathroom, she explained, and had forgotten the night-light. It was dark, was the problem, and she'd tripped on a stool.

"Where are you now?" I said. I was already late for work. Ms. Z was having an interview—filmed by someone for something—at an Upper East Side Starbucks.

"I'm near the stove," Grandma Lucy said. "I'm near the bottom of the stove, but I can also see the living room."

"The kitchen isn't on the way to the bathroom," I said. "You said you were going to the bathroom."

I never made it to Starbucks. I got a slew of messages from Ms. Z, as I'd known I would. Everything had gone wrong, and there would be hell to pay, and did I know that? Did I really understand that? I'd better. I'd be made to understand, I was assured. At a certain point she asked her housekeeper to keep leaving messages on my machine, once an hour, but the housekeeper's voice sounded defeated and a little jealous: I'd gotten out. She was still there.

Lucy wasn't unconscious, just unable to get up again. She was frail as a bird but hard to lift. If any part of her dragged across the floor, her thin skin tore and bled. "Be careful," she said. "Be careful with me, okay?"

I called my mother. "Things aren't good out here," I told her. "I think you should come as soon as you can."

She said she was finishing a case, and would I believe her—*please,* because it was true—that this case was a matter of life and death? She booked a plane ticket for the next week. I decided that Grandma Lucy would not spend another night alone. I'd stay on her purple couch until my mother came.

I told Ms. Z that my grandmother had died because this was the only way I could imagine getting the week off. I packed a duffel bag and bought, for once, a one-way ticket on the train. "You don't have to stay over," Grandma Lucy said. "I'm doing fine."

But she seemed pleased when I arrived. She'd made the couch as best she could, sheets tucked messily under cushions. I pictured her hands, quivering, trying to get it right. At night I watched ants crawl in a thin line from the cupboards, quiet and constant as leaking fluid. I drank cheap red wine. It helped the long hours edge away into sleep. One day a black crow dropped the corpse of a mouse onto the frost-slicked windowsill, and I swept it off with a broom, watched it drop three stories to the street below.

It was a week of bitter cold, dirty snow frozen all across the state, but our hours together had the dazed, loose-limbed quality of fever. Grandma Lucy was getting worse. She barely ate. I felt that I could see her body getting smaller across the span of hours. Still, I braved winter to fill the fridge with her favorites: green grapes, whole buttermilk, rice pudding, and seven-ounce bottles of beer that looked as if they'd been designed for the hands of children. She wouldn't eat much besides the pudding. The grapes were too tart, she said, and the milk too thick, like wet cloth draped across the inside of her throat. "I can't breathe when I drink it," she said. "It chokes me up."

Memories came without warning or context. "She slapped me once," she said. "Did you know that?"

I shook my head. I could tell from her voice, its somber hush, that she was talking about Matilda.

"I think maybe she could have killed me," she said. "If she'd been drunk enough."

"She had a drinking problem?"

Grandma Lucy paused, then shook her head, confused, as if she'd forgotten what I'd asked. "She was so beautiful," she said. "When she was young."

I found poems that might lend my life a sense of gravity. I read them in the near-dark, trying to pass the time so I wouldn't go to bed at such embarrassingly early hours. *When you are old and grey and full of sleep* . . . My throat was gritty with wine; anger rose like phlegm. How could anyone write those words once they'd seen aging for themselves? *But one man loved the pilgrim Soul in you,/ And loved the sorrows of your changing face.* What did young Yeats know about the bodies of old women, how their pubic hair turned ashen between the sticks of their thighs?

I couldn't look at my own vagina without imagining the labia wilting like a flower. I hadn't masturbated properly in weeks, and not for lack of trying. I roused dirty old fantasies from my adolescence—rich men paying me for sex, stroking their fat fingers along my spine—but I couldn't make them work anymore. My body felt pitted, flesh lingering hopelessly around a gutted core: the place orgasms had come from, before the sight of Lucy's body made them sputter dry.

* * *

I was a little drunk when my mother arrived. Grandma Lucy was asleep. I hadn't meant to be drunk, but she was two hours late and I'd started to think she wasn't coming. I opened the door and she hugged me, a quick pressure like a heartbeat. Her hands felt like paws of ice. "Jesus," she said. "You smell like wine."

"We had a little with dinner." My head was still thick with a dark sweet fog. I'd been napping.

"Mother's been drinking, too?"

"Just beer," I said. "Like always."

"She shouldn't be drinking anything." She rubbed her hands together. They were ungloved and bluish-pale.

"Cold?" I said. "It's worst in March, I think. You start hoping it'll get better, but it doesn't."

"I'm fine," she said. "I was outside for an hour at Howard Beach. Some problem with the A downtown."

She'd come all the way up from the city, saving money on a flight even though she had plenty to spare.

"You want some tea?"

"No," she said. "I don't." She picked up the empty bottle from the table and squinted at the label. "She really needs both of us, Stella. She needs us at full capacity."

"I needed to relax."

"Relaxing is never a long-term solution."

"It's not a long-term situation, Mom."

She set down the bottle abruptly. "Don't talk like that," she said. "At least not around me."

She started collecting things from the floor, books and magazines, and piling them on the table. Her own living room was perfectly neat. Even the kitchen was spotless. That was how she lived. I could remember her getting angry at my father before work, storming out the front door, yelling, "Come on, Jay, your crap is all over the house."

And I remember his reply: "I *live* here. My crap lives here."

Now she frowned at the piles she was making, rearranging them.

"It's been hard," I said. "I'm no good at this."

"At what?"

"At helping her get old, or stopping her from getting old, or whatever I'm supposed to be doing to help. It's too much, you know? All this falling down, all her drugs, all her daydreams and her shitting and everything. She's so *skinny,* Mom. You'll see."

Even in bed, lying down, swaddled like a baby in the direct line of her space heater, Grandma Lucy showed the skeletal lines of her decline. "Oh, Mother." My mother sighed. "Look at you."

Everything she noticed felt like blame: *I can't believe she lives like this,* looking at the mess, and of course I'd been looking at it for months. *What are all these drugs?* she said. *Where are the prescriptions?* I couldn't tell her because I didn't know. Grandma Lucy had filled them herself a long time ago, or maybe given them to Juana, but she couldn't remember the names when I asked. The bottles were empty in the cupboard, all of them jumbled. *Well, this is no good,* my mom said. *No good at all.*

She thought the whole place was depressing.

"She fixed up the inside how she likes," I said. I'd been hating it for weeks, all the bright matching colors, their symmetries like sutures stitching up wounds. But now I felt defensive.

My mom suggested I take the weekend off. "I'm here now. I've got things covered."

I saw her pulling up my sheets from the couch.

"You're not sleeping here?" I said.

"I'm sleeping with her," she said.

I couldn't imagine my mother sharing a bed with anyone.

"And what am I supposed to do?" I said. "While you're taking care of everything?"

"Why don't you take a trip with your professor?" she said. "Isn't that the kind of thing that makes you happy?"

I grabbed her wrist. "Why are you mad?"

She paused, considering her words. "It's gotten so bad. I just wish you'd told me."

"I did," I said. "I tried."

I called Louis from the train. Ordinarily, there would have been pride blocking my voice, getting in the way, but here I was, saying, "Take me anywhere," adding, "If you can get away, I mean."

"I'll see what I can swing," he said.

Crises made a difference to him. They could turn you into someone else, or they could become you. They were becoming.

He and his wife lived in TriBeCa, but he had a little cabin in Vermont near the Mad River Valley. That's where we were going. I think he told his wife it was a place where he could find himself—when really, of course, it was a place he brought women. I didn't kid myself. I knew I was part of a pattern. I'd been up once before, during the summer. The woods had been full of spindly mosquitoes, vicious in their veering, and moist heat that felt like the breath of a drunkard telling you a secret. I'd glimpsed important truths: I could tuck my pants into my socks or smear the stronger chemicals into my skin, but the bugs would always come around, and they would always leave with a little more of my blood; Louis would never make a life with me. These revelations were anecdotal and syntactically parallel: the trouble with insects, the trouble with expectations.

Now we were moving through the snow in his four-wheel-drive rental. He wanted to know everything about my terrible situation back home: Could Grandma bathe? Could she speak? Where could I see, especially, the outline of her bones? He'd made his life's work from crafting words about the broken bodies of women—he saw something sacred in them, something breathtaking.

"It helps," I told him. "Telling you all this."

"This is hard," he said. "And it'll get harder. You'll get yourself through it."

You will. I wasn't stupid. I knew what he would give and what he wouldn't.

We drove past strip-mall buffets and the skeletons of fallen barns. We stopped for lunch in a town called Windsor, at a pizza parlor with two windows. One said PIZZA. The other said & FUN. They were full of ferns. You couldn't see anything but leaves inside.

"This place used to serve pizza," I said. "Before a ficus ate the owner."

"Ah," he said. "Carnivorous plants."

There was a silence. He paused. I paused.

He said, "Should we eat?"

We ate pizza with pineapples and black olives. The marinara sauce was runny from canned juice. Each bite tasted saltier than the last. I didn't make any more jokes.

I called my mother from the edge of Windsor. Louis said we were about to go off the grid. My mom didn't seem worried that I'd be out of range.

"We're doing fine," she said. "I'm figuring out her prescriptions right now."

"I know the long red ones help with the pain. But they make her confused."

"I should go," she said. "I'm on the other line with the doctor."

When I hung up the phone, I saw Louis looking at me as if I were a child. There was a tenderness in his eyes I'd never seen before. He and his wife didn't have any kids. Weren't planning to, he said.

We stopped in a drugstore for supplies. I wanted to pretend the end of the world was approaching and we were shopping for our hideout bunker. He said we could always come back tomorrow.

He disappeared down an aisle and returned with a package of condoms and a tube of the kind of pain cream that heats your body until it doesn't hurt anymore. "The only thing better than getting head," he said, "is getting head with heat cream." He was trying to *lighten the mood,* a favorite phrase of Grandma Lucy's. I was happy he was thinking about oral sex, but I also wondered what that cream would taste like. Probably not good.

We took a dirt road into the woods. "My woods," he called them. He was a man who owned an apartment on Varick Street and a whole forest somewhere else. It got dark early, and we drank nicer wine than I'd tasted in months. It felt strange to drink with another person. I'd grown used to the feeling of drinking until I dissolved into delirium, its perfect silence, until I could feel absolutely unobserved.

Louis said he was curious about my love life. But he *was* my love life. He wanted to know: Was I seeing anyone else? I told him about trying to masturbate on Lucy's couch. He was interested in this. But I couldn't?

I was surprised by how quickly it could leave, all that hurt— how I could feel worse about Louis, closer at hand, than the memory of her face seizing up with pain, features twisted as if a big invisible palm had clamped her face and squeezed it.

I gave him head while he sat on the ratty plaid couch. I could see the cover of an old porn video stuck into the cushions. He forgot about the special cream and I didn't. I didn't remind him.

Afterward he said, "I want to do something for you," and we had sex on a shaggy rug the color of butter. He came, I think, and I didn't, I'm sure.

"Did you orgasm?" he said.

I said, "That felt nice."

I lay with my face to the empty fireplace. He wrapped his arms around me, and I could feel his chest hair against my shoulders. It made me giddy. It was the strong grip of a healthy body, nothing like Grandma Lucy's hunched back, her skin peeling onto the carpet.

"You really are beautiful," he said.

My heart skittered like mice under my ribs. He'd never said that to me before.

"Did you miss me?" I said.

He said, "I'm glad to be with you now."

I lay on my back and hugged myself to cover my breasts. I looked at him. The stubble on his cheeks caught bits of glow from the lamp. I wanted him badly. He didn't feel ashamed of anything he was saying. He owned trees! And he was not afraid of hurting other people. He made this seem like an important kind of bravery.

When we got back to Windsor, my phone told me I'd missed sixteen calls. They were all from my mother. I called her back, and she told me Grandma Lucy had collapsed. "Not like the other times," she said. "She had a cardiac event."

"What's that?"

"You better come," she said. They'd taken Lucy to Greenwich Hospital.

She was deep inside a coma by the time I got there. Tom had already arrived. I was the last one. My mother was holding a book called *Precious Hours* that was covered in flowers. It looked like a book you would buy at the hospital gift store. She was pacing the third-floor ICU when I found her. She looked tired, and there was a run in her panty hose the width of my thumb. "You're here," she said. "You're finally here."

I felt the sob rise, could do nothing against it. "She's dead?"

"She's on life support. Her mind is gone."

I put my arms around her. She felt like a little girl, so much smaller than I was. She smelled like stale sweat and, more faintly, like coffee. "I'm sorry," I whispered. "I'm sorry."

She told me she'd given Grandma Lucy some pudding. That was when it happened, all of a sudden, for no reason she could see.

"Pudding," I said. "She ate a lot of that."

She gave me a look, and I realized I'd interrupted her in the middle of a thought. "She told me I had a run in my panty hose. That was the last thing she said."

"I can't believe it," I told her.

Actually, I could.

"I'm just glad you're here. I'm glad we're all here."

It wasn't true, what she said. Matilda's name was never spoken in that hospital room, not once.

They say the body knows things, can sense presence even when the mind has gone. I wondered if bodies felt absence as well. I saw a shudder pass through the collapsing cage of my grandmother's chest, making her arms spasm as if they'd touched something electric. *"These are movements the mind doesn't even know about,"* the doctor said. *"She's already gone."* For a moment I imagined she was clutching the daughter she'd never mentioned, the one whose body was too far away to touch.

Juana arrived at the hospital in tears but didn't speak much. She stood by the window, holding a teddy bear she'd brought. Smoggy shafts of sunset filled the room and stained the linoleum floors like thin tomato soup. Cold air came through the cracked-open window and tapped our skin like fingers. There was a playground across the street. We could hear the squeal of rusty swings and the shrill voices of children calling fouls. There was a sweet, wrong smell coming from the cold breeze—like maple syrup. The papers said something about a factory disaster down in Jersey.

Tom pulled out his BlackBerry and searched for information about Lucy's condition. He wanted to know what had happened to her. *Getting old and dying* wasn't enough for the search field. He couldn't find specifics.

I stood by Lucy's bed and held her hand. A breathing machine went *clack, clack, clack* as it brought the air into her body, its plastic tube expanding and collapsing like an accordion.

I went to the bathroom and sat in the handicapped stall for nearly twenty minutes, just to be alone.

"Upset?" my mother asked when I got back. She was checking my eyes for signs of crying. I could count the number of times I'd done this in front of her. No matter what comfort she'd offered, there was always a desire lurking underneath her words, a hope that if I'd been crying, I would find the strength to stop.

"No," I said. "I wish I had been."

She hugged me then, with force. "Well, that's something I get," she said. "I've felt a lot of things in my life, and I've barely cried about any of them."

It was a bright day, a good death. That's what people say about a death like hers. She was old. It didn't hurt. I watched a nurse thread a morphine tube into the blue vein beneath her puffy skin. This marked the end of life support, the beginning of something called comfort care.

The smell of her room had two layers: soap and urine. Her face was bloated with fluids that came from her organs shutting down. Her chin swelled against the plastic collar of her breathing tube. The tube was no longer connected to anything on the other end. We tracked the beeping of her heart on a mint-green machine. Her deep breaths rattled and then stopped completely. I saw her chest deflate and then I turned away.

My mother unplugged the heart monitor before we heard the

flatline. I kissed my grandmother's forehead and smoothed back her matted white hair. Juana let out a startled cry—"Ay!"—and started sobbing.

The beeping was gone. The clacking of the breathing tube was gone. Juana's weeping was the only sound in the room.

Gone was the word my mother used about her sister whenever I asked, which made it sound like Matilda was the one who'd chosen to leave. Or else she used the word "estranged," which seemed apt: made strange to her own family. I pictured her living alone in the middle of an empty field, catching lightning with her fingertips, her body gone electric like the human maps she'd studied.

I was angry at my father for keeping the secrets of my mother's family, *my* family, during all the years of their marriage and its aftermath.

"It was your mother's secret," he said. "Not mine."

"But you knew she was out there somewhere . . . you probably knew better than anyone how hard it must have been for her in that family."

"You have to understand," he said. "Your mother never talked about her. Never."

"You never asked? You didn't think it was unnatural?"

"Your mother isn't a very sentimental person," he said. "You know that."

He'd once tried to explain some of the differences that had dissolved their marriage. "Your mother always wanted me to do more," he said, "and I always wanted her to feel more. That was most of it." He was full of brief statements about his own identity: "I am made of emotions. Emotions are my biggest addiction." He told me I could break his heart with a single cruel word. I reported this to my mother.

"I bet you could," she said, and I heard a note of satisfaction in her voice. She was different. She didn't depend on anyone. It seemed that other people's needs slid smoothly off her body, naturally and inevitably repelled, like beads of water coursing off an oily frying pan in the sink.

Tom didn't understand why I was so upset about Matilda. "What's the big deal with Mom not telling you?" he asked.

"It's not about my knowing," I said. "It's not *about* me at all. I just wonder who deserves to get cut off from every—"

"Maybe it was Matilda's fault," he said. "Have you thought of that? You don't know anything about her."

Tom wasn't callous, but he believed people controlled their own destinies. *You make what happens next,* he liked to say. I felt like "next" was something that happened all over me. I never thought I could shape it between my fingers like putty.

You could see the sculpture of Tom's life as something he'd carved. He'd spent his twenties making money in private equity. He'd left his big bank for a smaller boutique firm where he'd have more control over the cash. "If something goes wrong, it'll be on *me*." There was more pride in his voice than fear. He never had patience for things that didn't happen and people who didn't make them happen. Matilda was a person who hadn't happened. At least she hadn't happened to him. But now I felt, without being able to explain it, that she was happening to me.

I knew she must have been pretty, like my mother, maybe she still was, and this became part of my imagining. I conjured exotic lives and stuck the paper doll of her imagined body inside them: coastal mansions, distant jungles, cabaret shows in seedy strip malls. It did not matter where she was, only that her face glowed, luminous.

*   *   *

We planned a small memorial gathering in Lucy's condo. It was only a few friends—people who'd become, in recent years, more like pen pals. "This must be the new stove," one said. They recognized things from her letters. My father even came. He and my mother still got along surprisingly well. It seemed like their divorce had come as a relief to both of them. I sensed that he knew her better than anyone else. She wasn't known by many people.

When she criticized him, her opinions never seemed raw, only well considered and matter-of-fact. He was a deal she'd already gotten out of, but I was stuck with him for the long haul. "Your father always expected to be someone extraordinary," she said. "He wasn't prepared for how he turned out."

I told Ms. Z that I needed a few days away from work for my grandmother's memorial service. I'd lied about her death, and now the lie had come true. I needed more days.

"You don't have more days," said Ms. Z. "You have a job."

She had an important television appearance coming up: a daytime talk show where she'd be participating in a roundtable with a group of homeless teens. She needed me to do research: How many kids lived on the street in America right now? What had the president done to worsen their lot? Even Ms. Z, one of the most terrible people I'd ever met, knew our president was bad news. I told her I absolutely could not come to work. "Fire me if you have to" is what I said. She did.

I wanted Lucy's condo to look presentable for her service. I wasn't much good at cooking or cleaning, but I set out fresh flowers and smoothed the couch cushions. They'd stayed wrinkled from all my nights of restless sleep. Cleaning was a way of making things presentable for her, as if her ghost would come back as a finicky houseguest. I tried recipes from magazines, but they didn't turn out like their pictures. My wilted spinach leaves looked greasy and depressed. "Warm salad?" my mom said. "Interesting."

She rose during the meal and said a few words to our assembled guests. "It's only the body that goes," she said. "The spirit remains."

Near the end of the night, I saw her crouched on the kitchen rug, holding an empty Corona bottle from the recycling. She handed it to me like a relic. I wasn't sure what she wanted me to do with it. I set it neatly on the floor. "Matilda almost ruined this rug," she said finally. "Back in L.A."

"Yeah?"

She told me that Matilda had dumped cigarette butts everywhere, overturned all the plants and ground their loose soil into the knitted weave. "Just because she could," she said, shaking her head. Then she really got going. She told me how Matilda had run away with her English teacher during high school. "That was the start," she said. "The beginning of the end." My mom had already left for college. She felt guilty for being gone. "Not guilty for Matilda's sake," she said. "Guilty for Mother's."

She came home during the middle of the term to keep Lucy company, but Lucy said she wanted to be alone—moved onto the daybed and ate toast for breakfast, toast for lunch, toast for dinner. My mom spent her days brushing crumbs off the blankets. Sometimes Lucy didn't bathe for days. She smelled like old socks. This was a woman who had never worn a dirty sock in her life. Her fingernails got ragged from chewing. She'd always been so proud about presenting herself well, curling her hair and putting out a little bowl of salted nuts for guests. For weeks she didn't care about anything.

Matilda lived in Berkeley that year, tripping on acid and maybe protesting the war. My mom shrugged. "I don't know *what* she was doing. She didn't call us once. Then she showed up one day, broken by love."

"Broken by love?"

"Her words, not mine."

My mother knew those had been hard months at home, the ones after the return, even though she hadn't seen them herself. Matilda worked part-time catering gigs until she stopped working altogether. She started sleeping twelve hours a day, half her life. She wouldn't eat. Bottles of liquor went missing from the cabinets—Cristal, Pernod, Cointreau—and Lucy found her lying in bed in the middle of the afternoon, drunk and sweaty, sometimes asleep, sometimes awake, mumbling in a way that made it hard to tell if she'd been dreaming or crying.

Mom mentioned Grandma Lucy's will without a break in her voice. There was a clause that left a little bit of money to Matilda, enough to make it hard for her to fight the fact that there wasn't more. This clause had been my mother's idea.

I asked if Matilda was the kind of woman who'd start a fight about money. Was she that kind of person?

My mom pursed her lips. "We don't know what kind of person she is."

Our estate lawyer had found her current address, and he was going to send her a letter. The information placed her in a little town called Lovelock, Nevada. Bluff Estates, the address said, a neighborhood with a name.

"What kind of letter is he sending?" I asked my mother.

"Cordial," my mom said. "But not overly personal."

It would be a letter telling Matilda about her mother's death.

"You shouldn't say that in a letter," I said.

"Oh?"

"It doesn't seem right."

"And what should we do? Head out to the desert?"

"It's a possibility."

"Just understand my side of this? I don't enjoy feeling like a villain."

I didn't say: *You're not a villain*. I said: "I'm not making you a villain."

"Well, good," she said. "You always seem to think I am one."

I spent one summer during high school working for my mom's law firm. I was supposed to spend a month in Guatemala, building houses for a village in the northern jungles, but near the beginning of June some guerrillas held up an airport near Flores. The newspapers said they had a manifesto and a lot of guns. Their wives brought cold Fantas and tortillas to the hostages. The articles never said what their manifesto was about, but it said what kind of guns they had. I asked my mother if she thought it was safe.

"You're worried about guerrillas?" she asked, amused.

I shrugged. But I was.

Around the house, Tom made comments like: "You don't want to fuck with socialism." I didn't want to be scared of socialism, but there I was, a little scared. The headlines said things like: *Ambushed!*

That was when my mother suggested I could spend the summer working at her law firm. "Why make foreign countries better when you can help foreigners come here instead?" she asked. She was maybe kidding, maybe not.

I'd often argued with her social causes. "I think women should be able to cut their own vaginas if they want to," I told her once, because she was a crusader against genital mutilation. I couldn't stand the prospect of inheriting all her ideas about the world. They were rigid and particular, like armor that had been made especially for her body.

"It's not a question of *want*," my mom said. "It's a question of coercion."

Her certainty felt like a wall she'd built around herself—just like that, in the middle of a conversation—a sign that she lived in an entirely separate world more sure and steadfast than my own. She was a pro-choice woman who didn't like to hear other women going on and on about how much they regretted their abortions. I could never understand the ways she wanted to love me. She always flinched when I hugged her, as if she hadn't been expecting it, as if afraid of being crushed.

That summer I helped research the asylum case of a woman named Daro. She was a refugee from Senegal. Her problems had started when she resisted the cutting rituals of her tribe. She used her hands to show us, held her palms in a V above her crotch and then rubbed two fingers together. She fled her village—had been, she said, "run out"—and then suffered persecution at the hands of distant cousins in Dakar.

I transcribed interviews that my mother conducted through two translators: to French, then Wolof, then back again. Mom's voice was scratchy on the tape recorder: "Why do your cousins persecute you?"

There was a shuffling farther back, a circling game of telephone. "They think she have disrespected her village," the translator said. "But she did not want the knife for her daughters."

I went to my mother's bed that night and lay next to her. "You were right," I whispered. "It's terrible."

I wondered if she'd given me this case to prove a point, to show me how wrong I'd been. I'd told her something terrible and false about the world, about innocent people's lives, to show that I was not the same person she was. I remembered Daro's voice, the sorrow marking up her foreign tongue, and started crying.

"Don't cry," my mother said. "Just help."

So I tried: I searched Daro's name on the Internet. I typed: "Daro Izowede + persecution." And then: "Daro Izowede + defying tradition." The only thing that came up was a list of personal ads. Daro had made one before she left Dakar. It showed her face in profile—the thumb-sized photo, her long acrylic nails spread like a fan across her cheek. *My hello phrase is I am looking for a man to love I do not know the name.*

At the office I printed out pages of information from human rights websites. I highlighted all the parts that were about rural rituals, or rural violence, or sexual violence, or mutilation, or getting married. I made neat folders with neat labels. It felt good to stack them on my mother's desk. I said, "I hope these make a difference."

"They will," she said. She rose from her chair and shook my hand.

That summer she dated a younger man named Greg and got dumped. I don't know what broke between the two of them, only that I found her at the kitchen table one night, and she used that exact word: *dumped.* Her voice was blunt and ugly as a stranger's, but her eyes were clear and her speech was orderly. She never dulled herself with wine or heavy fits of crying. She only got sharper when she was sad, brutal and precise. "He thought he could make me hurt," she said. "He didn't even ruin my night." She was sitting there with her hands crossed on the table, staring straight at the clock above the fridge. "You don't have to stay and watch," she said. "It won't make me feel any better."

The next morning I found her in exactly the same place. This time she was wearing a suit and holding a steaming mug of coffee. Her eyes looked bleary.

"Do you have a hangover?" I said. I knew from television that this was what grief could look like: getting sad, then getting a hangover. Getting drunk, presumably, between. Back then, the Hangovers were just getting started. Tom had gotten a set of secondhand snare drums painted with sleek silver flames.

"Excuse me?" she said. "Do I *what*?"

"Are you okay?"

"You think I got drunk last night?"

46

"No," I said. "Of course not."

"You think that man *mattered* even one little bit? You think I need a man to make me happy?"

I shook my head, staying quiet. I was afraid of saying something worse. She asked me if I was ready for work. It was a Saturday. I wasn't dressed. I got dressed. *My hello phrase is I am looking for a man to love I do not know the name.* I wanted to tell my mother she wasn't alone. All around the world, people were looking for love. No one knew which name it would respond to.

On the way to the office, we walked through an alley that smelled like pizza and urine. We passed a homeless woman crouched in the shadow of a Dumpster. She wore blue mechanic's coveralls that had the name Pluto stitched across the breast pocket. She had a striped cloth wrapped around her head. Her skin was dark, like cola.

"Hey ya!" she called. "You girls spare any change?" Her accent was lilting and musical, inviting.

"Not today," my mother said. "*Not* today."

"That's bullshit," the woman said. She smacked her palm against the Dumpster. "Bullshit bullshit bullshit."

My mother stopped and turned to me. She said, "Never do what I'm about to do." Then she told the woman, "I don't owe you anything."

"You don't *owe* me? You never seen a day of this pain in your life, and you don't *owe* me?"

"You don't know what I've seen," my mother said. She unzipped a woven coin purse, probably knitted by a tribe, and turned it over the woman's head. Coins skidded off her scalp, her shoulders, and clattered against the pavement. The woman was silent.

My mom grabbed my arm. "Walk away," she said. "Now we walk away."

"Where do you think that woman was from?" I said. "What do you think happened to her?"

"It doesn't matter what happened. You can always make a choice to be a decent person."

"Maybe she is a decent person," I said. "That's what I was getting at."

My mother glared at me. She said, "I knew what you were getting at."

I pulled away from her grip and turned around. I saw the woman on her knees gathering coins, reaching under the Dumpster to check if any had rolled beneath.

I looked up Matilda's address on an Internet map. At first I thought Bluff Estates was a subdivision, but it was a trailer park. I brought up the address and kept clicking closer, scrolling back from the yellow skirt of desert that surrounded her grid of avenues. The trailers were arranged around cul-de-sacs, their neat rectangular roofs like the building blocks of children, leftovers placed in a splayed starburst of residence around the edge of town. Their edges fuzzed.

Did her trailer have a cactus garden? A swamp cooler? Broken windows? A family of mice under the crawl space? I felt my stomach seize up with every click, like a Peeping Tom, as if she'd suddenly appear at one of her windows, shooing me—a stranger—away from her sun-scorched home. Eventually, I got so close that the satellite image gave out, gave up, and offered a row of small blue question marks instead.

My parents got involved in something called Grief Work. My father made it sound like a social justice movement. But really, my mom said, it just meant setting aside time for what they were feeling. "Your father never has much trouble doing that," she said. "As we all know." I was surprised she'd agreed to join him. They were making collages every Tuesday in the pool house of a rabbi named Jeri.

"I really like her," said my dad. "But I'm not at all attracted to her." He said this like it was a marvelous good deed, something Jeri might have called a mitzvah.

"It's interesting to see your father impress a woman he doesn't want to sleep with," my mom confessed. "It's quite amusing."

My father brought back skeptical reports. "Your mother seems to enjoy herself," he said. "But she hasn't made a single collage."

I saw the twisting gears of epic grinding into motion behind his eyes. *Destiny is in the telling, not the doing*, he liked to say. Now he saw his chance. Mom was raw-nerved from loss and open to wonder. She might have a vision that could change her forever. He wanted to be part of it.

In the meantime, she came east to help me pack Grandma Lucy's possessions. "Couldn't trust you to do it by yourself," she said. "You'd save everything." There was honesty in her voice, a rueful knowing, that I appreciated. It felt good to be seen through.

She arrived like the last time, icy-fingered and determined. It was during a cold snap in the middle of May. We weren't done with winter yet. She had a plan that involved three boxes of garbage bags. "We're going to give away a lot of stuff," she said. "And we're going to *throw* away a lot of stuff."

In Grandma Lucy's closet, we saw a row of beer bottles filled with dirt. Each one was labeled—Maryland, Zurich, Rio de Janeiro. The columns of soil were colored dark rum, brown sugar, reddish clay. The Osaka dirt was jaundiced yellow, like a sick man's urine.

My mother examined one jar in her palm. "I can't believe he sent these," she said. After a moment: "Let's throw them off the balcony."

My mother was not always a fun person, but this—the throwing of a bastard's trophies from the balcony of his deceased and deserted wife—this was definitely fun. We watched the glass jars shatter on the asphalt below. We watched bachelor bankers emerge from their apartments and crane their faces up to the sky.

Later that night, I couldn't stop myself from sneaking outside and collecting some of the dirt that remained. I had to crawl under a black Mercedes to find it crushed into the pebbled driveway. I'd been a part of my mother's oldest anger, and now I was part of an even older remembering. I could be every face of this grieving all at once. I funneled the dirt into a single beer bottle and made a new label: *Osaka?* It said. *Maryland + Zurich + Rio de Janeiro?*

I waited until the last night of my mother's visit before I brought up the question of Matilda. I asked if the letter had been sent. My mother said it hadn't. They were still figuring out the details of the will. What did this mean? I asked. My mother assured me it was complicated. Legal stuff, she said. Legal stuff aside, I said, I really thought Matilda deserved—I had to pause. *What did she deserve?* I could not say exactly; something other than this.

My mother closed her eyes and rubbed her temples with her fingers. "Let's take a walk," she said. "I need to get out of this condo."

We fought while we walked. In the cold of early evening, in the middle of the state of Connecticut, we fought. We fought about faraway Matilda in her desert—whatever kind of woman she was, not yet grieving for what she didn't yet know. I told my mother it would be cruel to send the letter, almost unthinkable. I said: *I wouldn't want a stranger to tell me you died*. She said Matilda had *left,* did I understand that? When somebody kept leaving, over and over again, there was nothing to do but let her go. I'd been drinking wine and my face was warm with it; my mom had been drinking fizzy water and her face was smooth and white. Her features stayed perfectly still even when her words suggested she was very upset.

She couldn't understand how I could sympathize with a

stranger more than I sympathized with her, the woman who'd raised me. I said I didn't—I didn't know, that was all. I didn't know what to think. My mom said: *Go then. Find her. Be a hero.* I said I didn't want to be a hero. I remembered how she'd used that word when I was a kid, like it was shameful to depend on them. All I wanted was to see if we couldn't fix this thing at least a little. She said: *She'll make you tired, you'll see. She'll hurt you.*

I left angry—I left *her* angry, standing in the parking lot—but anger kept my hands steady enough to get my purse from the condo, to buy a ticket back to the city, to get myself on board and sit, knees together, in a nearly empty rail car. It was only once the train started moving that I grew unsteady, watching the darkened suburbs roll by, thinking, *How could a woman die—a good woman, a woman who loved as best she could—and leave this mess of bad blood behind, this terrible nest of angry, angry women?*

I breathed on the glass and traced figures. I wrote her name, *Matilda,* like a girl with a crush. I thought of where she was: Was it cold there? Was she alone? I knew it then. I didn't have to win the argument with my mother. It didn't matter if I won my arguments with anybody. I had an address. If I wanted to, I could find her.

$\mathcal{T}$ILLY

$\mathcal{O}$ ne winter Dora came home from college with all her nice clothes in garment bags, which was typical, and a pair of red eyes, which wasn't. She wasn't a regular weeper or a smoker of anything. Our mother had set the dinner table hours before she arrived. Our father had been gone for years.

Dora snuck into my bedroom after midnight, sat on my bed, and shook my shoulder: "Are you awake?"

Truth was, I was almost delirious. I'd been taking steady pulls from a bottle of vodka since dessert. We only had dessert when Dora came home, though she never ate any.

I knew most people started drinking with other people before they drank alone, but I went in the opposite direction. I loved the full heat of being drunk, like I was made of melting chocolate and spreading in all directions. I didn't need other people around to want that feeling for myself.

Dora told me she'd been with a man for the first time. It was hard for her to say it, I could tell. She never talked about things like that. I asked whether she'd liked it. She said it had been alright. She asked me whether I was drunk.

I asked about the guy. Who was he? Someone headed off to law school, she said, next fall. She hadn't heard from him since she left his bed. "What does that mean?" she asked. "You know about this stuff." I was seven years younger, but what she said was true.

I told her it could mean a lot of things, and I wasn't sure any of them were good. I asked whether she wanted to see him again.

"I want him to want to see *me*."

I nodded.

"I just wish I didn't give a damn."

"I don't see what's wrong with giving a damn."

"No," she said. "I guess you wouldn't."

In those days the house was quiet, like there was a funeral happening that no one could discuss. My mom didn't know how to talk to me. She was scared, I think, scared of the sadness that made me want to drink and sleep all the time, but she kept hunting for signs that I was secretly extraordinary. Sometimes I caught her reading the crumpled school tests that I'd thrown in the trash. Or else I'd open the bathroom door and find her in the hallway, as if she'd been listening to me singing in the shower. I had this feeling like her life was already done, and now she was waiting for mine to start. Made two of us.

There were always boys. Most of them I didn't even like that much, but they seemed like the easiest way to change my own life. After eleventh grade, I ran away to Berkeley with my American literature teacher, Arthur Boy. We joked about his name. He was my first real man. Mostly he wasn't a very funny person. *Save me from my wife,* he said. *From myself.*

We moved into a wooden rambler on Poirier Street. The house wasn't quite in Berkeley, but it was right across the Oakland border, with the artists and the full-time trippers. The summer of love had already gone stale. Kennedy died and then King died, the other Kennedy died, little Bobby!, and everyone felt a little lost. People were doing drugs for different reasons than they'd done them before.

The kid who ran the rooming house called himself Peter Pan. He sold drugs all over East Bay. Not just hash or acid, either, though I liked both of these and got my first dose of each from the jars lined on the rim of his bathtub, their glass the color of seawater.

Arthur and I dropped tabs in Tilden Park. He said, *Put your torso against my torso,* and his voice sounded like it was coming from beneath the grass. I tried to put our imagined hours on one side and our real ones on the other. Was there an earthquake so small we might have dreamed it? Was there a crow picking out the eyes of a squirrel? Did we throw stones at it? Did we kill it? Did we see its soul rising? It's a sputtering inside you when everything gets rearranged. It's amazing to share it with another person.

Peter P. was frying bigger fish, too. He was helping folks run off the rough end of the sixties and jump straight into harder stuff. Guys came back from the war and couldn't remember who they'd been before they started burning villages. One guy stumbled into our kitchen with a bloody gash down his arm. He'd broken one of our windows. He handed Peter P. a dirty twenty with the corner ripped off. "You fucker," he said. "Nearly killed myself for the cash."

Peter P. was holding a beer in one hand and a tuna sandwich in the other. He gave this man a little plastic Baggie. "Hey now," he said. "You got to stitch yourself up."

That night I told Arthur I wanted us to move out. "He's *killing* people," I said. I hadn't known what it looked like when your body needed something that badly.

"Baby girl," Arthur told me. "You don't know what's what."

I felt lonelier with him than I'd ever felt by myself. At home, at

least, I'd thought that leaving home would bring me somewhere better.

Arthur liked fucking in all kinds of places: on our little tar-and-gravel rooftop, in the hallway closet, in the bathtub. "This is just fine," he said, propping me up on the kitchen table. "A real fine-grained wood." I got the sense that he was homesick for his wife and all their nice things. One time in the bath I saw the door cracked open. Peter P. was standing there, watching.

"You fucker!" Arthur cried. "You goddamn pervert!" But they were both laughing, and I had the feeling that something had been arranged: *You wanna see how she likes it? You wanna see for yourself?*

I took a deep breath and told Arthur I wasn't just somebody to fuck. "What did you think we were?" he said. "A little family?" He was getting into a lot of harder drugs—they made him say things he didn't agree with a few minutes later. But they were still the things he said. That was the last time I felt betrayed by a man, I think. Afterward I expected it.

I left in the early morning, hitched a ride with an older couple down the coast. They drove a green van and bought me pancakes from a diner off the highway. The whole drive I practiced what I would say to my mom. I wanted to tell her what I'd learned. I wasn't looking for love all over the goddamn state anymore. I knew a thing or two about family.

Lucy came to the door in her blue silk nightgown, the one with orange juice stains across the lap. She looked older. She was older. She had her hand over her heart. "It beats all funny now," she said. "I think you did that."

It was one of the moments I loved her most, I think. Seeing her tired eyes and how they weren't looking at anything but me. Knowing I'd hurt her body by going away. This amazed me. It made me feel ashamed of myself.

"Oh, Tilly," she said, and started crying, and I wasn't sure why—because I was safe, because I was home, because I looked

like I was doing alright even though I'd been away, or because I didn't look alright, I looked wrong. I didn't know what I looked like, honestly.

I took her hand. Her skin felt soft, like well-worn paper.

"I feel beat up, Momma. I'm not doing so great."

"You're back," she said. "That's what matters."

In all the days that followed, she never asked me why I'd gone, only why I'd come back. I think it made her glad to hear how lonely I'd been.

"Dora says I should have let you figure things out for yourself," she said. By then Dora had moved to Boston, where she was going to law school. I wondered about that boy. Was he still in the picture? Sometimes she called the house, and we kept a certain silence balanced between us on the phone. One time I asked if she was happy. She said she was exactly where she wanted to be.

I didn't start school again, even though I only had a few months left. I got a job with a catering company, working parties. I liked making myself look pretty. I put my hair in two long braids down my back. Dora had taught me how. She always hurt my head when she did it, so I learned as fast as I could how to do it myself. I liked the way people looked at me at those showbiz parties. If you were pretty enough, people always thought you were hiding something. They got drunk and told me their secrets. I was good at listening. I got big tips.

My mother knew that money didn't come from nowhere. Money only showed up, she said, from someone wanting something. I told her I never let men touch me, which wasn't quite true. I just never let them pay for it. *All it takes is someone thinking you're a whore,* she said. *Then you are one.*

We lost track of that first moment on the porch—her paper hands, our wordless grip, the hope. We had terrible fights. She thought I didn't have much self-respect. "Or if you do," she said, "you do a good job hiding it."

Nearly every night my throat got swollen from crying. I poured the liquor down the ache, closed my eyes, and let the darkness swim. I brought home leftover booze from my gigs. I'd drink anything, but I got to like gin the best, tart and sweet and bitter at the same time. It did the job quickest, felt like, and sent flu pangs all across the surface of my skin. Everything touched me a little sharper when I was drunk—blankets, wood, smoky air, hairy carpets—as if they'd been tucked right around the shape of my body. The whole world fit, and I was folded inside of it. I had a few blind moments of peace before passing out. I woke to the liquor I hadn't drunk the night before. Drinking on an empty stomach glazed the inside of my body like a clay pot.

One day my mother found me like that, bottle perched between my knees above the covers. "Look at yourself," she said. "Just look." She grabbed my arm and pulled. "Get up, get up, get up!" She shoved me in front of my full-length mirror and held my shoulders, shaking. "You see *this?*"

I did see. I saw myself like someone from my parties might have seen me—a mermaid girl, barely clad. And then I saw the rest. I wasn't wearing shorts. The puffy letters of my sweatshirt spelled NEPENTHE, and there was a wine stain covering the N. I held the bottle with one hand. My cheeks were flushed and rough, like stucco, puffy skin around my eye hollows. My pupils peered out from their caves. My hair was thick and tangled, like the mouse nest we'd found in our garage when I was young: bits of rags and hair and strips of car upholstery. I'd been in awe of that nest, how it made a home of all our garbage.

Momma kept at me. "Do you see yourself? Do you?"

I grabbed the bottle and swung it against the door frame. I wanted to make her quiet. The glass splintered against the hard edge of wood. I held the ragged neck in my closed fist. I broke off one shard and reached to cut my thigh. In the mirror I watched the blood well from the slit. It came out thick, like the wine glaze was spilling out. The flow was quiet after the sound of splintering. I brought the shard up to my neck. I didn't know where to cut. I didn't know if I could.

She grabbed my hand and closed hers around it. The glass sliced my tight-squeezed palm. I felt the blood ooze between our fingers. I let my fist go loose. The shard dropped onto the carpet.

"I knew it," she said. "I knew you wouldn't do it."

That's when I turned around and slapped her. It sounded like a whip's crack. Then, very slowly, I laid my palm across the red skin of the hit. I wanted to soothe it. She cupped her hand over mine for a second, letting me, and then she shook her head and walked away. "Lucy!" I said. I yelled it. Then again, and again, until the sounds didn't make sense: *See, Lucy? Lu?* I just wanted her to turn around. I wanted to know that something else could happen after the dry crack of my skin on hers. It sounded like the end of everything.

Lucy said I had to move out. So I did. I left my pride in that house, and I missed it: the part of me that felt my mother's disappointment. It had some dignity, at least.

I slept with people I shouldn't have been sleeping with, for extra drugs or beds. I'd quit the catering gig, but I still hung out with folks I'd met at those parties, people who made comments about big hunks of abstract sculpture and asked me to give them head in bathrooms. Those pieces of art never had any people in them. That's what got me. I was going down on men and women, letting them inside me.

I made a little money on the Venice boardwalk selling necklaces I made. I must have walked fifteen miles a day hawking them to tourists. Skinniest I've ever been in my life, but it got me tired enough to fall asleep fast, wherever I was staying. I hugged my sore arms around my chest and felt the hurt close like an eye-lid—dark and quick.

There was a woman at the beach who showed me great kindness. She was nearly my mother's age and earned a living selling capes to passersby. Her knitting was like open fingers, letting wind and sand touch your salty skin. She used thick yarn in neon shades: blue jellyfish fringe, pale moon-rock green. Some were glow-in-the-dark, and in the twilight you could see the people who'd bought them, strolling the path, drinking soda from straws and shimmering like ghosts.

One day she came up and told me her name was Fiona. She wasn't a pretty woman but I liked looking at her face, all her features like knobs you might pull or twist to open the secret door of her speech. She had the skin of someone who'd spent her life in the sun. Her face was rough like cloth, sun-stained to the color of apricots.

"Where do you sleep?" she asked.

"Excuse me?"

"Do you have a place?" she said. "A lot of girls don't."

"I've got places," I said. "More or less."

Most recently, I'd been sharing a per-month motel room with a real estate agent who'd separated from his wife.

"Well, which one is it? More? Or less?"

"A little less. Recently."

She handed me a key. "Take this," she said. "If you're ever in a bind." She told me she lived on Rose Avenue. "Two buildings down from the greasy spoon," she said. "I'm the balcony with all the you-know-whats." She flapped her arms to make her capes shimmy.

"I should just drop by?" I said. "Whenever?"

She laughed. "You new in town?"

"This part."

"That's what I thought," she said. "You come by whenever you want."

She was a stranger, sure. She didn't owe me anything. But back then my life was full of strangers and no one else. I wanted to owe someone something, anything. I wanted to feel indebted.

Her balcony looked like she'd promised. Capes ruffled in the salty wind, their dark stacks humped like camels behind the railings. She wasn't home, but the living room had signs of her all over it: empty mugs with hardened tea bags, a vase of knitting needles that glinted silver in the moonlight. I tripped over the spines of open books, smashing their faces into the carpet. I curled up on the couch and woke to her voice. "Don't get up," she whispered. "You just rest."

Her place was full of mess and treasure: useless window screens propped against the walls, a row of old dog collars covered with glittering rhinestones, crumpled balls of paper pushed under the bookshelves. I smoothed one out and saw it was a paper bag from a doughnut shop. I smoothed another, and it showed a few lines of writing, maybe hers, that looked like the beginning of a letter or a song: *If that's your idea of heaven you can keep it for yourself* . . .

Fiona moved gracefully through the clutter. She knew where to find everything: the measuring cups, the old photo album, the remote control, out of batteries and wedged somewhere dusty. She already had a roommate, a guy named Drew, but he didn't come out much. He'd been in Khe Sanh, and this was one of the first things he told me about himself: *I was in Khe Sanh*. I knew Khe Sanh was in Vietnam, I told him, but I didn't know anything else about it. "That's all you need to know," he said. "There's nothing else."

I asked Fiona about Khe Sanh that night. What kind of fighting happened there? Did she know?

"Bad fighting, is what kind," she said. "It's all bad."

Drew's room was bare, like a jail cell. The only thing worth noticing was a carved wooden mask. It looked like it had been made from a palm frond. I asked him if it had been, and it turned out *yes*, it had, collected from a beach he'd visited on furlough. He had a beach towel spread flat below the window and a twin bed tucked into the corner. "It's been a long road to that bed," he said.

I bit my lip. I was a girl then, nervous around other people's pain. "From over there, you mean?"

"From over *there*." He pointed to the towel. "I slept so long on the ground, it was a hard habit to break. The floor felt better."

"What do you use it for now?" The towel had bright green stripes, as if someone had stripped a lime and laid down the skin in rags.

"Soaking up the sun. The window makes it real bright."

"There's a whole beach outside," I said.

He looked away. "I know," he said. "But I like to stay in here."

Sometimes we watched the news. Vietnam looked like a place where even the plants were alive, everything electric and crackling. Everyone had blurry faces and voices streaked with static like rain. The places had exotic names—Cam Lo, Da Nang—but all the battles sounded American: Operation Virginia Ridge, Idaho Canyon, Hamburger Hill. Every day I saw soldiers pacing the boardwalk with glassy eyes and heavy unlaced boots.

Drew didn't talk much about his year in the war. One time he said he missed the ammo belt on his M60, the way the metal felt under his fingers. He voice got ragged when he told me about a few nights in Saigon. "They had this great soup," he said, and I sensed there was a woman involved. I told him he'd be alright, but what did I know? Maybe next time he'd start crying and never stop.

Fiona said I could use the couch as long as I needed. But I was tired of other people being kind. I wanted to make something for myself. I put away the money I made off my jewelry. I took a part-time gig at a hot-dog stand. It felt like being part of a little world, that part of the beach, everybody recognizing my face and saying, "*Hel*-lo, pretty," even if it never really went past that. There was a crew of homeless guys who lived under the pier, and I brought them old dogs that had been burned or soaked in grease too long.

Fiona said I had a future in me. "You're gonna live some kind of crazy story," she said. "Hard to tell what it's gonna be."

I thought about what would happen if I saw Lucy—if she ever came down here, looked up, and saw my face. It wasn't likely. But she was still right here, same city and everything. How could I stop wondering: *What if? What if? What if?* She'd be ashamed to think of me like this—stinking of meat, just a few dollars an hour and nickel tips to show for it. *Do you see yourself? Do you?*

Drew told me he'd gotten his name because his mother doodled a little baby one day and found out three weeks later she was pregnant. "She drew me," he said. "Pulled me out of thin air like a magic trick."

He invited me to share his room. I said yes. I was getting tired of Fiona and her loneliness. I'd find her sitting on the couch with a dreamy look in her eyes, her hand rummaging in a bowl of popcorn. "You hungry?" she'd ask, and I'd take some because I didn't want to watch her face if I said no.

I moved my bag into Drew's room. "Don't worry about any funny business," he said. "I'll take the floor."

That night he crawled into bed. His bed. His words were gentle—"Do you mind?" he whispered—but he waited until I was asleep before he touched me, until I was too tired to speak or think, and I thought this wasn't the right way to treat another person. I remember thinking: *It's not gentle.* I rolled away and hugged my legs close to my chest. He didn't try again. I woke up to his moaning. He was clutching his left arm with his right hand, squeezing hard. I could see the white of his knuckles. "What is it?" I said.

"I'm bleeding," he said. "I think it's bad."

I ran my fingers along his arm, around the grip of his fist, but I couldn't feel anything sticky or wet. "Let your fingers go," I said. "I can't feel it."

His hand dropped away, but there wasn't any cut.

"There's nothing wrong," I said. "You're okay."

"I'm not." He moaned again. "You've got to keep the pressure or else—"

I realized then. I said: "You let go. I'll keep the pressure tight."

I knelt by the side of the bed and circled both hands around his upper arm. There wasn't anything wrong, but I held on anyway. I whispered in his ear, "It's getting better."

When he fell asleep, I let my fingers go slack, a loose circle like a bracelet dangling. Finally, I took my hands away and watched him rest.

Drew never paid for what we did together. But we made an arrangement that involved both our bodies. It was understood that I could share his room for free, and in return, he asked me to watch him while he touched himself. "I just want you to see it," he said. "I don't want you to turn away."

I cared for Drew, though I felt that he'd taken me into something I hadn't chosen for myself. It was better at night, the strange dark space of an empty room, but when I looked at him in the day, it made me sick to my stomach.

One time I found him sitting in the corner, arms clasped around his knees. He was wearing his big palm mask, and it made him look like a demon—the long curved chin like a comma, the eyes like slanted arrows. I stood there with my hand on the doorknob. He pulled off the mask and shook his head. "I'm sorry," he said. "I didn't want to scare you."

One day I woke up with cramps, a real motherfucker, my

stomach tied into a game of cat's-cradle. I vomited in a blue bowl because I didn't want to vomit in Fiona's bathroom. I'd already been such a burden. That night Drew came to bed and touched my forehead with the back of his hand. "You're burning up," he said.

I turned away from him. I wanted to keep the sickness for myself.

"You've got a lot of wanting," he told me. "But you don't say any of it. That's where the fever comes from."

He said his sister was like that, too, hot to the touch because so much happened under her skin. It was like an oven inside her. "You gotta be good to that kind of person," he said. "That kind of person especially."

I didn't say anything.

"You been good to me," he said. "I wish I could've been good to you."

I didn't feel sick, but I felt cleaned out and weak. I'd vomited everything. I knew what I needed.

I woke early the next morning. The sun through his window was bright and round and naked. I moved slowly so I wouldn't wake him. I packed a grocery bag full of odds and ends—a toothbrush, some clean socks, a coffee mug that showed the hills of Catalina like green knuckles under an orange sky, block letters saying: WHERE THE SUN IS ALWAYS SETTING.

My clothes had gotten mixed into Drew's neat piles. They smelled like the sweet bleach of his detergent. I tucked my saved-up money into the socks. I left Fiona a note that said *thank you*, once at the beginning and once at the end, and in between there was a phone number in case she wanted to reach me, my mother's number at home.

I took the 17 bus and got off near the old hardware store. I walked a mile uphill with the paper bag knocking against my knees. I could remember coming back from Oakland, sure she'd take me, when I thought the only thing that mattered was both of us wanting me home.

Lucy didn't answer in her dressing gown this time. She was wearing an old sundress with yellow stripes. It showed the sticks of her arms and the shelf of her collarbone. She'd grown thin and hard, like me. "If you knew how much it hurt me to see you," she said, "you wouldn't have come."

"I'm not drinking anymore," I said. "I stopped."

"That's good, Matilda. It's really good."

"I was thinking just a couple weeks. I could come back—"

"You scared me," she said softly.

"I'm not like that now. I won't be."

"You have things here. You should take them with you."

"Do you hear me? I want to come *back*."

"You have someplace to sleep?" she said. Now she was crying. "You have someplace to go tonight, right?"

I shrugged. "Sure I do."

"You mean that?"

I nodded.

"Then you should go there."

I touched her arm and she flinched.

"Please?" She looked away. "You should go."

I didn't go far. I sat on the curb a few houses down, just out of sight, and found the rolled socks in my bag. I took out one five-dollar bill and tucked the whole package back into place. I walked to a liquor store on Sunset and bought the cheapest gin I could find, then went next door for a liter of orange juice. I walked to the edge of the bluffs, found an empty bench in the middle of a weed field, and started taking one quick sip after another, going back and forth.

I pictured my mother reading one of her mystery books or lacquering her hair with bright auburn dye, the color stained in ragged peaks across her neck. I'd hated all her rituals when I lived at home, but now I tried to remember every one of them. The gin burned my sore gums. The ocean could have been the desert. It was a big field of darkness without any light.

The house was bright when I went back. The way light came out the windows at night reminded me of yolk coming out of a broken egg. I watched from the bushes for an hour, taking sips, and saw my mother's figure move through the living room. Her shadow bent to pick up something from the floor. Her head was oddly shaped, too tall, and I knew it was from a towel wrapped around her head. She would be different in the darkness, more broken. I took the gin and orange juice into my mouth at once, let the pool grow warm on my tongue, and then I took it all down, heard my wet throat swallowing.

I knocked and got nothing. I kept knocking, not in rhythmic bursts but continuously—*rap rap rap rap rap*—until she answered. The angle of the towel was tilted, threatening to topple, and her face was puffy underneath. She'd been crying.

"It didn't go right before," I said. "It went all wrong."

She sighed. "You're drunk."

"I'm sad," I said. "Tonight I'm really, really sad."

"You should go," she said. "Don't make me ask again."

"I'm not making you do anything!"

She stood there staring at her worn cloth slippers. She wouldn't raise her head. "I have nothing to say to you, Matilda. Not when you get like this."

My voice was a rubber band in my throat, pulled tight. I grabbed her shoulders and shook her whole body. The towel fell, and her hair dropped around her shoulders. When she looked up, her eyes showed nothing but a terrible shine, not tears but steel: hard blue shells hiding the hurt underneath.

"You're my fucking *mother*!" I yelled. The rubber band had broken. I wanted to shake the feelings out of her body so I could see them. *I have nothing* . . . She didn't have to say the right things. She could say anything. I'd listen to whatever she said.

"Please let go of me," she said. "Don't make me remember you like this."

I let my hands drop to my sides. It had come to this: remembering.

"You better get to where you're staying," she said. "You get there safe."

I shoved her backward, right into the screen door. My own mother and I did it.

She steadied herself against the door frame and whispered, "What made you like this?"

She turned around and went inside. She let the screen door slam. I watched all the living room lights go off, then the kitchen light, then the dining room. Her bedroom stayed bright. I lifted one huge stone and threw it at her window. It broke into bits of glass that caught the light. "You made me," I said, barely loud enough to hear myself.

I went back to Fiona's but I only found Drew. He told me she'd skipped town for northern Nevada, a little place called Lovelock. He looked scared and hurt. He wouldn't touch me, not even to shake my hand. I made him look me in the eye: "You're not a bad person, okay? Believe that."

I took a bus to Reno and got a job in an all-night diner owned by a guy named Phil. Philippe was his name, but everyone called him Phil because it pissed him off. He wasn't even French.

The Reno casinos were like toys built for giant children. One of them had a mural that showed pioneers in covered wagons, Indians crouched behind rocks, a campfire flickering with little lights. I hung out there sometimes, smoking cigarettes, because I liked the feel of history towering over me. It was one of the oldest joints in town, this place. Rumor was they'd gotten famous for a game called mouse roulette back in the day, where they put a mouse in a cage full of numbered holes and people bet on where he'd go. They tried to make noise that would make him change his mind. I bet the mice chose holes that already smelled like their parents or their brothers. I loved the idea of men going crazy watching some little guy decide which dark cave he should choose for shitting. It felt good to be in a town that didn't have anything to do with me. I woke up early and wandered air-conditioned lobbies just so I could see them empty.

One morning I was approached by a man wearing a pinstriped suit. He had a ponytail that reached his waist. He asked if I was in the business and whether I was represented. I remember that word he used: *represented.* Like you'd talk about talent or show business. He did this for a living. He was dawn-hunting that day, his word for it, hanging out in lobbies and searching for girls who looked lost. There weren't too many reasons to be a girl alone in a hotel lobby in the early morning. I told him I wasn't interested.

"Of course you're not." He smiled. "But just in case." He took my hand and wrote something on my palm with his blue pen: *Motel 6, Room 121.* "Just stop by. If you're curious."

The room was rented to an old man, a retired condiment salesman and unretired dope addict. He looked too poor to do the drugs he did. He wanted me to smoke his weed before he fixed himself up, and I said *fine, yes,* I would. The pot unbuttoned my muscles like a patient lover takes off your blouse. Then he took his little plastic tool box into the kitchen. *Come on back,* he said. *It's stir-fry.* He used a lot of slang, like he was proving something. He'd probably been a boy the other boys hadn't played with much.

I remember a dish rack next to his sink, stacked with washed beer cans and nothing else. He crushed one flat and cooked the drugs on its base. I watched him shoot it up, snap off the rubber tubing, and float right into space. His big beard dangled like dryer lint. He had his mouth open and his head tilted back like he was drinking something trickling from the sky. He offered to make me some as well. I shook my head. His voice got mean, and he whispered, "You've got to come here with me!" He tried to push the pipe into my mouth. He wanted me to need it as much as he did. So I took some, like I'd taken Fiona's burnt knuckles of popcorn, so I wouldn't have to see his expression if I refused.

His mouth tasted dry and sour when we fucked. Afterward he gave me some crumpled bills and pulled a Bible and a box of crackers from his nightstand drawer. I sat on the edge of his bed, legs crossed, and watched him eat. I thought maybe there was something he wanted to read aloud. But all he did was look at me, confused. "You're done," he said. "You can go now."

I started working for the man with the ponytail. He probably had a different name at home, but in the business he went by Bruce Black. He told me I was savvy. I knew I wasn't. He told me I was pretty, too, though by then I'd heard it from so many men—men on the verge of coming, falling asleep, kicking me out—that I barely heard. I couldn't see it.

Most of my clients were guys who hadn't ever hit the big time. I could see it in the way they moved, the way they fucked, in their occasional acts of cruelty. They'd had dreams crushed out like little fires over the whole course of their lives. By the time I met them, it was already done—not only the Big Chance but even the dreaming about it. Now they were traveling salesmen and real estate agents working subdivisions. A lot of them had habits. They were usually fair and sometimes even kind, and that made me feel grateful—which made me angry. I was feeling thankful just because someone treated me like a human being?

One was a diabetic with a wound on his foot that wouldn't heal. *It used to be just a regular cut,* he said. *But then the blood couldn't flow there.* For two years he'd been doing what he could to make it better. He wanted me to rub his pain cream into the skin around its puckered little maw, gouged right in the middle of his heel. I thought maybe he'd be one of those guys who wants to pay you for an ordinary moment, hand-holding or bathing, but it turned out he wasn't one of those. "Okay," he said, once I'd finished with his foot. "Now we fuck."

I spent my off-hours in casinos. Midday was when the hopeless cases showed up. I liked their stubborn dreaming. I watched what they ate, what they wore, when they started drinking in the afternoons. I watched the ways they got lucky, blowing on the dice or calling phrases: *Baby needs new shoes!*

The first guy who got rough with me, he wasn't the worst, because I didn't blame myself for him. I'd never seen how suddenly the switch could flip, my body pinned under his: *You think you have a say? You don't have a goddamn fucking say!* I blamed myself for the ones who came later. I should have learned by then. They were animals trapped in their own lives. When they saw me, they saw they could do anything they wanted.

One man left me bruised for days. He almost strangled me. He tried to do me up the back, and that was the reason he got mad, he said, but I think he was looking for a reason to get angry. The whole time he was doing it—pinning me with his knees, squeezing his fingers into my neck—he told me some girls had it worse: fingernails dug out, hands tied with cords, heads stuck underwater. Did I know that? How bad they had it? He made me say thank you. He pulled my hair so hard I felt my forehead drawn back. He whispered, *Say it.*

He paid me extra when I left. I was still catching my breath. I was scared that maybe if I tried to speak, I wouldn't be able to. Some part of my throat had been crushed. "You're one lucky whore," he said. "You know that?"

Once that kind of thing is born in a man, it can't ever die. It has to go somewhere. If it wasn't me, it might have been some woman walking down the street. I woke up with a bruise across my neck and thought, *Give me one good reason.* I only needed one. *Maybe now it won't be some other girl.*

Abe was one of my richest customers. Our first time, he stopped right in the middle, still inside, and it took me a second to realize he was sobbing. That's why his body was shaking. He pulled out and lay there without explaining himself. After a while, he said, "I almost had a kid a ways back. But she didn't keep it. We didn't."

He buttoned up his shirt and handed me my own clothes, neatly folded. This guy was big on keeping things equal. If he was dressed, so was I. When I'd arrived at his hotel room, he'd introduced himself right away, like he didn't give a damn about standard policy: "My name is Abraham Clay."

"Matilda."

My throat clamped shut when I said it. It belonged to my old life, this name. The sounds didn't belong here. They struggled against the difference.

Now he handed me a cigarette. "I'm going to smoke," he said. "And I'd like if you smoked, too."

Wind lifted the hair on my arms. A siren hollered from far away, then closer, closer—wailing louder, faster, sharper—until the sounds got slower, faded, and the ambulance was gone. "I make those," said Abraham. "My company does."

"Sounds important," I said.

He shrugged. "It's a living."

He told me he was getting a divorce. Not in Reno but in Vegas, where he'd lived with his wife. They'd fallen apart after she aborted their first pregnancy. He was almost sixty, but he'd never had a child. "I should have stopped her from getting it," he said. "It ruined us."

I started to say something back—*It's okay* or maybe *It's done now*—but he cut me off. He told me I should get out of Reno.

He said it sharply, and quick like he was trying to forget what he'd said about himself. He didn't know me, he said, but everyone deserved something better than what I had—didn't they? Didn't I think so?

What was I going to say with someone actually listening? It was like the sharp needle pains of hands coming back to life after the cold. If I focused on my thighs, I could make the muscles remember how he'd pushed them apart.

I slept in his bed. Every time the sound of a siren sailed through the night, I thought about the whole world he owned. I asked how many ambulances he'd made.

"How many wailers?" he said. "Probably thousands."

It took me years to go looking for Fiona, even though I thought about her all the time, and Lovelock was only a couple hours' bus ride from the depot in Reno. It was Abraham who finally convinced me to find her. I'd told him a little bit about my past, how Fiona was someone I still wondered about. "You should keep track of people who've been good to you," he said. His own life had a lot of loose ends.

Lovelock was an ugly town with a jail to its name and not much else. The address took me to a trailer park at the edge. Fiona's place was nailed to the ground with porches and rickety plastic stairs, great thick snakes of cables running into the hot, hot soil. There was a mat in front of the door that showed a kitten pawing at a couple of butterflies. It would never catch them. Everything was coated with dirt and sand.

Fiona came to the door so slowly I almost gave up waiting. She'd gotten fat. I thought maybe it had something to do with the brace on her leg. She explained about the injury. A big metal sign had fallen off its hinges and crushed her, she said, with letters the size of bread loaves. Her friend had been opening a clothing store, and she'd been helping hoist the sign. He ran the store now, Fiona said, but she couldn't help anymore. Her voice had an edge that hadn't been around in Venice. *Tower People*. It was a store for tall folks. Her friend was a short man, but he had a tall wife for whom he would do nearly anything.

I asked if she was still knitting capes.

"That?" she said. "That was a lifetime ago."

I paused. I wasn't sure what to say next.

"You want to come in or not?" she said. "'Cuz I need to sit down."

I followed her inside. She settled her body into a recliner and it made me sad to see how much relief it gave her. Like there was no greater pleasure she could imagine.

She wanted to know if I was looking for a place to stay. I hadn't been, exactly, but there was a reason I'd taken a bus out of Reno—I wasn't happy there either. I kept telling myself, *This isn't your real life. Not yet.*

"Well," Fiona said. "I've got a room if you need one."

It had been built as a breakfast nook, she warned, but there was room for a bed. Maybe I could a run a few errands in exchange? She had a hard time getting around with her bum leg and some extra weight. "Let me explain a few things about this town," she said. "Everything is out to fuck you over." I thought maybe she was going to explain another thing, but then she didn't.

She made me feel like I could actually do some good. I bought her pink carnations for her fold-up kitchen table, and twelve-packs of donuts to keep in her bedroom. She ate quickly, in secret—her pastries leaving a silt of sugar and crumbs across the sheets. I washed her endless supply of sweatshirts with their cheesy slogans: *PMS stands for Please More Sugar!*, or *My Heart's Locked Up in Lovelock*. I bought little green pills to flush out the worms from her kitty's belly, and a special kind of clear jelly she needed for a scab on her lips. It was an old wound that looked like a forever cold sore. She'd gotten it from chewing on a power cord when she was little. I tugged her shitty hose all around the trailer—it was knotted like a little girl's hair and so rusty it trickled red— and tried to water her withered garden. Fool's work. The plants wanted to die under all that sun. I finally let them.

Fiona didn't ask about my life or how I'd been living in Reno, but she said she had a lot of respect for my survival skills. She knew I'd been surviving somehow. If she ever got to know me well enough, she'd find out I'd been ruined like everything else, ruined by men and drugs and the sound of my own hand hitting my mother's face.

I think she wanted my company more than my favors. The little chores, we called them. We figured out small ways to pass the endless hours of our lives. We watched old black-and-whites and guessed which femme fatales would fall in love with the detectives, which ones would kill them, and which ones would do both. Sometimes we rooted for the Utah Jazz on television. They were the closest we had to a sports team of our own. We didn't talk about our most private feelings or our histories, but you realize there's a whole set of things to say to someone that aren't about you or the other person.

At least I was another beating heart in the room. That can mean something, I think, depending on your situation. One time Fiona pulled off my sneakers. "If you're running around all day for me," she said, "I want to see your feet." She took out a cream that smelled like peppermint and started kneading circles into the roughest patches—the back of my heel, the ball of toughened sole. "Just relax," she said. "You don't have to point your toes." She kneaded the joints until I felt my whole foot go loose, a bunch of minor bones caught in the net of my tough skin.

I reached for the lotion once she was done, but she stopped me. She said she didn't want another person to see her feet for the rest of her life. They showed her age.

"Plus," she said, "I'm not done with you yet." She stood behind me and massaged my back—with her bare hands this time, fingers twisting under the collar of my shirt—until I could feel the knots dissolving into muscle like lumps of sand.

When she kissed me, her scar brushed against my lips. Its edges were rough like sandpaper. "Is this okay?" she said.

"Yes," I said, and then I kissed her back, stuck my tongue into the warm well of her mouth. "I want this," I whispered. "I really do."

I started paying for my room once we got involved. I told her we couldn't get money mixed up in what we were doing together. I wanted to keep things separate. I was still doing jobs for Bruce a few times a month, taking the Reno bus. I told Fiona I was going shopping. "You never *buy* anything," she said. "Or else you never show me."

But once I started paying rent, I couldn't hide it. Telling her straight after all that time made me realize what a burden the lying had been.

"You know I don't judge," she said. "But I can't stand the thought of you sleeping with those guys to make my rent."

I told her I wanted to pay an honest price.

She made good money selling cosmetics over the phone, and she probably could have lived somewhere nicer than a trailer. But she'd given up on the world by then, assumed she was destined for ugliness and there was no use trying to get out of it. She had a comforting voice and worked with a headset. She leaned back in her yellow recliner and told women how pretty they'd be. *It's got this sparkle to it,* she'd say. *Your eyes will look like jewelry.* They must have imagined her young and thin, strolling inside some kind of greenhouse, running her fingers over tropical flowers to find words for all the shades of her eye shadow. When really, truth be told, every green was an impossible miracle under the bright white bone of our sun.

When I came home from one of the worst nights—*You're one lucky whore*—she nearly pulled out my hair, yanking back my head to see the bruise on my neck. I flinched from her grip.

"God," she said. "You're so afraid. You're so fucking *afraid*." She folded me into her huge warm body and rocked me back and forth until she felt better and I told her I felt better, too.

I was still seeing Abraham a few times a month. Sometimes we fucked and talked. Sometimes we just fucked. Even his smallest questions—what did I think of this weather? this kind of soda?— made me feel seen, as if there were more of me because I was something to him.

Fiona's leg was getting better, but the rest of her body was getting worse. I slept in my own bed most nights because it was more comfortable for both of us. It was a strange thing to be a woman with another woman, like a wave breaking across water. Everything was made of the same stuff, but still—there was an event.

I saw her body in pieces: thighs spiderwebbed with blue veins, a big belly loose with folds of skin. She had the kind of crimson stretch lines you'd get from a baby, but I never asked if she had kids. Once I found a scar hidden between folds of flesh.

"What's this from?" I asked.

"I got this nasty bug in my side," she said. "My friend had to dig it out."

I kissed the cut. I waited until she'd fallen asleep that night, and then I pulled off her thick white socks. Her feet were soft white paddles in the darkness. She woke up laughing. "Jesus Christ!" she said. She was groggy, sweet to me and playing.

My first orgasm surprised me. I'd come plenty of times—my body private between sheets, face muffled in the pillows, hand clamped between my legs—and I'd been with plenty of people. But the two things had never happened together.

She wanted me to tell her what I'd felt. I wasn't sure I could find words for it, but I tried. *This one felt like popping buttons off a shirt,* I said. *Those were claws scuttling around my womb. That was like custard turning thick on the stove.*

One time a bird got trapped inside our trailer, knocking its beak like crazy against the windows even though we had the door wide open. I felt sorry for it. I couldn't understand why it was stupid enough to stay. It was moving so fast it gave off heat, like a little lightbulb covered in feathers. *You ever feel a bird heart under the ribs?* I asked Fiona. It was gunfire knocking against toothpicks. *I want it out,* she said, and smacked it with a broom so hard it died. She wasn't the same woman that I'd met by the ocean.

I got pregnant during the summer. *Armpit summers,* Fiona called them, because it felt like her whole body was inside one. Some people call it dry heat. Fuck that. It doesn't let you stay dry anywhere, leaves you sweating all over everything.

Late in June, I spent the night with an asshole in Reno who kicked me out with no shower. He insisted we do it on the carpet because he didn't want to sleep in a dirty bed afterward. I left him buck-naked on his clean sheets and found myself waiting for a bus before dawn. His dried-up cum was peeling off my skin, crispy as doughnut glaze in my belly button.

It got hot fast, soon as the sun rose. I was sweating all over the bus seat, thighs smearing the rubber like buttered toast. I could smell my own cunt, which I liked because it was mine. I thought about that man's face—the way his cheeks shook back and forth, all wobbling and red—and it made me so sick I ran up the aisle. The driver was a big guy with a visor, sipping a Slurpee. I tapped his shoulder and told him to stop, swallowing as hard as I could. I pointed at my stomach in case he didn't get it.

He said, "Lady, we're on the highway."

I said, "You want this happening on the bus or off it?"

He pulled onto the shoulder, and I bent over the tar. The heat burned my knees when I knelt. I got the mess of vomit all over my teeth. It was pudding made of fever. What if someone drove by and thought I was praying?

I got back on the bus, and everyone was shooting me dirty looks. I was just another slut with a hangover. But the driver turned out to be a decent guy. He gave me some melted gum from his pocket and a little bell off the dashboard. "Next time you need a stop," he said, "just ring it."

One time I'd gotten sick and Lucy gave me a little metal chime shaped like a triangle. "Ring it anytime," she said. "I don't want you getting up."

I only chimed it once.

"What do you need?" she said. She smoothed my hair. "You want some ice?"

I shook my head. I just wanted her to stay.

I stopped at the bathroom in the Lovelock bus depot, full of the clotted smell of week-old urine. The walls were covered with phone numbers and scraps of slang. Some I couldn't even understand: *Jenny Razormouthed My Squad Car.* I'd felt my period on the bus, a warm wet seeping. Lucy claimed that all the women in our family knew it deep down before they started bleeding, but she never said "bleeding," only "it" or "that way."

Turned out my underwear was bleach-white. Which was funny because I'd been waiting for a couple weeks. I wasn't worried about getting knocked up, I'd had years of sex and nothing to show for it. But now I was waiting. I kept waiting for weeks, started throwing up nearly every day. I drank mint tea even though it was so fucking *hot* because it was the only thing that kept my stomach quiet. I finally bought a store test, not as fancy as the ones they sell now. The tiny pink cross was like the neon sign of a highway church. I pictured the fetuses I'd seen on television. Their skin glowed like dawn was breaking behind them.

I couldn't stop thinking about the bus driver. His fat smooth skin had made me want to touch it; his big fingers; that little bell. His eyes had been dark like television screens. This was all I had in the night: the big ghost of a bus driver behind my eyelids, the shabby kindness of a perfect stranger.

When I told Fiona, she gave me a big smile and then ashed over the arm of her dirty yellow recliner. "We'll celebrate," she said. "You'll buy champagne." Her voice was flat, but I was glad for the permission. I couldn't imagine an entire pregnancy without getting drunk. But here she was, saying, *Tonight, at least, we can have this.*

At the grocery store, I got pink champagne wrapped in cellophane, a big log of raspberry coffee cake, a whole rotisserie chicken in mashed gold foil. *Watch that junk,* Lucy would have said. *You're eating everything your little baby will be made of.*

We curled together on the love seat and picked chunks of cake with our fingers. We fed each other, our bodies so snug we forgot about them. We were weightless and warm. Fiona drank so much she fell asleep. She was too big to get tipsy, but when her blood got drunk, she was done, out cold. Snores so big they wobbled her whole body.

I had a terrible feeling in my gut, a stitch in my side like the kind you get from running. I was fabric somebody had ripped. There was a throbbing between my hips, and that's where I'd been torn. The hurt place was the same place my baby was growing. I drank a little more champagne—last time, promised myself— and then I found a bottle of gin. I got so drunk I wasn't walking straight. I banged my hip against Fiona's card table. One leg buckled, and all the food toppled onto the carpet. My hip was ringing like a funny bone. I lifted up my shirt and touched under my belly. "Sorry," I said. "Sorry."

I found the rest of the coffee cake, gouged where our fingers had been at it, and the leftover chicken. The ribs were mossy from carpet fuzz. I threw them away and took the gin into the hallway closet. I shut the door. Fiona wouldn't wake up, but just in case she did. I crouched underneath a row of dresses she kept from younger days, gowns that showed flashes of color in the dark: orange and green, a cocktail number in teal that she'd worn to nightclubs. I wiped my fingers on the carpet so I wouldn't get oil and crumbs on their fabric. They were one of the things she loved best.

I took steady sips. Kept swallowing. A stain bled across my whole life and I was glad for it, like someone had covered every memory with a blanket. I remember the swallowing getting stronger—that regular rhythm, like a clock—letting the spit pool and then pushing it back to swallow again: swallowing until there wasn't any room left inside me; swallowing until it got to feel like breathing. I drank until my throat hurt, and then I drank some more. I lost my edges. I wanted to throw up but I had this fear that if I threw up too hard I'd startle the baby, shake its bag or rip it open from heaving. I know you're not supposed to call it a baby—the little it, the absolute tiniest—but I felt that way about my son from the beginning.

Ever since I was a little girl, I'd imagined having a baby, painting a big room in a big house with blue stripes or flowers and hushing it—*sshh, sshh*—every night to sleep. And now this: no room to decorate, only a box built onto the side of Fiona's taken-roots trailer. I'd been with men while it was inside me, nothing more than a wad of clots and vinegar, I knew that, but all the same it wasn't fair. I'd messed up before I even knew I was messing up. I wanted to do this one thing right.

Some women clutch their momma stories close, the hows and wheres and whens of making another life. Lucy had told me how she'd started drinking water straight from the Atlantic Ocean when she was pregnant with Dora. She'd skimmed waves with her fingers and then cupped her hands to drink. My story was the ugliest one I could think of, vomiting on the highway and waiting to bleed in the desert, eating myself sick between the outsize dresses of another woman's brokedown dreams.

I knew Abraham was the father. It was the only way the timing worked. But I didn't want to explain this to him, to say, *this other man was too early, this one too late,* to admit how many men there'd been. I stopped going to Reno altogether. One day he called me. "Bruce told me," he said. "I want to know if it's mine."

I told him yes, I was sure.

He'd been thinking long and hard, he said, and he wanted to adopt. Only if this was something I wanted also. He thought he could give this kid a decent life. "Not like you couldn't," he explained. "Of course you could." But there was the question of money.

I told him I needed a few days. We got off the phone and I couldn't think of a single good reason I should raise the baby myself. I wanted him so badly but everywhere I looked, every part of my own life, made me hate the idea of bringing a little person into the middle of it. I was still drinking. I knew it was wrong, and some nights I was good—some nights I ate a plate of pasta and forced myself to fall asleep before I could stay awake long enough to get drunk. Other nights I'd say *just one.* Just a glass of wine or an inch of gin. And then I'd find myself lying flat on the bed, ceiling gone all swimmy, holding my belly and saying, *I'm sorry. I'm sorry. I'm sorry.*

One morning I woke up on the bathroom floor. I couldn't even remember how I'd gotten there. My face was flat against the tiles near the toilet. Had I been throwing up? I couldn't remember that, either. I called Abe right away. I told him okay. He should raise this baby. I went to Reno every three weeks, and we saw a doctor together. I sat on the paper-covered table, and Abe sat on a chair and watched. There were so many questions. *What are you eating and how much and are you feeling sick? Do you feel any cramping any kicking any sudden blood rushes when you stand too quickly?* I tried to answer as honestly as I could. But it was hard: Abe was right there, watching. I lied about two cigarettes in the third month and made up a banana for breakfast every day. I lied about the drinking. Of course I lied about the drinking. I couldn't stand to imagine Abe's face. If he could have seen the long nights, how I filled the curve of my belly with sweet long pulls of gin until the baby must have nearly drowned. Some mornings I woke up with crusty cheeks and I knew they'd gotten that way from tears. I got so drunk I couldn't even remember crying.

The doctor's office had photos of what happened to babies when their mothers got drunk: their sloppy little faces, wide mouths and wet-clay noses. But they seemed far away from us, Abe with his solid body standing proud next to mine. It was his baby more than ours—he had the rights, we had a deal—but still, he took good care of my body because of what I held for him. I wanted to keep that feeling, at least. It was the only good thing I had left. *Your wife looks beautiful,* one nurse told Abe. *A big beautiful boat.* He smiled and put his hand on the small of my back.

Fiona didn't like my trips to Reno. "If he cares so much," she said, "why doesn't he come here?"

I said he was busy, which was true. How could I explain how desperately I'd pleaded: *You can't come here. Please don't.* I didn't want him to see how I lived.

I pictured the forming skull inside of me, a tiny ball of cookie dough that would someday hold the gray of brain, wet knuckled eyes, spidery lashes. I wanted to put my ear next to my own skin just to hear both liquid pulses: one in the heart and another in the gut.

Sometimes Fiona looked at the bulge in my stomach like the

devil had put his seed there. We didn't sleep together anymore, and we certainly weren't doing anything else. One night we tried, near the beginning of my last trimester—our two large bodies lying on her too small bed, our forehands touching, her hands fumbling past the lump of my belly to get her fingers under the elastic of my underpants. I turned away. "Let's try to sleep," I said.

She wanted to know if something had changed. I told her everything had changed. My privacy wasn't mine anymore. It belonged to me and him. I knew I'd only have him a few more months. I didn't want her hands or her breath on the skin around his home.

During the eighth month I found a note. *Rent is covered for the year,* she'd written. I stopped reading. I sat down with a cup of orange juice. After one sip I felt the need to pee, the pang running through me like electricity. She'd left for good.

I knew she wasn't coming back, but in my head everything was still *Fiona's chair, Fiona's fridge, Fiona's closet.* My water broke in her shower. I took a towel from the rack and felt the water coursing between my legs, as if the nozzle was still running. *Okay,* I thought. *Here we go.*

The nurse at the hospital asked if I'd come alone. I told her I had. *Qué linda,* she said, and stroked the hair away from my face. I was already pretty dilated. Her shift ended at midnight, but she came back in jeans and a light pink sweater and held my hand. She counted through the contractions: *uno, dos, tres . . . treinta y ocho, treinta y nueve, cuarenta . . .* I learned the Spanish numbers higher than I'd ever known them before.

I remember wanting to scream and also wanting to shit. I remember they gave me shots for the pain, but I don't remember which ones. I remember feeling like I couldn't do anything more until my body gathered up and said: *Yes, you can. You will.* I remember pushing with secret muscles tucked between my spine and crotch.

His body was purple and quivering with the force of his screams. When they lifted his head I was the first one who saw his face. His forehead was creased like he was worried and the skull looked soft as putty. His mouth was a round hole where the crying came from, opened wide enough to push folds of skin over his eyes, lips stained dark like he'd been eating blueberries. I thought: *Here he is.* The one thing I would never regret.

TELLA

We left for Lovelock in the early morning. Tom sat in the passenger seat of my Camry. "This little shitkicker of yours," he said. "I wouldn't trust it past city limits."

But here he was, coming along. "If you're planning to do this," he said, "you shouldn't do it alone."

It was the part of him I could count on most: not knowing what he would choose or want. He was carrying a letter to Matilda from our mother. She'd been intentional about this, and very clear. It was for him to carry, not me.

On my road map, Lovelock was nothing more than a bump on the red vein of Highway 80. It was hardly a pinkie finger north of Reno. Sherman, the lawyer, was sending his notification in a week. I wanted to reach Matilda before his letter did. Sherman's voice had the feel of bleached fabric, and he referred to Matilda as the "severed member," as if she were a thumb.

The freeways were nearly empty. I thought of the other drivers with their knotted stomachs, fingers jittery from coffee and hooked around steering wheels. My own hands were clenched tight, my fingers curled into claws, knuckles flooded white as if they'd been steeped in milk.

The outer suburbs looked desolate outside our windows, the bleary outlines of a dream we hadn't woken from: long strip malls full of auto dealerships and outlet stores. These towns had names like Rancho Cucamonga and Diamond Bar. Their parking lots lasted for miles.

Tom slept beside me. He'd gotten our mother's delicate looks, the beakish nose and long lashes. The tendons of his neck pushed taut against his skin like the strings of an instrument you could play. He was the kind of man you'd see and think, *Now, there's a smooth operator. A real heartbreaker,* but then he'd surprise you by stammering or blushing, tripping over his words or a chair leg.

He hated my timid driving. Nervous Nelly, he called me. My brakes made a horrible grinding sound. We felt them like ragged kneecaps, bone sliding against bone. Tom didn't have patience for people slowed by their fear—their ambivalence, or their shitty cars, or their cowardice. *It's your responsibility to figure out what you want and pursue it,* he'd told me. Now I was finally driving fast and he wasn't even awake for it.

Tom had always been strange to me. Though I sensed he felt strange to everyone. I'd seen him once with a girl in our basement. He was holding a switchblade, snapped out and gleaming, but he wasn't hurting the girl who had her head in his crotch. He was cutting the underside of his own arm, where the skin was hairless and pale. It was a big knife. He was drawing it back and forth like the bow of a violin. His mouth opened to an O—he gasped abruptly, like a hiccup—and then he smiled. She kept going. But he was done. He leaned back and closed his eyes.

I didn't know what it was about, but I knew it wasn't about her. I could never trace the sources of his hurt or desire back to other people. They were closed circuits that began and ended with him.

One time he took me to the pier at night—not *to* the pier, quite, but underneath it. The salt-sodden planks were studded with barnacles that reminded me of Forklift, our spaniel, Tom's spaniel, her skinny rib cage bumpy with pink nipples beneath the fur. She had so many! Even though we'd spayed her young.

In the dark down there, chattering men swathed like babies parked their shopping carts and jammed their wheels with sand. They used beeping canes to look for underground gold. Tom handed me a plastic bag full of nuts and bolts. "We're going to plant them like seeds," he said. "Everywhere we can."

I did it because his invitations were scarce and precious, but for years I thought of those bundled ghosts, gripping their machines with rag-mittened fingers, pausing patiently to dig up our burials, disappointed every time.

We stayed in a peeling-paint motel off Highway 15. Guys in jogging suits bummed cigarettes from other guys in jogging suits; boys carried unplugged televisions in their arms, holding plastic bags of chips and candy between their teeth. Tired-looking women emerged from some doors and disappeared into other ones. I thought of Alice, who would have known how to tell stories about this place. She would have enchanted it.

In our dingy room, Tom pulled out his BlackBerry. The buttons glowed in the darkness, sending messages everywhere on earth. He typed with speed and purpose.

"What are you doing?" I asked. "Buying a company?"

He smiled. I'd found the right thing to say, and then I'd said it. This was a good feeling. Sometimes I was afraid it was the only good feeling I had left.

I convinced him to go swimming. I wore an old shirt and boxers I'd stolen from Louis to remember him by. Now they were going to smell like chlorine, not like a man, and they weren't going to remind me of Louis so much as they'd remind me of myself, missing him one night in a motel pool in the middle of nowhere.

I felt proud to watch Tom's body gliding through the dark hide of the water, to see him living inside these moments I'd imagined into being. He ended up staying longer than I did.

Back in the room, while he was still in the pool, I found Tom's backpack. It held three energy bars, one bottle of water, and a brown folder marked MEYER ACCOUNT. There was an envelope with Matilda's name written in cursive. Mom had written on a piece of card stock with her own name embossed in gold at the top.

> *Dear Tilly,*
>
> *I hope you have found a life that brings you happiness. I have never wished you ill, though I know you often thought I did—and told me this, so many times—but the truth today, as ever, is this: I wish you only the best. Though I hope you realize this letter doesn't imply a desire to communicate with you further or otherwise resume our relationship. I didn't want there to be any confusion.*
>
> *All best,*
> *Dora*

I watched Tom sleep that night: chest moving up and down, mouth open. His nostrils flared slightly, and his hands made loose fists. He was powering up, gathering secret energies for the day to come. During kindergarten, the only way I could fall asleep was if he slept on my floor. *No skin off my back,* he'd said. One time I woke up and saw his eyes, close and staring, bright whites in the dark. *You breathe faster than any other human being,* he whispered. *I counted.*

* * *

Lovelock looked like a mining boomtown that hadn't ever boomed. The main streets were named after Ivy League colleges.

They were hard to tell apart. There was a billboard that quoted *Time* magazine calling Lovelock the Armpit of America. Someone had spray-painted underneath: *Thanks for Noticing,* and over that: *Thanks for nothing.*

We had nothing but an address in our pockets and the long hours of the day in front of us. "Let's wait until tonight," I said. "She's probably working anyway."

"We can do it how you want." Tom shrugged. "I don't think Sherman found out what she did for a living." He seemed relieved as well. Neither one of us was ready to find her, and neither one of us was ready to admit it, and our biggest consolation was that we could agree about this without having to confess it explicitly.

We found a rusty trailer with a flapping wooden sign that said *Visitors Here!* as if a flock of tourists were trapped inside. At the desk, a woman named Shelley paused her game of solitaire to tell us about local attractions. There were silver mines somewhere, collapsed. I pictured them like toothless gums around the hole of an old man's mouth. The courthouse, she explained, was one of only two round courts in the nation. Apparently, an innovation could be remarkable simply because no one else thought it was a good idea. One thing was clear: There wasn't much to do. We would have to work hard to avoid what we'd come for.

Shelley suggested someplace called Rye Patch Reservoir. She squinted at Tom. "Bring sunscreen," she said. "You look like you just crawled out of a cave."

The reservoir was bright and large. The heat made us sleepy. We drank orange soda and watched sparkling flakes of light ripple across the water. We got bored, and then we watched a family get bored nearby. They tried to entertain themselves with plastic pool noodles in the water but finally broke down and ate their sandwiches two hours before noon.

Tom was antsy. Shelley had been right about one thing:

His skin was going to burn, and then it was going to peel right off his body. My own face felt achy and flushed. We didn't last long. Back in town, we found a diner called the Cowpoke Café. Flies hovered above thumbprints of dried ketchup on the tables. When I swatted them away, their bodies felt still and hard as pebbles. The waitress grinned at us. "Hey, city kids," she said. "Y'all hungry?"

Tom ordered curly fries that came in a plastic wagon. It was a specialty of the house, we'd been told; it came with two settler dolls perched on its hard front seat. The fries were a nest of deep-fried snakes ganging up on them from behind.

Tom tried to fold his napkin into a swan. Its wings kept wilting. The regal neck collapsed like a noodle. Tom kept at it. We didn't talk about what we weren't doing.

Our window faced a dingy Laundromat and a gift shop called *Charming Isn't It*. One of us would make a remark. Tom made a remark: "That store should pay for some punctuation."

"Aren't you charming," I said. "Question mark."

Dusk came late. The wind was dusty and hard against our eyes. We waited for sunset before we drove to her trailer park, where the streets' names suggested orchards: Peach, Pear, Fig. The driveways were full of cars that had been junked for parts.

Apple Lane was the farthest back, right up against the desert. Matilda's trailer was more elaborate than most. She'd added a little porch with a barbecue and a dirty white cooler. We paused outside her door. Tom gave me a look as if to say, *Well, it's what we came for,* and I knocked.

We heard a woman's voice—hoarse from sickness or yelling—coming from inside: "I'm not coming out again! I won't!"

"We're not . . ." I called back, leaning closer. "We haven't been here before."

The woman who answered looked like a bloated version of our mother. That was the first thing I thought: *Somebody has swollen our mother,* as if the parts of her face had been soaked in water for a long time. Her hair was pulled into a long braid, dusty brown threaded with silver, and her skin was specked with large pores. She had a belly hanging over the waist of her jeans. She wore a pink shirt that wasn't long enough. She looked like someone from a television show about the American poor, about *white trash.* The moment I thought the words, I shook my head—physically shook my head—to get rid of them again.

"Yeah?" she said. "Can I help you?" Her words were slurred, her voice smoke-wearied.

"Don't close the door," I said. "We're family."

"Whose family? What do you want?"

I smelled something terrible. At first I'd thought it was from the breeze, maybe garbage, but now I realized it was coming from inside. I realized it was coming from her body—not her breath but her body. It was liquor. Her eyes were glassy, and she tripped as she leaned away from the door. I stepped forward and took her elbow.

Tom gave me a look like: *What are you doing?* I widened my eyes back, daring him to speak. "Think about this," he hissed.

I tightened my grip on her elbow and walked her inside. *There's always somebody falling, isn't there? And you catch them.* Her skin was leathery around the elbow, furrowed into dusty wrinkles, and mottled with white sunspots that reminded me of dandruff. The smell was like waking up to the aftermath of parties in college— arms flung over the edge of a couch, strange boy curled behind my back, looking onto a sticky floor littered with crushed cups and reeking of vodka, tequila, rum.

She pulled her arm away. "Who are you?"

"We're here because we're—" I paused. "We're—"

"Just let me go," she interrupted. "I'll get myself to bed."

It was barely seven. I turned her around to face the living room: two pink love seats, a television set whose crooked antenna looked like spread legs. There was a pair of jeans dangling between the rabbit ears.

"I'm sorry," Matilda mumbled. "It's not a good night, is all." I glanced back at the doorway. Tom was standing there. I beckoned him inside. Matilda twisted around. "Are you a friend of Abe's?" she asked. Her voice was lighter, almost hopeful.

"No," said Tom. He looked nervous, shifting awkwardly from foot to foot. I motioned again. He stepped inside.

"I don't know what you came for," she said, flat-voiced again. "But you should go."

Her face was shiny. She needed some water and maybe a cold rag. I turned to Tom and made a twisting gesture that was supposed to suggest faucets. He shook his head and said to me, quite loudly, "I don't know what you're talking about."

I helped Matilda sit. She crossed her legs and then recrossed them. When she moved, her motion had the quality of a drowning woman flailing, as if she were struggling for purchase against surfaces that refused her grip.

I glanced into the kitchen and saw a garbage can piled high with paper towels. A plastic bottle stuck out like a broken limb. I walked closer. The kitchen counter was nearly empty, just a row of plastic tumblers and a couple of limes. I picked up a lime and saw a dark patch near its tip, like a sore. It felt pulpy.

The plastic bottle in the garbage wasn't liquor. It was tonic. I noticed a row of small porcelain cats perched above the toaster. Each one was engaged in some kind of winter play: building a snow-kitty, drinking cocoa with impossibly mittened paws, unpacking stockings by a tiny fire. I walked back to the couch, where Matilda faced me, staring.

"We're Dora's kids," I said. "Your sister, Dora."

"I know who Dora is," she said. She brought her finger to her mouth and bit her nail. I could see the ragged cuticle fringed in red. Here she was, years later, chewing her fingers just like her mother had done—until she hit the quick, tore the edge, drew blood.

She settled her hand carefully onto her lap, as if it were an object she was trying to balance. She was visibly shaking. She said, "It's been a long time." Her voice was full of something thick and wet—phlegm in the throat, the mossy undergrowth of tears.

Tom sighed. I glared at him. "Tom?"

"Your name is Tom?" she said. Her gaze was full of sudden longing. "You look like him."

I started to ask, "Like—"

But didn't finish. There was a knock at the door. It sounded powerful enough to tip the entire trailer.

Nobody moved to answer it.

"Tom?" I said. He stood there for a moment, silent. I said again, "Tom. Answer the door."

He opened the door. There was a small man in an overcoat standing outside, short and bald, with his hands clasped between his legs. "I'm sorry," he said. "I didn't know. . . ." He pulled his coat tighter. "I'm interrupting." He didn't sound anything like his knock. It must have been an effect of the trailer, how it echoed, turning every outside noise into an act of God. We must have sounded like that, too.

Next to me, Matilda put her head in her hands.

"Who is this guy?" I asked. "Do you want him to leave?"

"Yes," she said. "I want him to leave."

I got up and joined Tom at the door. The man looked sheepish, squeezing his hands together as if working up the courage to speak, but he didn't look like he was going anywhere.

"You should go," I told him. "I'm sorry."

"Is she in there?" he said. "She's in there, right?"

"She'd like you to leave," I said. "We'd like you to leave."

"She can call me when she's back," he said. "I know she will be."

I reached across Tom's chest and closed the door. I turned to tell Matilda he was gone, but she was gone, too. "Matilda?" I tried.

"We should leave," said Tom. "She doesn't want us here."

"Did you *see* her?"

"I saw," he said. "I think we should go."

"Matilda?" I called again. I started down the narrow hallway. The walls were full of photos in cheap plastic frames: A young boy held a net of frogs, his expression stiff and sorrowful; the same boy stood at the edge of a cliff at sunset with his arms spread open toward the camera. The sky was like cherry sherbet behind his bowl-top haircut. There was a prom shot: the same boy, recognizable but older, with his hair gelled and his arm draped awkwardly over the shoulders of a pale girl in a mint-green dress. He looked miserable. He looked, it was true, like Tom.

"Matilda?" Nothing.

There was a closed door on my left, probably the bedroom. I knocked—silence—and then opened it very slowly.

It was a closet, not the bedroom. I could see dim shapes: bottles glinting on the floor and the ghostly ribs of a turkey carcass. There was a small stool tucked into the corner. I could pick out flies buzzing in the blackness. The mess rotted quietly, like a festering wound. I pulled a cord. A naked bulb sparked dirty light into the dark, showing an inflatable mattress covered with plastic bottles: empty handles of gin, too many to count. The air reeked like a drunk's breath. There was a pink blanket bunched into one corner, the kind of candy shade a child might choose.

I felt someone behind me. It was Matilda. "Leave it alone," she said.

I closed the door. "Can we just sit down? Just for a second?"

"You should leave," she said. "I'm tired."

She was carrying a plastic tumbler full of something clear. She took another sip, wrapping both her palms around the plastic like a little girl. She was a stranger still, but here were the raw wounds of her eyes, like bandages had been pulled off them.

We sat on the couch. Tom stood by.

Matilda rubbed her temples with her fingers. "Maybe you should come tomorrow," she said. "I'm so fucked tonight."

Tom nudged my back.

"There's something we came here to tell you," I said. "Something we should say right now."

"You're her *kids*?" She shook her head. "Jesus."

How could I tell this woman that her mother was dead? Saying it wrong seemed unforgiveable, but I couldn't think of how to say it right.

Tom cleared his throat. "Your mother is dead."

Matilda shut her eyes and shook her head again.

"She's dead," I said. "We're sorry."

"Sorry?" she said. "You're sorry?"

"I am. I mean, we are."

"Please leave," she whispered. "Like I said." She tipped back the cup and took another gulp of gin, dropping ice on her foot. She didn't seem to notice. I bent to pick it up. "Don't touch me," she said. "Don't *touch* me."

She wanted us to leave. Maybe I wanted to leave. I hadn't made her life, after all, only found it. "Get out," she was saying. "Get out get out get out get out."

I hesitated. I could feel the letter with my fingers, its cool paper, but I didn't pull it out. It had been written to another woman. It was meant for someone who'd run away from hell, but this woman was living right in the middle of it. Our mother hadn't seen this woman, with her cheap blue jeans and her twisted cotton shirt, her glassy eyes, her lurching body. She didn't know a thing about this woman's life.

"I want you to understand," I said. "We thought maybe you'd want to see us."

She was crying like a child. She pawed her tears away in rough swipes, slapping her cheek with open palms to wipe them back into the skin. "I wanted to see you," she said. "I didn't want to be seen."

Outside, I leaned against my car and waited for Tom to speak. He was watching me like he had something to say. What I wanted, more than anything, was to drive away and never come back. Her eyes lingered with me, their hopelessness—like she could see herself as we saw her, feel the force of a disgust we'd done our best to hide. But maybe owning that disgust and sharing it—following it to the furthest places and then following it back again, still clinging—could make up for all those lost years, could turn our plodding silences into the stuff of family.

"Okay," Tom said finally. "Why didn't you give her the letter?"

"You're asking about the letter?"

"Yes," he said. "I am."

"Did you *see*? Did you see what I saw?"

"I got the gist."

"She's got a closet, Tom. Where she drinks. Just a cheap mattress and a pile of empty bottles. There was a stool like somebody had gotten punished."

"She's an alcoholic, Stella. She's clearly got a problem. It doesn't mean—"

"I think she has a son. There were pictures of a boy. That's who she meant when she said—"

"I looked like him?"

"I think so, yeah. But this closet, Tom, I'm telling you, it was something from a fairy tale. Where the bad witch lives."

"The letter was the reason, Stella. The whole point of being here."

"It wasn't my reason."

"Then what?"

"I wanted to tell Matilda her mother was dead, to her face, end this absurd silence. You don't even know what that letter says."

"Neither do you."

I dropped my cigarette and crushed out the glow.

"Isn't that right?" he said. "Neither do you?"

"I wanted to see what we were carrying, okay?"

"But it wasn't *yours,* Stella. It's that simple."

"That doesn't matter," I said. "It's not the most important part."

He shook his head.

"I shouldn't have—"

"You've always been terrible at your own life," he said. He sounded tired. "You're so greedy for everyone else's."

"What's that supposed to mean?" I asked him. But I knew what it meant. There was an emptiness that I filled with other people's secrets. He was right. It was true. It had been true for so long that I couldn't really imagine another kind of life.

In our motel room, Tom switched on the television, and a cop show flickered into focus. A fat woman got hustled off someone's porch. She was hoisting a big cooler of Gatorade. Her shirt slipped off her shoulders, and we saw a flash of breast, no fuzzing. It was cable. From the doorway behind her, a thin man was yelling something about divorce. A voice-over said, "Looks like somebody messed up!"

Tom laughed. We could be easy together every once in a while. We'd had a few good times I could remember. Once he'd given me a jester's cap. *Do a little dance,* he'd said. *Make me laugh.* I rattled my bells to make them jingle. I shuffled my feet. I stuck my hands on my hips and swung around like I was spinning a hula hoop. I got on all fours and scampered like a dog. He clapped harder. My head was down, but I could hear him laughing. *Stella Jester,* he said. *Stella Jester, don't you stop.*

Tonight I wanted to make things right between us. "Let's celebrate," I said. "Let's toast this day going the *worst* possible way it could have gone."

"How Stella of you," he said, smiling slightly. "But we don't have anything to toast with."

"There's a mini-mart down the block."

"After all this? The mini-mart?"

"And I want you to pick up a chaser, too."

On TV, the woman chucked her cooler over the railing while her husband stood by, whistling. Tom stood up. "You better tell me what I miss," he said. "What will happen to this marriage?"

He left the door ajar, but I didn't get up to close it. I sat back. I switched the channel. There was a show about sharks. It wasn't about sharks that were alive. It was about sharks that were dead, and the dead animals you could find inside them. Fishermen cut open their gray bellies to show pink-muscled chambers of jellyfish, silverfish, condom wrappers, metal cans of oxygen. They found octopus tentacles and the bright orange wristbands of deep-sea divers.

When Tom came back, the TV screen showed a pulpy tub full of brine and pickled human remains. "Jeez!" he said. "Divorce is worse than I thought."

I muted the program. "What did you get?"

"I wanted gin, but it felt like bad juju."

He'd gotten whiskey. We filled the motel's plastic cups with amber fingers and drank them quickly, clamping our throats against the heat. We watched fishermen bloodying their arms as they searched for scraps that might pinpoint the identities of the dead.

* * *

I woke with a hangover, eyes glossed and lashes flecked with bits of sleep. Tom and I eyed each other guiltily, like strangers who'd just slept together. We'd have to talk about the night before, though neither of us wanted to.

"I'm staying out of it," he said.

I told him I was going back to her trailer.

"But why would it—" He cut himself off. "Okay."

I stood there silently.

"But give her the letter, yeah? She has the right to see it."

Matilda was strangely animated when I arrived. She kept rubbing her fists with her eyes like a child waking up from a nap, and I wondered whether she'd taken any pills since I'd seen her. Her eyes were red like beets. She had a look that I recognized from my mother. It was a look that suggested emotions happening just past your line of sight: a grief so deep you'd never be able to see it, a love so fierce it could swallow itself completely. The expression never lingered on my mother's face, but Matilda's didn't flick over the feeling so fast. Her eyes were fixed inside that grief, the twist and wrench of it. It turned her whole face into a grimace. Her breath and body still stank of gin.

She didn't invite me inside, but she didn't tell me to leave, either. I shut the door behind me.

"You came back," she said. I couldn't tell if she was glad or surprised. She smoothed her denim skirt. I felt her gaze on me: my chino slip dress, stained with half-moons of sweat, and chartreuse ballet flats. I was stucco-colored and tasteful, suburban before my time. What did I look like to her? We were quiet.

"So here's what I'd like to know," she said.

"Ask anything."

"What did Lucy get sick with?"

"She didn't get sick. She just got old."

"But what happened, exactly? Did you see her?"

"It was everything," I said. "Falling down, falling asleep, just generally, totally, falling apart. She had this pain on her skin."

"Were you there when she . . . Did you see her die?"

"I did."

"Did it hurt?"

"Not as much as it can."

Matilda bit her lip. She knit her fingers together and cracked her knuckles one by one, all down the line. "I don't even know which parts to ask," she said. "I don't even know where to start."

"You want to know the last thing she said?"

"What?"

"She told my mom she had a run in her panty hose."

"You're shitting me!" She paused, then smiled. "You're not."

I shook my head.

"Goddamn," she said. "She was a stickler. Straight up to the end."

She was still for a moment. Then she started laughing. She laughed so hard her whole body shook. It was so sudden and wordless it felt private. I looked away, embarrassed, and when I looked back, she was still shaking, but it was a different kind of shaking—more of a shuddering—and it wasn't from laughing anymore. She rocked against the couch and hugged her chest.

"What do you need?" I asked. "How can I help you?"

"I do it in the dark," she said. "I can't stop."

I stayed quiet. I let her keep going.

"I turn off the lights and take little sips—just little sips one after another. Then I sleep and I wake up and I think maybe, I don't know, it's stupid what I think, but maybe if there's a door I can close . . . that maybe, I don't know, it's a kind of an ending."

"Other people have this problem," I said. "People get better from it."

"You don't have to say 'this problem,' like I'm an idiot," she said. "I know what's wrong with me."

ing my gaze. The crying had opened something in her the way heat might loosen a sealed envelope.

I trashed the hollow turkey cage first. I found another pile of food, farther back in the shadows: a paper plate caked with ketchup packets and blisters of hardened cheese, an old TV-dinner tray that held the pink husks of shrimp, their tail veins dangling like loose white threads and their shells like fingernail cuttings, crackling and clicking. I smelled old meat and the genital stench of yogurt. There were bags of candy wrappers and crumbled muffins. I touched their grease-bled paper, my fingers feeling for what her fingers had done.

I piled the bottles into bags. Their loose-screwed caps leaked gin onto my fingers. Matilda sat on the couch and watched me going back and forth through the living room, my hands full of empty bags and then my arms full of bulky ones. When I was carrying out the blanket, she stood abruptly.

"Here," she said. "I'll take that."

"It's fine. This is the last of it, practically."

"Please," she said. "Let me take something."

She took the blanket. She folded it neatly on the couch and told me to stay put—would I wait for one second?—while she got something from the back. I waited. She returned and handed me a folded piece of paper. I smoothed it flat. There was a check taped to the middle section. *For Tilly* was written above it, and then below, *You made it!* The check was for thirty thousand dollars. "This is from my son," she said. "For when I'm sober."

That's when she told me about Abe. *My demon miracle,* she said. Her little boy. She'd been working as a prostitute in Reno, and his father was one of her clients. He was a good man, she said, but it wasn't a good situation. "My son's a good man, too," she said. "He works hard."

I remembered the mattress, the furled blanket. I didn't say anything. "What do you want?" she said. "You want me to say I'm like an animal in there? Is that what you want?"

I bit my lip. I said, "That's not what I want."

I felt sick. I sat there silently, trying to keep the foulness from rising.

She said, "You look ill."

I went outside and crouched down, retching onto the hard white dirt. The ground was brittle and crusted from the heavy sun. Nothing came from my mouth except a thread of yellow spit. I looked up. I saw her watching. "I'm sorry," I said. "I didn't mean—"

"She would have hated it, you know."

"Who?"

"Lucy. She would've *really* hated it. How bad it's gotten." She was crying now, softly. "It's a problem I have."

"There was so much," I said. "So many bottles."

"It's never enough."

She was crying harder. I wanted to say, *It'll be okay.* But it hadn't been okay for years. And what could I do to change it anyway? She'd wake up tomorrow in this place—full of the memory of that mattress, the memory of her mother, the memory of that man, whoever he'd been—knocking at her door. The smell might leave—might leave her body and her closet—but it would take a while, and everything else would stay the same.

I took the car into town and came back with supplies: garbage bags, bleach scrubs, air fresheners whose names suggested change and movement: Lemon Breeze, Citrus Flow. I asked Matilda if I could do a little cleaning. She nodded without saying a word, grinding her fingers into the hollows of her temples, barely meet-

It was quiet between us. *Prostitute.* The word felt large, another presence in the room.

I said, "So you were . . . ?" I couldn't finish.

"Not for a while," she said. "It's been five years."

"But before?"

"I'm not proud."

"I just . . . ," I said. "I didn't know."

"I stopped because of him." She pointed at the check. "Because of Abe. He's been supporting me so that I could . . . well, so I could stop."

I could smell it on her breath—not last night's gin but this morning's. It rose from her tongue like smoke.

"My son's been sending checks for years," she continued. "He's a big-time banker in San Francisco, got so much money he doesn't know what to do with it, and a mom living dirt-poor in the middle of Nevada, and what's he supposed to do? It was the best way he could think of to help me out."

I nodded. She told me that he'd called one night and heard it in her voice, how bad it had gotten. He just *heard* it, she said. And I knew exactly what she meant. Now he was done with her until she got clean for good.

"No more money until you give it up?"

"He won't even talk to me. Not until I get better. Until he sees it for himself."

"Sees it?"

"He has this idea about my coming out to him."

"He wants you to live with him?"

"He's lonely," she said. "I'm sure that's part of it."

I tried to imagine a grown man begging his mother to live with him. I imagined their conversation the night he'd realized. *Baby boy,* words slurred, *I'm all alone in the dark,* her cell phone the only light.

I took the letter from her hands. It had been folded and refolded so many times the creases were soft, the paper had gone weak in them. The name on the account was Abraham Clay, and the address was on Harrison Street. The handwriting was neat and cramped, as if great effort had gone into each letter: *You made it!*

"He calls you Tilly?" I said.

Just like Dora did. I still had her letter in my purse.

"Him and everyone," she said. "Everyone except my mother."

I need Matilda where's Matilda she had ideas about ginger.

Of course. Everyone except her.

I asked if she was close with her son.

"Yes and no," she said. "I don't know him very well, if that's what you mean."

I waited.

"But he's the only thing I've ever done that ever . . . Well, he turned out okay, is all I'm saying. Even if I was never much of a mother."

She explained about his father, Big Abe, and all his money. I could smell the gin between her words like punctuation marks. Turned out that ambulances were good business anywhere, but they were especially good in Vegas. Casinos meant heart attacks, knife fights, elderly dreamers collapsed on plush carpeting. Abraham was a shrewd wheeler-and-dealer who'd landed in the rescue business.

Abe had grown up with his father but lived with Tilly for two weeks every summer. "Those were our weeks," she said. "Just the two of us."

She glanced at the kitchen, and I could see it—just a flash of it—this wild, desperate hunger in her eyes. It wasn't even noon.

"Let's leave," I said. "Let's take a walk."

If we were going out, she said, she wanted to change. She put on white pants and a matching blue shell and cardigan. She combed her hair and let it go loose. Her breath smelled like mouthwash. She took a couple of aspirin before we left, said she got headaches from the heat.

Walking the streets of Lovelock felt like being trapped inside a wheezing body during those moments before the end, everything dragging its heels to slow down for good. I heard the flapping of the tourist sign against the metal of the trailer, the windy *clack, clack* of the breathing tube doing the work of Lucy's lungs.

We talked about New York, a city she'd never seen, and I gave her the whole parade: the guys playing handball outside the stop at West Fourth, the famous cupcakes that smelled better than they tasted—*But they smell so good,* I said, *don't get me wrong*—and the time I dropped an air conditioner from my bedroom window. I told her about watching one rat eat the remains of another rat on the subway tracks while the A train rattled closer.

"You're good at describing moments," she said.

That was just it. I couldn't remember my life as anything but these snapshots, small gestures of sight or reaction that were supposed to suggest the larger truths of my existence.

"Do you know many people?" Tilly asked. "Your stories don't have any people in them."

"I know people. Sometimes I think I know too many."

She turned to look at me. "You're very clever," she said. "Just like your mother."

I didn't know what to say to this. I didn't know what it meant for her to say it to me. "I'm not happy there," I said instead. "In New York, I mean."

Here was one of my larger truths: I was lonely, was the long and short of it. I could talk for so long without saying it outright, but it was always there.

"Then maybe you should leave."

She took me to the famous round courthouse. It was round. She showed me padlocks dangling from long metal chains in the town green. "People lock up their love," she explained. "It's local tradition."

"Oh?"

"It may seem stupid to you," she said. "But to some people it means a lot."

We got hot dogs from a vendor on the green and ate them with our fingers. She showed me the town's history like she was proud of it. I guessed she probably was a little bit; this was where she'd spent her life. In any case, there was a bronze plaque: George Lovelock had been a Welsh pioneer following rumors about silver. Local legend claimed he dipped a knife in quinine every morning and licked the powder off the blade just to prove he could. He wasn't sick, not once, until he got so sick he died. This was typhoid, 1907. His last night on earth, he was deep in delirium, carrying a candle into a mine shaft. *His career was its own justification and eulogy.*

I told her about losing my job back in New York. She hadn't even asked what I did for a living. "It was a terrible job," I explained.

"Most of them are," she said. "You gonna get another one?"

"To be honest, I'm not sure what I'm doing next."

"I bet your mother loves that."

My laughter came out like an animal noise, frantic. I was nervous. I still hadn't shown her the letter.

"Dora was always big on planning ahead."

"Don't worry," I said. "She still is."

"What did she think about—you know—about your coming out here?"

"My mother?"

She nodded. She looked genuinely nervous.

I reached into my purse and felt the envelope. I said, "She didn't know what to think."

"Back when I knew her, she always knew what to think."

I pulled out the letter. "This is from her."

She read it in front of me, standing still. I watched her face. Her expression didn't change. She handed it back to me. "So that's that," she said. "There it is."

"She can be hard sometimes," I said. "I know."

She sighed. She was looking off into the distance. She ran one hand through her long silver-streaked hair. The air was getting cooler. The desert was darkening around us. "You know what I need?" she said. "I need a drink."

By midnight, we'd ended up back in the park. The courthouse gleamed white like a tooth in the darkness. We were on the grass with a liter of Gordon's. There were only a few fingers left, glittering like jewelry in the bottle. I was tipsy, but I knew that Tilly had drunk most of it. It was hard to believe an ordinary woman's body could hold so much liquor.

We lay back on the dirt and looked at the stars. There were probably constellations up there somewhere—a question of perspective, really—but my vision wouldn't stay in focus long enough for me to see them.

Tilly's voice was clear and forceful in its drunkenness, thoughts without bodies coming from the nearby darkness. "So what's your big hope?" she said. "Ten years from now, what do you want?"

I thought about this for a long time. My head felt heavy. It was full of liquid that had turned to gel. Answers were trapped in there like bugs in amber. I said finally, "I'd like to do something that gets me out of myself."

"Why's that?"

"I get tired of being stuck inside my own—"

"You're free," she said. "You've got your whole life left."

"I hate when people say that."

She smiled. "I used to hate when people said it to me."

I knew it wasn't right, what we'd done. I'd seen her darkness, and now I was part of it. But it felt so much better out here, two women in the open night. It was easier to speak with our faces in the moonlight, my tongue loose and warm. This was a kind of bravery, too.

I asked about her childhood. What about her summers? I'd heard about the Cape. *You heard about those?* From Lucy, I said. So she talked about the Cape. It seemed to bring her pleasure. I asked her about the bath full of dying sea creatures. Was the story true? Yes, she said. It was. One time Dora pulled the legs off a starfish, and Matilda got angry. *You put that star back together!* And so they arranged its pieces and glued them together to give it a proper burial in the sand.

Tilly told me about the summer she got sick, with a fever so hot she dreamed without sleeping. Lucy gave her a little silver bell and cooled her skin at the tide pools, trickled a sponge full of seawater all over her hot forehead. I imagined my mother collecting specimens the next day, filling a jar with old fever water without knowing, she couldn't have known, how her younger sister's sweat had steamed against the stone-cold Atlantic, found sleep for good.

My mother hadn't known the moments she'd missed between her sister and her mother, and this made me sad for her, for the girl my mother had been.

"I'm off to piss," Tilly said. "I'll be back."

"Out here?"

"Well, the courthouse is sure as fuck closed," she said. "So I guess that means the bushes." She lurched a bit, back and forth, and held the bench for balance.

"You okay?"

"Yeah, yeah," she said. "I'm fine."

Now the stars were clear and sharp. They weren't swimming at all. I was coming back from drunk. The cold was helping. If I squinted, I could see a lobster raising two of its claws toward the moon. It was fighting itself.

Tilly's body hit the ground hard. "Ow," she said. "Did you hear that?"

"Hear what?"

"My ass hitting dirt."

"Yep," I said. "I heard."

We were quiet. I tore up clumps of grass and wiped the dirt between my fingers. She drank the last of the gin. "Well, fuck me," she said. "That's no good." She poured a trickle of liquor into the soil. "I'm trying out here," she said. "It might not look that way, but I am. I've been trying for years."

"It'll be a good change when you move," I said. "A new start."

"A new start!" she said, suddenly loud. "I've fucked up more of those than you could count. I'm always doing them alone."

That was when I first thought it. I couldn't even see it clearly until I suggested it to her—out loud, a little drunk—like a dim constellation, far away, resolving itself against the glaze of my drunk eyes.

"What would you say," I said, "if I said we should move out together?"

It was a long time before she spoke. Then: "I'd say we don't know each other at all."

"What would you say next?"

"I'd say it could be a disaster. I'd say it's not my apartment. I won't have any fucking idea what to do with myself once I—"

"Neither will I," I said. "I'll pay rent until I find a place of my own."

"I'm gonna be starting all over again. It's gonna be a shit show."

"Maybe I could help."

She looked at me and raised her eyebrows. "Can we get one thing straight?"

There was a blade in her voice that I recognized from my mother: *Stella, you come here,* grabbing my arm just before she yelled at me for something terrible I'd done: soap in the fish bowl, crumbs in the bed, getting pregnant by a married man.

"I don't need someone taking care of me," she said. "You think I'm a wreck. I know that. You think I can't see it for myself?"

I took a deep breath. "I never said you couldn't. I just thought—"

"I know," she said. "You want to help."

I stood and brushed the dust off my jeans. "Forget I ever said it."

She patted the ground again. "Sit down already," she said. "Sit down. I just need to know this one thing."

"What's that?"

"Tell me you're not doing it for my sake. And we'll go. We'll do it. You just tell me you're not doing it for me."

"Easy enough," I said. "I do everything for myself."

We called a cab and it dropped Tilly first. She'd stumbled twice on the pavement. I wanted to make sure she got up the stairs to her trailer. And she did, all three of them, without tripping. This was her home. She knew it drunk. This was probably how she knew it best.

The shower was running in our motel room. Tom hadn't closed the bathroom door, and all the mirrors had thick beards of steam. "I'm back!" I yelled.

The plumbing went quiet—always a gathering sound to my ears, like the water was inhaling—and Tom emerged in boxers and a white shirt. He told me he'd taken a flashlight and run into the desert. Then he'd stopped and switched off his light. "It was dark as hell out there," he said. "It was like another planet."

"Neat," I said. I waited.

"How was she?" he said. "How was it?"

"It was good."

"Good."

"Tom?"

"What?"

I told him about the move: my big idea. I told him about Tilly and her son and his big empty apartment—how he was lonely and she knew it, and she was killing herself and he knew it, and there was this crazy plan that maybe they could do it together, for a while, try to make what they'd never had when he was young.

I couldn't stop talking. The more I talked, the more crazy and wonderful it seemed, this plan, so full of hope and absurdity. She was scared to start something new and so was I, truth be told, but I was even more scared to keep doing the same thing for years, trying to explain to other people why it didn't make me happy.

When I was done, Tom asked, "Are you drunk?"

"You think it's silly. You think it's absolutely crazy."

"You can't be serious about this," he said. "We met this woman yesterday."

"She's not a stranger."

"But she *is*. Don't you see? This isn't even about her. You know that as well as I do."

"What's it about?"

"Come off it, Stella. You think Mom didn't know how to be a mother, so you keep trying to play mommy with everyone else—the whole goddamn world, your own grandmother, and now—"

"This isn't about Mom. It's about me. This is my life."

"You don't have a job," he said. "You don't have any money. You've got funny stories about how you live, but that's pretty much it."

"That's exactly what I'm saying. I want something else."

"So play it out for me, Stella: You guys move into some rich apartment with her banker *wunderkind* and you play twelve-steps nursemaid, is that it? You lash her to the bed while she cries out for hooch and tells terrible tales about our terrible mother? While you listen carefully? You keep your crucifix in the pantry?"

"Well," I said. "Somebody's been reading his Al-Anon Bible."

"I don't know a thing about Al-Anon," he said. "I'm just afraid of what you want. You want to see her whole life change in an instant? You want to hear her say thank you?"

I was quiet.

"Well?"

"When did you get so bitter, Tom?"

He sighed. "This is for real?"

"I hope so."

"You've always wanted to turn yourself into a story," he said. "I knew it would get you in trouble someday."

When a young woman leaves New York, a woman of a certain age and promise, it feels like a verdict delivered at the end of a trial. *How long did you last?* someone asked, and the others pretended they did not think of it this way, but honestly they did—lasting meant duration, a mark of weakness or strength. I'd loved the city the way I loved boys, without pride. Maybe it had only loved me for a moment, but I'd kept loving and loving—walking those crowded streets, fumbling for another touch.

"I don't understand why you're doing this," my mother said. "But I suppose I don't have to."

"We're not starting a life together," I said. "It's just a holding pattern. A way to get to know each other for a little while."

"This isn't about her," she said. "It's about you walking out on your own life."

"I'm living my own life."

"I hope you don't think you can save her. I know you want to try."

"That's what Tom said."

"Maybe he was right."

I didn't say anything.

She sighed and asked, "How are you getting out there, anyway? Is there a plan?"

We were driving a U-Haul west. I sold my furniture, flew out to Lovelock, and helped her pack. Tilly didn't have many possessions, but she was very particular about keeping them safe—those cats in their winter mittens, clutching cocoa mugs the size of toenails. It turned out all the cats were gifts from Abe, one each Christmas. "It was habit," Tilly explained. "He probably couldn't think of what else to get." There was room left in the U-Haul once we were finished loading it. "I thought I had more stuff," she said, apologetic. "I guess we didn't need a whole truck."

The drive was long and hot, blurred into hours of sore-limbed fatigue and soggy french fries. We measured time by the gutted rumbling of our truck's broken fan and the growing rashes of sunburn across our window-facing cheeks.

The salt flats took our breath away, weather-bleached and lunar along their crusted shores. They looked like they shouldn't actually exist but then they did, for miles and miles. It was like the world had been dipped in a vat of bleach. Tilly had seen them before, hitchhiking in a truck full of feed-lot chickens with a guy named Pat. He had an Adam's apple that stuck out like a doorknob, and he liked cracking dirty jokes to see if she'd flinch. She'd hated the sound of his voice everywhere, and the gusts of chicken-shit stink. Now she pounded the dashboard with her fist: "I knew they could be this good!"

I imagined how those years must have felt to Lucy—knowing Tilly was out there, not knowing where she'd gone. She'd made her daughter's hurt young body, the one so prone to these abandonments. She'd seen that body ache. She'd known it well.

* * *

At a rest stop, we saw a trucker rattling vending machines with his fists, scratching his own arms in fits of panicked flurry. Tilly recognized what he'd done to his teeth and skin. "He's probably tweaking," she said. We watched him suck his open sores. She whispered in my ear, "He wants to get the last meth from his blood."

We stopped at a motel that took the desert wind like a beating. The air moaned past our windows and rattled their glass. The lobby walls were hung with oil paintings of sailboats, windmills, puppies in cowboy hats. I skipped dinner and slipped into bed with an ashtray and a pack of cigarettes. I still enjoyed this sometimes—going to sleep hungry so I'd wake up feeling light, falling asleep in the foul smoke.

The phone rang once, twice. I picked it up. The line was dead.

A few moments later, it rang again. I picked it up: no one. It was either a wrong number, or else it was Tilly. She was sleeping in a room downstairs.

Her door was unlocked. I pushed it open. "Hey," I said. "Did you call?"

There wasn't any answer. The room was perfectly untouched except for a paper bag crumpled at the foot of the bed.

"You don't have to stay," Tilly called from the bathroom. "I'm feeling better."

"Better?" I said. "What's wrong?"

I heard the toilet flush. The long mirror behind the television showed a sliver of the bathroom. Tilly was kneeling in front of the toilet. I walked to the bathroom threshold but couldn't force myself farther. "I'm sorry," she said. "I didn't mean for you to see this."

It smelled like vomit and corporate jasmine. She'd sprayed an air freshener. The odor reminded me of Lucy—not how she usually smelled but how she'd smelled one time when my mother took us out to dinner. "I know Dora's used to fancy restaurants," she'd said. I guessed it had been a while since she'd seen one. Her eye shadow had been absurd that night, too dark, her floral dress bright and starched around her shoulders.

I ran a hot bath. I wasn't sure if baths were good for drunks—maybe they only deepened the fog of the liquor, bled out the mind through the pores—but I wanted to give Tilly something nice against her skin. The bubbles scattered like beard stubble across the water. She soaked while I watched a true-crime program on TV. *She filled a bath to bring them back to life.* The show was about an alligator farmer who'd been murdered. Everybody thought it was his stepdaughter, only fourteen, but nobody had any proof. They all knew he'd been raping her anyway. Not raping, exactly, but whatever you call it when somebody says yes but doesn't know what's good for them.

Tilly took so long I was afraid she'd fallen asleep in the water or passed out from the heat. I knocked on the door to make sure she was okay. Her voice came back a moment later: "You can go. I'm fine."

Later, I would learn to recognize this—the hope that if she waited long enough, I'd simply go away. More than anything, she hated looking like a fool.

She came out in a clean white bathrobe. Her hair was dark from water, the twined colors of stained wood and steel gray. She jerked one hand through its dripping nest.

"I can comb it," I said. "If that's easier."

I'd never had a younger sister or even a girl cousin, anyone.

She didn't reply but sat on the edge of the bed, like she was giving me permission, and I sat cross-legged behind her, running a comb through each section until it hung perfectly straight down her back.

"What happened?" I asked her.

"It felt better," she said, "and then it didn't."

I pulled her hair from the teeth of the comb and gathered the woolly tumbleweed in my closed fist.

"I just thought . . ." She paused. "I thought, *once more*."

I ran my palm along the slick curve of her scalp. "It's all brushed out."

"You're good at that," she said. "Dora always yanked so hard."

"Yes," I said. "I know."

I found her naked in bed the next morning, sheets flung aside. Her face and body were covered with a jaundiced sheen. She sat up slowly, tapping her fingers against the blanket. She balled one hand into a fist, then shoved it under a pillow. I realized she had tremors. She was trying to hide them. "Well," she whispered. "I guess we should hit the road." I could hardly look at this woman: skin pale, eyelids fluttering, hands scuttling like animals across the bedspread.

"No," I said. "We're going to do this here."

Four days, I told her. No liquor. I gave up my room upstairs and moved into hers.

"You're not supposed to stop cold," she said. "You know that, right?"

I saw the look in her eyes—like a net she'd fling in any direction, at anyone, just to get what she wanted: the clear sauce, the warm silk of it down her throat. I thought about that word *drunk*, its funny vectors—as if she had been the one consumed, sucked down, polished off. Her lips were brittle as corn husks.

She had a hangover and a bad case of the shakes. Her mouth was so dry it hushed her voice. "It's like my throat is stuffed with moths," she whispered. I was coming to learn that she always had a clear picture of what could happen inside her body, even when she was hurting it: tumors clustered like blueberries in her breasts, liver flushed and spongy from toxins, liquor trickling through her veins like an old man's urine. She had a language. Her words were ugly, but they were the ones she meant.

I went to a grocery store to pick up food and bottled water. I asked the woman at the cash register, "What's the vitamin for detox?"

She gave me a look like I was crazy.

"I'm sorry." I fumbled for my credit card. "Never mind."

"Hold on a sec." She picked up her intercom. "Paging Freddy." Her voice boomed loud. "Freddy, counter sixteen."

A man showed up a moment later. He had big hands and a pistachio-shaped scar beneath his eye. He'd come from the meat department, according to his badge, and his smock was stained with blood.

"Freddy," the woman said. "This girl wants to know about a *detox* vitamin?"

He folded his arms across his chest and looked at me kindly. "That's B1 you're looking for," he said. His eyes were full of pity. "Good luck."

I sat in my car in the parking lot and couldn't bring myself to turn the ignition. I thought of our motel room—Tilly on the bed, not knowing what to say—and I felt tired and taxed, ridiculous. I pulled out my cell phone and stared at it for a long time, flipping it open and closed again. I wanted there to be someone, anyone, whose name came easily to mind.

Louis picked up before I even heard the phone ring. I wasn't ready for his voice.

"Stella," he said softly. "I thought you were moving."

"I have," I said. "I am."

There was a pause. I could hear honking and then the wail of a siren, the sounds of those streets.

"How are you?" he asked.

"I've been better."

"The thing is," he said.

He and his wife, they were having a baby.

Just past midnight I woke up to flushing. The bathroom door was open. Tilly was sitting on the toilet, her cotton shirt clinging to her body. "I had a dream," she said. "You wouldn't believe." There'd been a dog, she said, pawing at her arm like it had buried bones beneath her skin—as if her bones were *its* bones, buried away—and now it was digging them back up. "My whole arm was shredded like string cheese," she said. "That's the last part I remember."

She was blinking very fast. Her skin was pale but her cheeks were flushed. Her hair had the ragged quality of fur. *She's a woman,* I told myself. *A woman.*

"You should sleep," I said.

"I can't."

I turned to leave. I felt guilty. I felt tired.

"Stella?" she said.

I turned back.

"Did you have to piss?"

I nodded.

"Then go ahead," she said. "I'm not a cripple."

"Thanks."

She walked slowly. I steadied her elbow. "It'll get better," I said. "Tomorrow's another day."

"Another day," she said. "I can't wait."

I woke to find her lying in a fetal position, clutching her stomach. She stayed that way the whole morning. "Something is *wrong* in there," she said. Her sweat made patterns like Rorschach blots on the sheets: a stag with broken horns, an infant with two heads, a syringe stuck in a thumb.

She said she wasn't hungry, but I made food anyway: hot-pot noodles, soup in the microwave, macaroni and cheese from a box

covered in cartoons. "Can you take that stuff outside?" she asked. "The smell is making me sick."

She accepted salted crackers, butter cookies, nothing else. She took the vitamins I fed her every morning. I hid the bottle and told her they were pills from a doctor.

"What can I do?" I said. "Tell me."

She sighed. "I'm not supposed to go off it like this."

I shook my head.

She was so goddamn bored, she said. She was losing her mind. She wasn't used to all this time—hours after hours after hours of this wide-awake and breathing. Maybe I could distract her?

"Tell me stories like that woman," she said. "The one who told them for all those nights."

"Scheherazade?"

"Yeah," she said. "You be her."

I told her about my own problems. At least they weren't hers, I told myself, and the truth was I hadn't talked about them for a while. I missed them like old friends.

I told her about starving myself for two years straight, waking up so hungry in the middle of night that I snuck down to the basement of my dorm and found a jar of peanut butter in a Dumpster. I crouched down and stuck my finger into the jar and licked it clean, over and over again, until I caught sight of a mouse running past a crumpled plastic bag and thought, *This is when I stop*. I couldn't bear the thought of those empty hours without sleep or company, the hours that kept repeating themselves in front of me.

I told her about skipping breakfast and getting dizzy from early-morning cigarettes. I told her I'd done eight miles on the treadmill every morning. I could hear the old pride creeping back.

She didn't say anything. I couldn't tell if she was interested or in pain. I didn't know what was happening inside her body, only that it hurt.

"What did your family say?" she asked. "Your mother?"

"She helped," I said. "She tried."

I want to be proud of you, she'd said. She said the starving was the most confusing thing I'd ever done.

I showed Tilly a college ID from that year. Her breath came out in a long sigh. "You can see it in your face," she said. "You look sad."

"I don't even know why I still keep this in my wallet."

"You don't?" she said. "I think you do."

Telling her these stories, the old fear returned—the fear that nothing would ever feel as good as that pride had felt. One day on the subway, during the worst of it, I caught a glimpse of myself in the darkened glass: a pair of ghoul eyes peering sideways above my cheekbones. I watched the other people on that car—the old man with his violin, the woman with a slouching baby, and thought there was no way a stranger could see me without thinking, *She's given up on something.* All of them were coming up with stories about what made me look the way I did. I switched positions and clutched the pole from another angle, this way they could see me from all sides, the stick of my profile and the protrusions of my shoulders.

When we broke into sunlight on the other side of the river, pushed up from our underwater tunnel, I lost my own face in the darkened glass. I looked around at the strangers, and none of them was looking at me. They'd been looking before, hadn't they? *Maybe I'm going crazy? Could I be going crazy?* Nobody was looking; there was only my sick useless need for them to see. I raised my hands to cover my face *oh my God* and then the subway lurched and my hip banged into the seat and I clutched the hard plastic for balance.

"You better sit down," the old man said.

"I'm sorry," I said. "I'm sorry."

He was only a stranger. And there I was, crying harder, still standing. He shook his head and handed me a pack of tissues and shuffled off at the next stop, the hospital that specialized in ears and mouths and throats. What kind of help did he need? Back then I hadn't even wondered.

One time I saw a thin girl, even thinner than I was, fall to her knees in the bathroom of our dorm. Her legs were twitching. She had broomstraw hair and the glassy startled eyes of an animal smoked out of its burrow. She was splashing water on her face, and then her knees just buckled. I thought, *This is where it ends up.* The body forgets how to stand.

I'd fallen in bathrooms of my own, several of them. Once I flushed a toilet at Revere Beach and woke up in a puddle of wet sand and urine. Blackouts took the moments of my life and hid them from my sight. I thought: *This is being sick. This is wanting it.* Years later, finding Lucy on the floor, I remembered the chill of piss and concrete on my skin. I saw her fluttering fingers and thought, *This isn't wanting anything. This is dying.*

At the Central Square T-stop on an icy morning, I tripped on the long steps leading underground. I'd been dizzy because I was always dizzy. I only felt stable when I was lying down. I felt the crush of bodies and then I felt my own body, surging with darkness like syrup, and I tasted something sweet, like saliva before vomiting, and felt the hard edge of the step, the bruising pain across my cheek, the metal tang of blood in my mouth. I heard someone say, "Her foot's twisted."

I closed my eyes. I wasn't dizzy anymore. I was lying down.

I opened my eyes and saw a pair of white sneakers, then a woman's face. "Listen to me," she said. "Your mouth is full of blood."

She helped me to a coffee stand near the turnstiles. My ankle was already starting to swell. I was wondering how I'd run the next morning.

The guy behind the register was a balding man with braces. How did that happen to a person, both at once? It didn't seem fair.

"She needs a bathroom," the woman told him.

"Bathrooms aren't for the public, ma'am."

The woman whispered in my ear, "Smile."

I smiled.

"Go ahead," he said. "It's right in back."

I lifted one hand to my lips. When I pulled my fist away it was smeared red. Years later, I'd sit in front of Lucy with her wool skirt, prim and proper despite the way age had turned her body into rotten fruit. *Strangers being nice never make anything better. They just make me feel alone.*

The woman bought me coffee and a chocolate doughnut. She wanted to get my blood sugar back, she said. The coffee was hot against my hurt lips. I picked at the doughnut with my fingernail and sucked the crumbs off my finger. I did that a bunch of times, until there was a row of little nicks across the top. The woman watched me quietly. She pursed her lips. "I see," she said finally. "So that's what this is about."

I broke off a little chunk, placed it on a paper napkin, broke off another chunk and placed it on another napkin. I actually did things like that. It's funny to remember. Not funny, so much. Something else.

I knew that lots of girls with my problem needed to be convinced they had it, but I'd known from the beginning. I felt I'd chosen it, wanted it, though I knew I could never admit this to anyone. I watched my collarbone getting sharper. I counted my upper ribs obsessively, like tapping piano keys to play scraps of song. I kept a fat black book where I recorded the number of calories I'd eaten each day. Years later, when I came across that book and threw it in my mother's trash bin, I felt a sense of pity. It contained the worst parts of me, and now they didn't belong to anyone.

I was writing poems about food, essays about food, doodling pictures of food. If people had blogged back then, I would have blogged about food. I did everything you could do with food except eat it. I liked the bit in *Ulysses* where the guy remembers getting fed: *Softly she gave me in my mouth the seedcake warm and chewed. Mawkish pulp her mouth had mumbled sweetsour of her spittle. Joy: I ate it: joy.*

This wasn't a feeling but a remembered feeling. *Me. And me now,* he said. There was only the gap between, the longing. I could remember myself larger. Now I felt like a single point on a vast plain. There wasn't another body for miles.

The third day Tilly got her energy back. The sweating was worse, but the shaking was better. "Now it just feels like the flu," she said. "It's coming out through my skin."

Her appetite returned and I took this seriously, like a gift had been given to both of us. I peeled an orange for her. I bought a salad.

She watched a lot of TV. I could tell this was part of her usual routine, because she already had her favorites—reality shows about teenagers, about animals.

"Let's go for a walk," I said. "We need some sun."

We walked from parking lot to parking lot. We must have walked a mile without hitting any sidewalks. The outside world smelled like tar and car exhaust. Everything was gleaming, hard light shivering off dirty metal hoods.

"Scenic," she said. She wanted to go back. She felt sick. She wanted more stories.

About my disorder? It was just one story over and over again. Every day was the fucking *same.* I got the feeling Tilly understood that.

It was barely six. It wouldn't be dark for hours. We had the whole night to dissolve. At first I'd thought she could sleep her way through the worst of this, but that was before I'd heard her nightmares. Maybe it was better, I thought, to keep her awake as long as I could.

I could tell her about boys, I said. I'd known a few.

In the beginning there was Josh, my tenth-grade obsession. I was obsessed with his Judaism, at least, the thickness of it—years and years layered around this ordinary boy, shimmering off his glasses and braces, onionskins of history and myth. He invited me to his seders and we dipped eggs into salt for the sadness of our ancestors, his ancestors, and I pretended to hate gefilte fish even though I didn't, because hating was also part of the ritual, a dislike passed down through generations.

My first real boyfriend was a surfer-depressive named Carl. He signed his notes *Peace and love*, but above this signature he wrote things like *I will infect you with the hardness of my soul*. He lived with his biological mother and her asshole husband and their surprisingly delicate offspring: deerlike twin boys and an eavesdropping little girl who wore bells around her ankles that sang the high, clear notes of her trespass. Carl took me miniature golfing but liked to stretch himself taut with speed right before-hand, flick his mood so he was twanging like a rubber band all night. "Motherfucking windmill motherfuckers!" he'd say, kicking obstacles. His eyes got wet and hungry like they were searching for something—maybe for my gaze, probably something beyond. Back then I thought he was being melodramatic, inventing little pegs for hanging up his make-believe pain. Later, I saw it differently. He might have been making up the pegs. He wasn't making up the pain.

There were pseudo-intellectuals during college: a physicist, a philosopher, a chemical engineer–cum–Japanese historian. There was a poet I met during a summer writing workshop, when a July tornado danced through our town and destroyed two city blocks. Cars flipped into trees, but nobody died. My fellow students wrote poems in response. They wrote: *Mother Nature I've got questions!* They wrote: *Why our yards? Why our cars? Why our bars?* My poet sent me a text message: *I saw the funnel cloud! It was green, green, green!*

New York held a string of one-syllabled men: Max, Dan, Scott, Pete, Steve. They were easy to list in retrospect. I dated a banker named Paul because this was what jaded girls did, we dated bankers, and he did what was expected of him: fed me desserts across the tables of expensive restaurants, invested too much ego in his work, never showed much feeling. But when I left him for good, he cried right in front of me. He pretended it was only allergies, pollen, the luck of the season: spring.

I liked the ache that crept into his voice during those final moments. He was willing to let me hear it. I was terrible then. I could only feel another person's pain as something hurting in myself. For some people that's empathy, but for me it felt like theft.

Tilly listened patiently to my catalog. She rubbed a cool damp cloth across her cheeks, her neck, the dip of collarbone where moisture had gathered.

"You've turned them into little servings," she said. "Like appetizers."

I pictured her working one of her catering jobs years ago, a sad-eyed girl offering pigs in a blanket with her slim fingers—another helping and another, always another.

"That's fair, I suppose. I've practiced."

"What I want to know," she said, "is what hurt."

So I told another story. This story was about finding a downtown clinic during an autumn cold snap and letting a woman suck the small bud of an embryo from my body.

* * *

I found out I was pregnant from a drugstore test. I watched the cross appear over the bowl of Ms. Z's toilet. Even though I wasn't showing yet, wasn't anywhere close, I felt heavy with the sprout of tissue, the little boy or girl who wasn't either yet.

It was Louis's baby. But Louis had his doubts. "Aren't you sleeping with a few guys?" he asked.

I shook my head.

"Oh," he said. "I thought you were."

I waited for something else.

"Well, it's obviously your choice," he said. "I want to be absolutely clear about that. It's your body."

"You want me to get rid of it, don't you?"

"I didn't say that," he said. "Did I?"

I shook my head.

"Did I?"

"I thought—"

"You keep it or you don't. I don't *want* you not to. This choice doesn't have to do with anyone but you."

Which made the choice for me. Which made it his choice in the end.

The day of my abortion, the sky smelled like smoke. It was cold. Wind carried the sunlight like noise. The glare showed cigarette butts like rusty gadgets on the ground, soaked by rain and dried again. A homeless woman tapped my knee as I walked by. Her lips were chapped and pink like candy. "Hey, lady," she said, "you wanna help another lady out?"

I gave her a ten-dollar bill. I knew I'd remember this day for the rest of my life, and I wanted to remember being generous.

The Planned Parenthood clinic was in a dingy building off Third. On the sidewalk outside, two old men bundled in sweatpants and knitted sweaters leaned against the brick walls with handmade signs. You Never Met the Baby You Are Killing, said one. The men looked cold and tired. I was ready to snap at them if they said anything to me, but they didn't. They just stared as if waiting for me to talk to them.

The receptionist was a woman with hair woven in tight rows against her scalp. Her nails were long and painted with acrylics. Each one showed a tiny ocean frosted with sunset. Her thumb held a leaping dolphin. "I'm Luella," she said. "How can I help you?"

"I'm here for an abortion," I said.

"A termination?" She handed me a clipboard and a pen with a chewed cap. I wondered about the woman who'd chewed that cap. Had she been nervous? Had her choice been harder than mine, her fetus larger inside of her, its limbs more shapely?

The waiting room was full of anxious teenagers and people without health insurance. I passed a bearded man who looked up and checked me out before he went back to the dirty personals section of his magazine. I sat across from a boy in baggy jeans who listened to his headphones with half-shut eyes. His posture was remarkably upright. The chair next to him held a white purse and a gold quilted jacket—his girlfriend's things, most likely. She was probably in there right now, getting what I was going to get.

There was a crate full of children's books by my feet. FREE, said a sign. PLEASE TAKE ONE OR MORE THAN ONE. The boy took off his headphones and picked up a square hardcover called *The Big Moose's Dictionary for the Big, Big Woods* and laughed nervously, waving it in my direction. "Pretty funny, right?"

I nodded politely.

"I mean, a kid's book, here."

"I knew what you meant," I said, and looked away, and wished immediately that I'd been kinder. I felt sorry for this boy, who would get rid of his sadness before he even realized its size, and I felt even sorrier for myself—here alone, with no nervous boy-child wondering what was happening to my body.

I filled out forms: my age, my last period, my method of payment. Did I want to see the ultrasound before the termination? I paused. I checked yes.

I went to the bathroom in the waiting room, which I soon regretted. Later, I had to squat over their plastic cup for nearly ten minutes, waiting for a trickle large enough to stick inside their metal cubbyhole. They took my urine and my blood, and then I went into a small room where a woman strapped a condom onto what looked like a large plastic dildo. This was the vaginal ultrasound, for fetuses so small they wouldn't show up through the belly. I saw the sound waves resolve into a grainy image on a television screen, the dark jelly bean of a could-have-been against the gray wash of my uterus.

A white-haired woman showed me into a small consultation room. She had weathered skin and calloused hands. Her table was covered with small jigsaw puzzles that showed birth-control methods and the structure of the cervix. "This is your choice," she said. "That's the most important thing."

Her voice was full of pride and fear. She'd fought for all this. She was old enough. And I was the female body she'd fought for—invaded by science, waiting for a pamphlet. Her brochure said: *Our Bodies, Our Choices.* There was a section called *Everybody Has a Choice.* Another called *Living with Choices.* The woman on the front cover was made of orange ink lines. Her sketched eyes were full of hope. She was going to get better.

I couldn't tell this woman, *This is about a man.* It was supposed to be about me.

"I'm going to explain the steps of the procedure," she said. "So you know exactly what's happening inside your body."

"Thank you," I said. "I'd appreciate that."

There wasn't much to explain. Just the things they did: the suction straw they inserted, the cannula, it was called, like a pastry; and how long they did them for—not long, it seemed—to suck everything away; and what they did to make sure I got through it: the sedative first, through a needle in my arm, and then something local into my cervix.

There was an interior lounge where we, the pregnant women, waited. When we stood or changed positions, our gowns rustled like dry leaves. Nobody was showing yet, but I pictured their ghostly bulges. Some of them were just girls. I imagined their bellies as small nests made of organs webbed with bloody veins. There was an open secret between us. We were all there for the same reason, and women spoke plainly about their situations: The guy didn't want it, case closed, or else he was flipping out because he couldn't stand the thought of someone killing his baby. "He's going crazy," one girl whispered, "he won't stop leaving messages."

These women talked about their cravings and their morning sickness. I realized that some of them really thought of themselves as pregnant, even though they wouldn't be soon enough, while I'd never thought of myself as anything but a woman getting closer to an abortion, carrying this weight until it lifted.

Each time they called a name, the other women looked around, wondering who it was. They'd shared the length of their terms and the nature of their cravings, but not their names. No one knew who was who. When my turn came, I stood and smoothed my gown, grabbing the back sleeves so it wouldn't show my bare legs, goose-pimpled and jittery.

In the operating room, a short bald man stood up and said he'd be doing my procedure. He didn't offer his hand. I noticed his scrubs had a small circle of blood on the breast pocket—as if a pen had leaked or a woman had bled. It was the size of a pickle cut crossways. I couldn't stop staring at it. "Looking for my name?" he said. "It's Rosengeld."

He fitted my feet into place and smiled down at me like you'd smile at a beautiful painting. My toes nestled for purchase in the stirrups. Then he tested the machine—its ragged hum pulsing once, then again, before he shut it off—and unwrapped a new plastic tip from a sealed plastic bag. Another man knelt beside my right arm. "You're going to feel a sharp prick," he said. "Then everything will get blurry."

He was right. Figures melted into voices. I could hear a general buzzing above and around me, and it had a quality like warmth, like a serious conversation after several glasses of wine. I felt hands pushing my legs apart, and then I heard the whirring start again, and then I felt a cramping pain drawn out like a long moan, but I didn't feel like stopping it, even though it hurt, and I vaguely understood that this was what the sedative had done. It had not protected me, exactly; it had protected me from wanting to protect myself. It felt like tree roots had wrapped around my womb and gripped it tight.

In my peripheral vision, I saw a tube full of blood, a red thread drawn through the plastic, and I thought, *This was mine. It was his.*

What had the brochure said? *You live with the choices you make.* I would live with this, not the fetus but the memory of sucking it away. It was mine, this plastic tube and its whirring, like an animal emerging from the paper gown, the hooded darkness of my crotch. I'd done things, and now these things were going to make me hurt.

I came up slowly, which was a good thing, because the procedure ended before the hurting did. They wheeled me into a recovery room where women sat in blue reclining chairs against the wall, like patients in a hair salon. A man with green eyes and a long beard handed me some ginger ale and a few crackers. The pains were like sutures holding me together. Each one ached along its seam. Another cramp tugged at these seams and cinched them tighter, like my whole gut was a drawstring purse. I asked the bearded man for a pain pill. "In a few minutes," he said. "Get something in your stomach first."

I sat there for a while, I'm not sure how long, until the same man stood beside me and cupped his hand over my shoulder. He offered me orange juice and a paper bag with two jars of pills, some Advils and a rattling case of antibiotics. There was a pamphlet titled: *What to Expect After Your Procedure.* In little letters beneath: *Electric Vacuum Aspiration.* There was a column called *Physical* and another called *Emotional.* I clutched my paper bag with two fingers, knuckles large and quaking. I felt the paper softening from my palms.

Before I left, Luella made sure somebody was taking me home. "You need an escort," she said. "You know the rules."

It was true; I had been told. I said somebody was coming. But this wasn't the case. I would duck into the deli two doors down alone, and buy one of those cookies as large as a fist, and sit as long as I needed, until I felt better.

"That's good, honey." Luella turned back to her computer screen. She didn't want to break open my lie; she probably got it all the time. Her nails clicked the keyboard. She wouldn't be the one who saved me from my own life. She was just a stranger with an honest smile. She was someone's daughter, maybe someone's sister or someone's mother—maybe all three—and she'd heard all kinds of terrible stories about how much it hurt to be a woman. I could see it in her face, the insistent beauty of her painted nails, that she still believed in the end of the day, the possibility of getting there. She'd already heard so many tales about aching. I could tuck myself into them like body hollows left on mattresses, easily, without saying a word.

Tilly was quiet for a long time. Her skin was dry and smooth but her eyes looked weary. Finally, she said, "That's a terrible thing, getting rid of a baby."

"It wasn't a baby," I said. "It wasn't even a fetus."

"A fetus," she said. "That's what I meant."

"You think it's wrong?"

"I don't know about wrong," she said. "I think it's terrible."

"I just wanted things with him to turn out differently, that's all. With Louis."

"Who knows who that little baby would have been?" she said.

I frowned. You Never Met the Baby You Are Killing. I wasn't sure what to say.

Tilly rolled toward the wall, her voice barely audible. "I'm sorry to keep you talking."

"Are you upset?"

"Let's sleep."

I rubbed her shoulder under the blanket. The gesture felt awkward. My fingers rubbed unsteadily against the fabric. I said, "You seem upset."

She sat up. Her expression wasn't kind. I couldn't tell what it was. "Let's leave tomorrow," she said. "I couldn't stand another day."

She insisted on driving. Her face was puffy but her eyes looked bright and ready, squinting against the sun. She said it felt good to press the accelerator pedal. She'd never owned a car, she told me. Could I believe it? A little bit, yes, from the way she drove.

Just past the state border, we saw an RV stalled in the middle of the Mojave Desert. There was a cardboard sign propped against the back fender that said Free.

Tilly pulled over without asking or signaling. An older man emerged from the door and eased down the steps, gripping the handrail. He was wearing a shirt with a huge tiger's face, the open jaws spread over his belly.

"What's free?" Tilly asked.

"I've got hot springs," he said. He banged his fist against the trailer. "And this piece of shit if you're interested."

"Hot water?" I said. "Sounds terrific." It must have been a hundred degrees, as they say, in the shade.

"A whole pool of it," he said. "There's a natural spring up that hill."

He showed us where he meant: a scrubby slope rising away from the highway, pinned in place by a few gnarled trees. The ocean felt a thousand miles away rather than a hundred; it was just a notion somebody had had one day in the middle of the sand, an impossible act of imagination.

We followed dirt switchbacks to the pools: a tub of murky water breathing curls of steam, circled by fake rocks. Tilly took off her shirt and then shimmied out of her denim skirt. Her bra was the color of an old photograph, that sepia, and it barely kept her long breasts from swinging out. She tap-danced across the concrete. "It's like a stove!" she said. "You'll burn your toes!"

She was right about the ground. But the water was hotter. We held our bodies perfectly still under its surface. Even the smallest movement made tiny unbearable currents, like boiling threads, against our skin. Tilly gritted her teeth. "I'm barely here," she said. "I think I melted."

The hill behind her was covered in cacti, their broad paddles studded with needles that stuck like pins into the rippling warmth over the land.

Tilly dunked her head under. "All I wanted was a little peace from the heat," she said. "This state is just as bad as the last one."

She took the curves of Highway 1 with a grim face, slowing for each long bank around the cliffs, but sometimes we got a view, wide and rustling blue, and I could see her faintly smiling. We were tired. We watched the fog burn away. The land was full of dingy, infinite mysteries. The roads were lined with produce shacks. There was an island barely bigger than a shopping mall, tethered to the coast by a thin bridge whose distant dirt heaved flickering oil flames against the blue sky. We passed broad hills that rolled steady and seemed to die a little in the furrows, their grass baked brown like too much sun had pooled there. We saw a whole flock of blackbirds rise from the land and make a shape in the sky, wing to wing, that was larger than any of them would have been able to imagine. "How do they know what to do?" Tilly asked. "I never get that."

We didn't stop much. There was one time we saw dolphins, another time we bought pistachios. Mostly, we listened to folk music and tried to keep our truck steady on the curves. Tilly wanted to make sure I hadn't told my mother about her work. I hadn't.

"Good," she said. "Like I said, she wouldn't get it."

I thought my mother understood a lot of hard things—more than you'd guess, from the way she spoke—but I couldn't think of a way to say this to Tilly, the one she'd hurt most.

"How did it start?" I asked. "The prostitution, I mean. If you don't mind my asking."

"Not having any money," she said. "That was most of it."

She told me about wearing secondhand pants that smelled like other people's privates and eating meals made from diner condiments: creamer and ketchup, salt and pepper on crackers. "I was *poor*," she said. "Not artsy poor. Poor poor." She told me about the men, how she still heard their voices. Some of them were time bombs, she explained. *Tick tick tick.* Just waiting to explode.

"Did you ever get hurt?" I asked.

"There are things you shouldn't tell another person," she said. "You can't take them back."

I told her it didn't matter about taking them back. I wanted to know.

"It's not for your sake," she said. After that she was quiet.

The cliffs got steeper and the turns got sharper. She hugged the road and went slower. Other drivers honked and she cursed them loudly. I cursed them too. She bit the edges of her nails until they bled. I remembered the mocking lilt of Tom's voice: *Nervous Nelly.* So she was one, too.

TILLY

Harrison Street wasn't what I'd been picturing. There were strip clubs flashing neon signs and homeless guys sleeping behind Dumpsters, hiding from fog so heavy it felt like rain. The sky was gray like raw shrimp. The trees on the street looked dead but their roots looked alive. They pushed through the asphalt like tapped veins showing for needles.

But it was funny, you could tell the apartments on these blocks cost serious money. Their walls were the color of crayons, salmon pink and mint green, with big glass windows and patios full of ferns. It had been my hope from the first day, the first neon cross on the pee stick, that my kid would spend his life in places I could never afford.

He was waiting on the sidewalk, leaning against a big steel door. I double-parked our truck and climbed down without killing the ignition. Here he was, my boy. He looked just like his father, too much skin for his body. He smiled, very tight, and said, "I'd hug you, but I'm sweaty."

"Do it anyway."

He laughed at this, though I hadn't meant it as a joke, and

135

squeezed me with his dangling arms. They were paper-white and skinny, knobs sticking out of his elbows. Every time we talked on the phone, it sounded like he was pacing across his office or his living room, and his face showed it, full of worry that couldn't walk itself away. His face was gaunt: sharp cheeks, big skull, wet eyes. I kept him close for a long time, running my palms along his shoulder blades, then down his bumpy spine. I'd made every part of him.

He pulled away gently, like I was a fragile toy he was putting down. I heard Stella's door slam shut. She'd come around the side of the truck. I followed his eyes, following her body getting closer.

"Abe?" She shook his hand. "It's good to meet you."

He seemed restless. "We should get everything unloaded."

Our things didn't amount to much: a few boxes and some garbage bags. I'd thought bags would be easier to stuff into tight spaces. I'd left a lot of things in Lovelock because I never wanted to see them again, but I'd made Stella help me pack the kitty statues and all of Abe's little projects. I'd labeled that box CATS, writing the word in careful letters, once on each side.

"We should be careful with this one." I pointed. "It's fragile."

Abe lifted it easily. "Come on," he said. "I'll show you up."

"I guess I'll drive the truck back to the rental," Stella said. "We can't just leave it in the street."

"You know the drop-off lot?" Abe asked. He couldn't hear the irritation in her voice, or else he wasn't responding to it.

"No," she said. "But I have an address."

What did she want? She wanted an offer, or at least attention.

"Okay, then," he said, turning back to me. He gestured up a set of concrete stairs. I followed like a bum, garbage bags slung over my shoulders, up to a courtyard full of plants I couldn't name: pink flowers, towering fronds, sturdy fingers of green. Stalks of bamboo lined the stucco like wallpaper. "The garden is communal," Abe told me. "You should use it whenever you want."

The wooden benches were straight, their paint unchipped.

They didn't sag the way benches sag after enough people have sat on them. I couldn't imagine sitting there alone.

Abe gestured to an open doorway off the courtyard: his place. We walked into a two-story living room that was almost completely empty. There was a plastic lawn chair propped in front of a flatscreen TV, and boxes stacked along the walls. I saw a kitchen made of steel and marble and a loft above it. There was a spiral staircase.

"Is that your room?" I asked. "Up there?"

He shook his head. "Afraid of heights. Always have been."

I'd never known this. But I suppose it made sense that I hadn't realized. I'd known him in a flat town, full of strip malls and single-story trailers, no heights for miles. I could remember something about his father forcing him onto the tallest roller coaster in Vegas, but I'd never been sure which part he'd been scared of. He'd cried just telling me about that shaking coaster, how the city lights went blurry from distance—he was so far *up*, like a terrible bird—and how his tears blurred everything even more. I thought he'd been afraid of the speed, or maybe of his father, who was never a cruel man, just had a lot of hopes and only one son to carry them.

Abe set down the box. "My room is back here," he said, and took me to a small room behind the kitchen. It was bare and bright, with a swivel chair, no desk, and a mattress on the floor. A laptop sat on the floor with its plug trailing behind it, like a dog on a leash. There was a tie rack on the wall, draped with shimmering bands of blue and green. There was a book on the pillow and a half-eaten bar of chocolate stuck like a bookmark between its pages. I bent closer. The book was some kind of science fiction; I saw a red planet floating in the middle of licorice space. Even as a boy, Abe liked all that stuff. He got impatient when I mixed up aliens from different movies.

Behind me, he said, "It's kind of a bedroom-slash-office. It's not fixed up."

"You don't have an office at work?"

"I do."

"But you needed another one."

"I needed another one."

He'd been living here for three years, I knew from the address on his checks, and it still looked like this—barely unpacked, just a bar of chocolate to mark his place.

"The loft is for Stella," he said. "Until she finds a place of her own. And there's a whole basement for you. More privacy."

He showed me downstairs: a bathroom, laundry room, and bedroom. There was more furniture down here than anywhere else in the apartment—a matching bed and dresser, a braided red carpet, a small writing desk with one lonely glass paperweight. I didn't have any work to do at a desk like that. I had only tiny cats to arrange across the wood.

Abe set down my box. He touched his lower back briefly as he stood straight again—a moment of ache. It had been a couple years since I'd seen him—his last business trip to Reno, something to do with a tire recall—but he looked older than I'd expected.

He kissed me on the cheek and said he needed to run. Literally run. He was late and wearing sneakers. He'd bring up the rest of the boxes but then he had to take off. He was supposed to be at a meeting that had started an hour ago.

"You coming back for dinner?"

He checked his watch. "I'm not sure," he said. "You shouldn't wait." He grabbed an apple from the kitchen counter and headed for the door. He turned around before he left: "I'm happy you're here," he said. "I really am." Then he was gone.

He'd said, "Don't wait," but of course we did. I drank too much water, needed something in my mouth, anything. Taking pee breaks broke the waiting into smaller pieces. If there'd been a clock, we would have listened to it ticking away the moments, but there wasn't a clock, or maybe it was packed away too deep to hear. Abe's boxes lurked around us like strangers.

"God," Stella said. "It's good to be out of New York."

She started talking about why and kept going for nearly an hour—why she was so glad to be done with it, why it felt good to be alone out here. *Alone* was her word. She didn't apologize for it. Her old friends, she said, were smart about everyone but themselves. The streets of the city were full of trash and strange fluids, green milk, dark oil. People bumped into you, hard, and didn't even notice that they'd touched another human body. The bottom line was, the whole city made her tired. It made me tired to hear about it. She was scared about leaving everything, and I got that, but I also knew you couldn't start living in the new place until you said *fuck-all* to the old. I was never good at this, either.

I switched on the TV, but the screen stayed black. It wasn't plugged in.

"You could call him," Stella said.

"I don't want to bother him."

"Well," she said, "I'm fucking *starving*."

So we went looking for dinner. I wanted barnacle food that would grip the inside of my stomach. All those years of liquor still needed sponges—something doughy, something fatty—to soak up what was left. The mist made our skin wet and turned our fingers into cold rubber. The streets were empty. Stella shivered. "It's like a ghost town."

I got the sense she didn't mean *ghost town* like an empty place but like a place full of ghosts, and it was true: the bums were all around us.

We walked past skyscrapers and triple-story clothing stores. There were coffee shops bigger than my whole trailer. We didn't like the feel of Market, so we turned onto a side street and ducked into a crowded noodle shop. It smelled like cooked meat, and the air was warm and heavy like it might turn into greasy raindrops. A short guy with a mustache shoved two menus into our hands and pointed to a table squashed into one corner, under a painted dragon. Stella sat down and asked for water.

"I thought we were going back to eat with Abe," I said.

"Sure," she said, standing abruptly. "I forgot. Of course."

"You take this or stay?" the man asked.

"We'll go," said Stella. "We're going."

"Wait outside," he said. "I come ask what you want."

We stood outside, and through the windows, we watched other people dip their chopsticks into noodle piles. We wanted beef soup, both of us. We didn't know what to get for Abe. I thought maybe he wanted chicken. When he was a little boy, he liked little-boy foods—sloppy joes, mac and cheese—which were cheap, and two weeks weren't long enough for him to get tired of them. His nannies always made him eat vegetables at his dad's, he complained. It made me sad to think of: it was their job and they took it seriously, these women; and I was his mother, feeding him junk from cardboard boxes.

We walked home in the dark and stumbled over the sidewalks, broken by roots. I'd called Abe to say we'd gotten him chicken soup. He said he'd be late. "You guys should eat."

"I'll wait," I said. "I want to."

"Don't wait."

"Will you say hello, at least? When you get home?"

"You might . . . You'll probably be asleep."

"Then wake me up. Doesn't matter when."

I put his food in the fridge and wrote *Chicken for Abe* on the paper bag, though there wasn't much to get it confused with. The shelves were empty. I also wrote a note that said *Chicken for Abe in here* and fixed it with a magnet onto the fridge door. There was a calendar of photographs hanging from the side of the freezer, black-and-white highways stretching into the distance. It was still on February. Abe hardly lived here. He'd said as much in his notes: *I have a second bed at the office.* I always thought it was a little joke. I'd looked over those notes for hours, trying to figure out what kind of guy he was—what would make him angry, what would make him laugh.

Stella and I opened our soups and ate them straight from the plastic, mangled beef floating in blisters of oil. I squeezed four packages of hot sauce into my bowl. I dumped chili flakes until my soup looked like an aquarium full of fish food. I slurped the broth loudly. I wiped my runny nose with balled-up tissues that smelled like my own hands. Stella watched. Her own eyes were teary and anxious. "Spicy enough?" she asked.

"It's just right," I said. "I want to taste it." I shoveled noodles into my mouth, long worms of burn, until tears ran down my cheeks. My skin felt flushed. It was good to cry.

"Are you enjoying that?" Stella asked.

I nodded. I blew my nose again. I took another clump of noodles. They looked like a dying jellyfish I'd found on the Cape way back when, its tentacles tangled on the sand, its clear body glassy and heaving.

I wiped away my tears with one fist. My hand was dirty and I could feel the hot paste smearing onto my skin. I didn't care. Stella looked nervous. I'd seen this look before: Were we still okay? Or had something gone wrong?

"What if this doesn't work?" I said.

"This?"

I put my chopsticks on the table and drank the rest of my broth from the bowl. My throat burned like sunburned skin in the shower. Stella picked up the wet chopsticks so they wouldn't stain the wood.

"I mean this place," I said. "I mean everything."

* * *

Abe woke me up, squatted close to my face and whispered, "I'm home." He smelled like toothpaste in the darkness.

"Turn on the light," I told him. "Let me get another look at you."

He was only thirty-two, but his face made me think of an old person's wrinkled palm. His eyes were big greasy almonds, full of hurt like a woman's.

"You're a real worker," I said. "Like your dad."

"I never thought I'd turn out like him."

"He was a good man."

"He didn't make your life easy."

"I didn't make it easy."

He looked away. I touched his cheek with my fingers, the skin stretched between his bones like a drum. "You look tired," I said.

"I am," he said. "For years now."

I sat up and we talked, just for a few minutes. But still, it was a start. He told me he wanted me to fix up his place. Make it a home, if I was willing. He slipped his credit card into my hand and I woke up the next morning to find it tucked under my pillow, showing the raised letters of his name: *Abraham Clay,* like his father. He sounded like a prophet or a swindler, someone who could change the course of history.

I was ashamed to put my clothes in the polished wooden dresser Abe had chosen for me—mainly baggy sweatpants and T-shirts with the letters faded nearly to nothing. I shoved everything deep into the drawers and told myself, *Soon enough.* I'd buy new things. I was planning to get a job and a little spending money of my own.

The important stuff took longer to unpack: my cat statues and the box of Abe's art projects—marker drawings of all the slot-machine fruits, a flower made of poker chips. Every piece was terrible and precious. I kept them in a drawer so he wouldn't see them and get embarrassed, for my sake or his, along with some letters he'd sent. One had a picture of a big red planet with crayon scrawled so thick it crumbled off like dandruff:

Dear Tilly,

   Here's a picture that I made of Jupiter in Ms. Coomb's class. Ms. Coomb said it looked just like the real thing and I said how do you know you've never been there. But anyway I hope you like it. I know you're always asking what I'm going to be for Halloween. I am being James Bond this year, from the movie with the egg-jewel not the movie with the big tarantula. Youll probably make me show you in the summer anyway.

   Love,
   Abe

P.S.—Do you think we will ever find life on another planet (not earth)? I have a bet with dad.

Outer space stuck with him. He'd taught me the order of the planets and all their information. He knew the real statistics but he made up other ones just for us. The biggest exports of Jupiter were asteroid visors, rocket hubs, and star crushers. In July he made a solar system out of Popsicle sticks. It was a team effort. We ate the Popsicles together, and then he used them for satellites. To me, it looked like a bunch of basketballs had been turned into skeletons. I said, "You can really see how hard you worked."

   The last night of his visit, I found him standing over a bulky trash bag in the kitchen. "Who was I kidding?" he said. "It looked terrible."

   I felt left in the lurch. We'd been partners in a way, but he hadn't asked me before he wrecked it.

* * *

Dry days were long. The hours piled. Clocks moved slowly. The minutes of my life stretched out like the salt flats we'd passed, blanched and flat, so endless I could hardly stand to look at them. So much had changed—this new city, Abe close—but I still woke up each day and tried to figure out what to do with myself. The empty hours were questions I was being asked: *What now?* And: *What next?*

I started unpacking Abe's books from the boxes in his living room. I didn't ask if I could do it, I just did. I organized them by height so they wouldn't look like jutting teeth. Stella came in from her shower, wearing nothing but a towel, and found me arranging. Sometimes I found it painful to look at her body—the seagull wings of her collarbone, her smooth back—because my own body looked so tired and worn. She was pretty like I'd been once, but she knew it better than I'd known it about myself. Standing in her towel, she had a stillness. She wasn't trying to look any way right then, she just *was.*

"You're just putting them on the shelf?" she said. "You're not putting them in order?"

"In order how? Like a library?"

"Alphabetically, I meant. I've just never thought . . ." She paused. "They're fine how they are."

"Oh," I said. It had never occurred to me.

I started all over again. I took them down and made twenty-four stacks. Abe didn't own so many, nothing under X or Z, but when you spread them out, they covered a lot of his floor. Their covers showed glowing mountains, creatures with blue or silver skin, spaceships that looked like giant metal insects. There weren't enough shelves to hold them.

I found a few planks of wood in the alley, wiped them clean with a wet rag, and stole a stack of bricks from the courtyard that no one was using. I made a couple of shelves. I put the books in a row.

"I like it," Stella said. "Looks very hip."

"You think so?" I said.

She nodded. She did.

It wasn't much, but I was pleased.

That night I woke up to a loud crack, then a patter of heavy thumps. I checked my watch. It was two in the morning. I went upstairs and saw Abe crouched in the dim light. My shelves had broken, and the books had spilled everywhere. "I knocked into it," he said. "I'll put it back together." He was putting the books in piles. He wore a light gray suit. His briefcase leaned against one thigh. He'd just come home.

He ran his fingers up the spines of one stack. "Can I ask you a question?" he said, amused. "Are these in alphabetical order?"

"They were," I said. "They're not anymore."

"I've never . . ." He paused. "Thank you."

He started laughing then, crouched on the floor. "It's kind of silly," he said. "All these trashy books, and you put them in order, and then I . . ."

I started to see it, too—all these stupid ways we tried to make the world make sense. I held my knees against my chest and laughed. I watched my son laugh, too.

Stella and I walked the neighborhood, *our* neighborhood, every morning. It gave us a reason to wake up. There was a cat in the apartment next door who cried all night, every night. She sounded like a little kid getting hurt. Maybe she was in heat. If so, she never seemed to be out of it.

Abe was always gone before we got up. He left his dirty cereal bowl in the sink, brownish milk with a couple swollen flakes of bran.

I liked spending time with Stella, but sometimes she was hard to be around. I felt like she wanted to dig something out of me. She especially liked to hear about the Cape. It didn't surprise me that Lucy had talked to her about it. They were some of our best times, the two of us.

"She said something happened with a boy out there," Stella said. *Something terrible*, she would have been told. That's what Lucy would have said.

"With Nick," I said. "That's what she meant."

"There was a scandal?"

"Not exactly."

"But . . . he hurt you?"

"I hurt myself."

Stella got quiet. Sometimes when she shut up, it was sudden; she could tell that she'd asked too much. Lucy never asked, either—about Nick, what really happened—because she didn't want to know the truth. He hadn't forced me, not really. The truth was he hadn't done anything wrong.

I'd been eleven but I'd wanted it, if you're allowed to say that. I liked his hands, like beaten sails, even though he was just a boy, only a few years older than I was. Until that summer, my breasts had been flat little sugar cookies under the bright pink triangles of my bikini, and now they were huge and unexpected, bulging out the fabric and large under his fingers.

His mother was a little bit crazy. She sat quietly behind the register of the family five-and-dime and knitted finger puppets with black cross-stitches for eyes. That woman was *ruined,* my mother said. Absolutely ruined by a man. He'd been a banker from Boston, rich and married. There was an affair one summer, an abortion one fall. She'd walked into the Atlantic with paperweights in her jeans but hadn't had enough heartache, or guts, to go through with it. The whole town knew. Nick was good to her. He fed her oranges piece by piece and put her knit creatures in the windows.

One day the two of them, mother and son, took me to their favorite beach. It felt very private between the three of us, more private than the part of him that came inside me. We built sand castles. Nick's mother helped me make a tower. She cupped her hand over mine to let me feel the right shape. She'd carried a basket of tuna sandwiches and cans of grape soda. We ate in silence. The waves were loud. "This is what we do," Nick told me. "We don't talk much."

The first time he put my hand on his erection, he whispered, *Feel how big it gets*, but I hadn't known what size it was to begin with. We had sex in the dry-goods aisle.

There was a terrible day when everything came apart, his friends catcalling when I walked by the five-and-dime with Lucy. We were already the poorest folks in Chatham of all the summer visitors, already shamed. Nick just stood there, saying nothing and admitting everything. Lucy saw him and she knew. She pushed me at his mother, sitting all mute and peaceful, and I could hear her voice get distant, like she was miles away: *Do you want to end up like her? Do you? Do you?* That broken woman stared me straight in the face and took my hand and held it for a moment, so I knew it wasn't all bad to be where she was, even if it looked that way.

Stella asked about Dora. "Don't you think about her?" she said. "Do you miss her?"

I told her the truth, which is that I'd never really *gotten* Dora, but she was my sister and there were things that happened in our lives that only happened to the two of us.

"Yeah?" said Stella. "Like what?"

I told her about our grandparents' farm. It had been Lucy's parents', the only grandparents we'd known. They had a big grove of orange trees. We played our cop-and-robber games in the endless rows. Gramps had a pair of big white poodles he sent to find us when it was time for dinner. Those dogs were like curly-haired ponies. We waited until they found us, and then we followed them home. There were long moments when the whole world went quiet and it was just the four of us running through the trees.

Me and Dora had so many years of being young together, but it felt like she was somewhere else for most of them. There were a few stories I kept coming back to because I couldn't think of any others. We went camping near Mammoth Mountain, and a bear broke into my backpack because I hadn't put my candy in our special metal drum. We could hear his claws clicking through the plastic wrappers one by one. Dora unzipped her sleeping bag, and I crawled inside with her. *That was pretty stupid,* she said. *You know that?* But she held me until I fell asleep.

Another time we found a dirty woman's shoe on the grass by the sidewalk. It was alligator-skinned, with its tall heel stuck in the mud. We spent hours making up stories about how it got there. Mostly they were stories about love gone wrong. I was better than Dora at inventing them. I'd say she'd been running away from a jealous former lover or dodging a jealous wife's baseball bat. Looking back, funny thing, it hurt more to remember the good parts. Stella had a phrase she used once, *the salted wound of memory.* She talked like a professor, but sometimes she could hit the feeling just right.

Stella helped me pick out furniture for the living room. *Furnitures,* little Abe used to say. As in: *You don't have all the furnitures.* There were years he wouldn't even call my trailer a house. But he was always careful not to spill anything.

The first thing we bought was a green sofa set from a store we'd passed on one of our morning walks. The matching armchair was enormous. If you curled the right way, you could fit your whole body between the arms. I pictured Abe's bony legs folded into the cushions . How often did he just relax? What did he think about? I imagined all of us shooting the shit—talking about the weather, or his latest space book, or our fuckup president. I wanted to be the kind of person who had something useful to say about politics. It was hard to imagine nights or whole days without being drunk. It all seemed endless.

The guy at the furniture store insisted that delivery was free. We could make a donation if we wanted. He showed us a brochure for something called Haitian Smiles. The front cover had a Haitian child who wasn't smiling, and the back cover had a Haitian child who was. I paid for the chair with Abe's card, but Stella insisted on making the donation. She said: "I'd like to contribute something."

I knew she was already paying more rent than her room was worth. She'd decorated the loft like she was planning to stay for a while, draping fabrics all over the walls and bed. Abe hadn't gotten much furniture for her. "Of course he didn't," she said. "I'll be leaving anyway." She'd gotten a job working nights at a bed-and-breakfast on one of the fancy hills, Nob or Russian, on a steep block covered in pastel wooden houses.

She was looking to help. That much was clear. She wanted to help Haitian kids, her whore aunt, everyone. She was still trying to figure out what her life was becoming, like it already had a shape and all she needed to do was squint hard enough to see it.

Every week for months, we got something in the mail from Haitian Smiles, a free calendar or a despairing letter, all of it addressed to Stella by name. I cared about them, too, those smiling and not-smiling thin folks down south; they just didn't know it.

I didn't get much mail of my own. When I moved, I only had to send my new address to one person. Fiona was a faithful pen pal but sometimes it took a while for her notes to make it to me. She wrote from the Florence McClure Women's Correctional Center, just outside Vegas, and her correspondence had to get approved every time.

Years after Lovelock, she'd been involved in a meth lab with a couple good-for-nothing kids. *It was a stupid idea,* she wrote.

Hardly my first. But prison had given her a lot of time to think about what mattered. *You were one of the people I loved most. In all the times and places of my life.* Apparently, she'd lost weight. *You wouldn't believe my fingers,* she wrote. *Like a skeleton.*

She signed her letters: *Your good friend since 1970, Fiona.* She'd always done that: friends since 1970, even in 1971.

I sent pictures of Abe at all different ages. I got them color-copied. *You aren't in any of your photographs!* she wrote back. Which was true. My favorites were the ones that showed him alone: splashing in a little plastic pool outside my trailer, standing sullen in his ghost robes. Every summer I asked him to show me what he'd worn for Halloween the year before: a stuffed parrot and plastic cutlass for his pirate outfit, one of his father's suits and a martini glass when he was Bond. He always complained—he was hot in his suit, he felt stupid—but he did it anyway.

Fiona wrote that she had a pet parakeet named Toe Picker living in her cell. *He looks like a pile of scrambled eggs,* she wrote. *He's always hungry.* She was part of a special program where inmates trained animals—lost, wild, abandoned—and gave them to other inmates so they'd have some company. Fiona learned a lot: how to feed baby squirrels with an eyedropper full of milk, how to love Jesus with her whole heart. And she was still learning. She mentioned that a few times. *It doesn't ever stop.*

In Toe Picker's case, he'd had a good home until his owner got so old she died. Before she died, she'd been a woman without arms. So you got: Toe Picker. He was trained to eat from toes, and it made him afraid of hands for good. You couldn't put out your fingers without him pecking. *Not pecking for a snack,* she wrote. *Pecking for blood.* I remembered how she'd gone after that bird in our trailer. But now she loved this one. He didn't see her as a criminal, she explained, because he didn't know any better.

I don't see you like a criminal, I wrote her. *Maybe I could come visit?*

Her letter back was short. *You can't see me like this.*

I wanted to believe she didn't mean that. I wanted to believe in all the other things she'd said: that her life had gotten rough, but it wasn't over yet, she didn't feel ashamed of the person she had become, she treasured what she was learning, something new every day.

I bought a blue pantsuit for my first job interview. This was part of the plan: little changes, one at a time. I was applying for a sales position at a clothes store called Sweet Sixteen. The clothes were supposed to be for girls, but they didn't look like anything a little girl should wear—fake leather coats with fur collars, sparkling tops that drooped under their sequins.

Stella and Abe helped me do a practice run before my interview. "It's a mock," Abe said. That was the term they used around his bank. Stella was supposed to play good cop and Abe was supposed to play bad cop, but I thought Stella's questions were meaner.

"What brought you to retail at this point in your life?" she asked.

I cleared my throat and said, "It's never too late to learn."

"Yes!" said Abe. "That's exactly what they're looking for!" He wasn't very good at going for blood. He asked, "How would you handle angry customers?"

Stella poked him with her pencil—the sharp tip, not the eraser—and shook her head. "Not like that!" she said. "Harder questions."

The manager was a woman named Tina, pretty but prissy, who wasn't particularly nice or mean. She just seemed bored. She chewed a big wad of pink gum the whole time. Her questions came all at once: *What do you like about stores what do you like about clothes what's one time it was hard for you to get along with another person and what did you do about it?*

She raised an eyebrow when I talked about the entertainment industry in Nevada, but she didn't ask about it. She shook my hand and said she'd be getting back to me.

I ran into her outside the entrance, on the sidewalk, holding a cigarette in one hand and a lighter in the other. She had a granola bar trapped between her two front teeth like a rodent. She was thin, that girl. But not so pretty in the sunlight.

She jerked her pack in my direction and raised her eyebrows. I don't think she was expecting me to say yes, but I did. She kept the granola bar between her teeth while she flicked her lighter under my cigarette.

"Thanks," I said.

She took a drag and looked up. "Off the record," she said. "What did you mean by 'entertainment'?"

"Off the record?"

"Yep."

"It was a long time ago."

"You were a hooker?"

"Yes."

"Really?" She put her hand on her stomach. Not like she was sick. Like she was hungry. She looked eager. "Did you like it?"

"I wouldn't say I liked it," I said.

She called me three days later to say I hadn't gotten the job.

"Good riddance anyway," Abe said. "You can do better than retail."

"I thought it might have been alright," I said. "Just something to get me started." I felt ashamed to know he'd thought so little of what I'd wanted.

He smiled at me like you'd smile at a child with a ridiculous dream: owning an entire country or making a castle from hot dogs. I knew that kind of smile. One time I'd smiled at Abe like that. He'd had this plan to build a baseball field on the moon. "The homers would fly so *long,*" he said. "Can you imagine?"

* * *

I tried to be useful. I bought things I thought Abe would like: neon signs for his walls, a round glass lamp that might have come from a spaceship. Stella gave me advice about style, sleek lines, colors. Abe said the lamp was nice, but I didn't have to spend my whole life fixing up his place. He didn't want to keep me from my job search.

I bought more bookcases, done with making them, and finished unpacking Abe's boxes. I found his collection of poker manuals, with titles like *Hold'em Up, Partner!* and *Five-Card Games in Five Days*. His father had spent three decades, half his life, getting good at that game. There were also books about dominoes and, of course, the sci-fi, now in order: Alfred Bester, Ray Bradbury, Arthur C. Clarke. He ran his fingers along their spines. "I like them in order," he said. "It's growing on me."

He recommended a book called *Cold Fires* when I asked for a suggestion, and I gave it an honest shot. It started with a planet that had been covered in darkness, I got that far, and a hero whose name was full of X's and Q's. I couldn't even pronounce it in my head. I thought of Abe coming home from work—all alone, before we got there—and reading about deep-space battles that lasted for centuries, that could darken worlds for good.

I liked TV shows better. I didn't have to picture everything for myself.

Stella had plenty of advice about jobs. If I invented a few proper nouns, she said, names and places, I could probably get a waitress gig. But I'd seen those girls. They were her age, not mine. That wasn't how I wanted to turn my dreams into reality, I told her. I didn't want to lie.

Dishwashing was what I had a shot at, experience-wise, and restaurants always had dishes that needed washing. But I knew people would feel bad about hiring an old woman for that. It would be like pushing your mom into the back room and making her clean up your mess. There was something about my face that seemed too tired for all that. Like: *You listen, okay? I've come a long way. I've seen a lot.*

Abe meant what he said, *You can find something better,* but I could tell he wanted me to find it sooner rather than later. His disappointment filled the house like gas. *How are you?* he'd ask, and I could tell he was a little scared of what I'd say.

I worried that he was sorry for this whole idea, my coming out to live with him in the first place. We hadn't found a way to be easy with each other. His bedroom was right above mine and some nights I heard him shuffling around for hours. It sounded like he was dragging a heavy sack across the wood.

One night I found him watching television in the living room. "What's on?" I asked him. "Anything good?"

He whipped around, handing me the remote. "You can use it if you want to."

I sat down. "I came up to watch it with you."

He tapped his fingers on the fabric. "You must get bored all day," he said. "I wish I could—"

"I'll find something, baby boy. Don't worry. I'm looking."

"And you're doing alright with . . . with all the rest of it?"

"I'm still sober," I said. "Have been since I got here."

"That's good," he said. "That's what I thought."

We were silent for a few minutes, sitting. "There are tons of groups for this kind of thing," he said. "You could check one out. It might help."

"I'm not sure," I paused. "I don't think—"

"I could go with you." He was looking at his fingers, staring. He wouldn't look at me.

"You mean that?"

"I do," he said. "I would."

One weekend I overheard him talking on his cell phone. I was in the downstairs bathroom. Not spying or anything, just peeing. "It's better this way," he said. "At least I can see that she's okay."

It didn't make me sad to know he thought of me as an obligation. I knew that much already. It made me sad I didn't know his friends, even their names, the ones who heard his confessions.

We found an open meeting listed in a ballet studio above a comedy club. The sidewalk was brightly lit and full of smokers, funny men and addicts, and the upstairs was an empty room multiplied by mirrors. There were long exercise bars along the walls and a folding table set with lemonade and cookies, spread with pamphlets called *44 Questions, Is A.A. for You? Questions and Answers on Sponsorship.* There was a poster tacked up that said: LIVING WITH CHOICES. Everyone was nice. Too nice, felt like. A woman gave me her telephone number and said, "I'm not asleep when other people are. Call whenever you want." We chatted about the weather, the strange warmth of fall, the difference between here and Nevada. I was proud and sad to hear Abe saying, "I'm here for my mother."

The meeting started with the whole group speaking together: *God, grant me the serenity,* etc. I'd heard it before, but I didn't know the words well enough to follow along. I looked at Abe. His lips were moving, but there wasn't any sound coming out.

An elderly woman walked to the front of the room and leaned her cane against the podium. "I'm Sarah," she said. "I've been sober for fifty years, six months, and three days."

Everybody clapped. People hooted, whistled. She was home.

"You might wonder what I'm doing here after fifty years. *Fifty years,* I said. And six months. And three days. Because it never gets any easier, is why. That's the bad news: I'm still coming. But the good news is: I'm still coming."

The applause started up again.

"Save your clapping," she said. "I'm old. My story's long."

It started when her husband ran off and left her with a baby girl. She'd always liked to drink, been a bit of a party girl when she was young, ended up with a party boy who did things like skip town the first chance he got. But it was only when she realized what her new life would really be like—no husband, no family, no future, only the daily work of this baby—that she really got bad. "The baby would cry all night," she said. "And I wouldn't even hear her." She drank wine alone in her kitchen, stole it when she was too broke to buy it.

Next to me, Abe was taking notes on a pad of paper. *Afraid of the reality,* he'd written. *The dream of disappearance.* No one else was writing anything.

Sarah's rock bottom had to do with her baby. I'd sensed it would, we all did, with a growing feeling of fear. One night Sarah didn't notice her daughter had crawled out of the apartment. The police found a tag on her pajamas, what she'd been wearing, and called Sarah to come pick her up. That was when Sarah realized she'd have to go to the police drunk. She tried everything—two cups of coffee, a cold shower, running through the streets until she lost her breath—but it didn't make much difference. She was too far gone. She showed up at the station in a clean outfit and talked as steady as she could. "That officer looked me in the eye," she said, "And he *saw* me. He saw what I was."

Abe had stopped writing. The last phrase on his paper was *rock bottom,* underlined three times. He caught me looking and covered it with his arm.

Sarah told us about the long road back. She drank tomato juice every night and did her step work in a tattered journal that she held in front of us: "My second baby." She went to meetings, did service, found a higher power she could trust. "People talk about God," she said. "But I felt like it was my mother's ghost. Wouldn't leave me alone for a goddamn second."

Laughter. The woman next to me clapped so loud and long, I thought she'd rub her hands raw.

"I spent a year without my child," Sarah said. "So I could spend the rest of my life with her."

Others around the room were leaning forward in their chairs, listening and nodding, eager to share once she was done. Their eyes were full of pain and victory. Here they were—making coffee, calling each other, swapping lives—and I hadn't done much since I'd gotten sober, just learned the TV schedule and watched the clock.

Abe was fidgeting beside me. I turned to see him putting on his coat in his chair.

"I've got to leave," he whispered. "You should stay."

I grabbed his arm harder than I meant to. "You're going?"

He didn't say anything, just stood and walked through our row, apologizing to the people who let him pass—twisting in their seats or pulling back their knees. "Sorry," he said. "Sorry. I'm sorry."

I stayed until the end, but I didn't stick around to talk to anyone. I didn't want to explain myself or why he'd left. I wasn't even sure myself. I knew there was a world I lived in—every night wanting, just *wanting,* my whole body aching under it—and he would never live in that world. He didn't have to. He wouldn't want to. He'd gotten out into the freedom of an empty night. I could follow him, and I did, but I couldn't find him out there, and I knew that, too.

I borrowed Stella's computer to search job listings. One called itself a "starting sales" position with a small agency, but it turned out you had to go door-to-door selling knives. Another listing said: *You Want to Save the Dolphins? Then Do It!* and claimed to pay twelve dollars an hour. You had to collect signatures on the street. I tried for a few days but hated shifting from one aching heel to another, watching every person glance up quickly and glance away again, hoping I wouldn't speak to them. You only got paid the full amount if you got enough names.

One day Abe came home early and found me standing by the TV. I'd been on my way to the microwave with a frozen pizza, but I'd gotten interested in the program along the way. Men were using whale songs to trick lost calves into coming home. My hands were cold under the cardboard.

"I found a couple listings this morning," I said. "I'm gonna call them after lunch."

"In general," he said, "you want to call before five."

It was almost four-thirty. I hadn't noticed.

He glanced at the screen. "You into this stuff?" Like it was trash.

I nodded, hurt. He must have known this about me, must have remembered all the programs he watched when he was little. "The show got me all distracted," I explained. "That's why I lost track of time." I held up the pizza. "Nearly got frostbite."

He took the box from my hand and put it on the counter. "You curious why I came home early?"

There wasn't anything about him that didn't make me curious.

He said: "I found you a job at my bank."

I was quiet for a moment. Then I said: "Because I couldn't find anything on my own."

"It's not like that. It's only a temp thing, but it's a good start."

"And you think I'd be okay at it?"

"It's not for specialists. I think you'd be fine."

Abe had become this kind of man, very polite. He used to hurt my feelings when he was a kid, and now I almost missed it. At least when he was willing to hurt me, he didn't feel like a stranger.

One time, he must have been seven or eight, he got mad because I made him do some chores around the trailer. I'd decided to make it more of a home, even if it was only for two weeks. "I don't want any chores," he said. "This isn't the place I live." He wouldn't take out the trash. He wouldn't even eat a bowl of cereal. He just sat there with his favorite stuffed animal, a green and purple dragon named Smoke. It had a curly tail and hard plastic eyes you could *rap-tap-tap* with your fingers. I could still hear his little voice. *He's not like other animals. He makes the fire in his belly.*

This was his first day, and those were usually the hardest, our starts and endings. He'd brought flannel pajamas from the city, covered in squirrels and too hot for summer, and a chocolate mouse that melted in its foil. His fingers pushed its ears right into its head. "Well, now it's ruined," he said, voice flat, and threw it in the trash. "Don't you have to go to work?"

I left him sitting there while I cleaned houses on the other side of town. I never went into Reno while he was visiting, so I found temp work with a maid service. I scrubbed another woman's tile floors while my son sat in my house thinking, *This isn't my home. This isn't my home.* But I got back to find him standing in the kitchen with an oven tray of unbaked cookies. He was holding his dragon. "Smoke is baking them," he told me. "It'll only take a couple centuries."

He was kind that day. He was willing to try.

We celebrated my new job with dinner. We had to eat after midnight because Stella had a night shift. I made a green-bean casserole that Stella probably knew as well as I did. It was one of Lucy's recipes. The secret was cornflakes.

I took a nap at eight and woke up at eleven to put my casserole in the oven. Nobody was home. I set the table and waited. I got up eventually and wrapped my hand in a dishcloth and pulled out the glass tray. Abe came up behind me, very sudden. "Careful with that," he said. "Those towels aren't thick."

He said he was going to meet Stella at her parking lot. He walked her home most nights. I hadn't known because I was never awake. I wondered what they found to talk about.

When they came back, Stella tossed a salad. "Something simple," she said, but it looked like a dish from a restaurant: green and purple lettuce, sweet pecans, pears sliced so thin you could see right through them. Since she'd started working, she'd learned a few things about how to make a home. She poured herself some wine and drank it fast, invisible sips as she whisked oil and vinegar. She looked up once and caught me watching. "Sorry," she said. "I wasn't thinking."

"No," I said. "You should do what you want."

"But still," she said. She poured me a glass of sparkling water for her toast, which was to me. Her salad was rich and oily. I dug for pecans. We tore chunks off a loaf of bread and dipped them in the dark swirl of our dressing. Stella talked about work stuff, gourmet coffee and designer bedspreads. "Nothing like the pleasures of material comfort," she said. "They're fabulous."

The night felt good—my new job, my old son, my niece, our home—and its parts gave off strong flavors in the heat of that table, like crushed tea leaves in boiling water. I was steeping. Our faces were flushed and open. I asked Abe about the bank. "So what does it *do* all day?" I said. "The people in it, I mean."

"He hates to talk about his work," Stella said. "I thought you knew."

"Oh," I said. I hadn't known.

Abe spoke sharply: "Now it's Tilly's work, too."

Stella raised her eyebrows.

"I don't know exactly what you'll be doing," he told me. "But I know you'll be working in the high-asset side of things. The clients with the big accounts."

Stella brought out three pieces of coffee cake in little plastic sandwich bags, leftovers from the inn. "It's just pieces," she said. "We give the rest to the maids."

Abe shook his head politely, *no thanks,* and got up to pour himself a glass of water. He said he had a conference call.

"It's two in the morning!" I said.

"London," he said, and thanked me for the casserole.

I told Abe I'd been wanting to wake up next to the ocean, and he said he could make this happen. Maybe we'd camp on Angel Island? This was where the Chinese people had stopped before they made it to Chinatown, with its lobster tanks and red paper dragons. One time on Stockton I'd seen a bathtub full of frogs and thought, *Now, these are a people I'll never understand.*

We went out to the island on my last weekend before work. It was full of palm trees and there was a large white building that looked like an insane asylum, with poetry scribbled on the walls in Chinese characters. The letters looked like a pile of sticks had fallen down, brushstrokes crossed in all directions, making tents for other brushstrokes to crouch under. There were plastic translations pasted next to them: *The waves are happy, laughing 'Ha, ha,'* read one. Another: *The barbarians have two wests / this one and the one / we came for.*

There was a photograph of a Chinese bride propped against the wall. Her face was all shades of gray, hair gathered into a tight bun that pulled back the skin of her face. She was waiting for a boat, or else the man she was supposed to marry. I turned her to the wall. I wanted to give her this, after all these years: a little privacy.

Abe and I took turns with the backpack while we explored. I liked knowing that our things were jostling together inside: sunscreen and water bottles, a bag of pretzels. Somewhere down there, our extra shirts lay close and folded.

Before twilight we set up camp on the shore. The water looked shifty and terrible, flashing back the gray sky. Sunset hadn't come yet but I knew the clouds were too thick for a good one. The water was like a lurking old man with his whole body spread as far as we could see. "Want to swim?" Abe said. "I wouldn't watch."

Even if it was a joke, I didn't like him thinking of me like that, my old body wrinkling in the cold water. I imagined easing through the darkness with a bottle of Potter's, could practically feel it coming through my body, unlocking the catch at the back of my throat. I remembered getting high with Arthur, how he'd pounded his fist against the ground like he was knocking on a door. "Are you down there?" he'd called. "Can you hear me?"

We lay back on the sandy grass. Waves were sliding over waves and hissing back again. Abe pointed at the stars. "I can see a puppy up there," he said. "A spaniel with . . ." He laughed.

"With what?"

"Straight above the second tree," he said. "Can't you see the body of a dog, four legs and then . . . a penis?"

"Christ." I laughed. "You're right."

I couldn't see it at all.

My fingers felt hard and full. The tips were red from cold. My breath was steaming out in puffs. It carried heat from my throat and the wet bag of my organs farther down.

"Was Stella right?" I asked.

"About what?"

"Last night. She said you hated talking about work."

"It's something I told her. And I meant it."

"But?"

"Now that you'll be working there . . ." he said. "It's different. We can talk about it, if you want."

He told me about the buildings. The bank owned twenty floors of one skyscraper, he said, and twenty-five floors of another one. It seemed a shame they didn't have an entire building. I didn't understand much about his world, and I was ready to accept that. My main priority was not being afraid to ask questions.

Abe launched into a list of the people I should watch out for. Turned out his division was full of crazies. I probably wouldn't be working with them, he said, but just in case. There was Joe

DiFranco with a drawer full of porn. "Most people are using web-sites these days," Abe said. "But not him." I didn't like to hear Abe talk about that kind of thing, as if he used websites, too. He told me about Demetrius Sloth, whose name still got jokes.

He thought you could learn a lot about people when you saw them staying late.

"Like what could you learn about you?" I said. "I mean, if you weren't you."

He laughed. He said he ate chocolate bars to keep himself awake, was one thing. He could eat four or five in a row.

He asked if I remembered the time I caught him eating sugar in the dark. He was maybe ten years old.

Of course I did, I told him. I'd found him striking his spoon into the hard bag. He explained the sugar was full of mountains and valleys, its own planet, and he was eating the whole world. He whispered, "I'm shoveling."

If he ate too much, I'd warned, the spiders would crawl into his mouth while he slept, because it was sweet. He'd smiled and taken another bite. I'd tasted some once he was gone, just to fall asleep with the same toothache.

"I kept my mouth wide open when I fell asleep that night," he said. "I wanted to catch a mess of spiders and name them after us."

"And did you?"

"No."

There was a long silence.

"Abe?"

"Yeah?"

"Do you still get that thing at night? Where you can't move?"

I remembered these most of all, the night terrors. They struck him suddenly, like stomach flu, and I'd wake to hear him calling my name, complaining that his limbs wouldn't listen to his mind anymore. *Like dead animals attached to all my endings.*

"I get it after dreams now," he said. "Only bad ones."

He climbed into our tent and left me alone by the edge of the ocean. The bay water was full of moon. I felt the night all over my cold arms. The days of my life stretched out like a series of wrapped presents, who knew what they'd hold? Strange nights like this one.

When I came into the tent Abe murmured in his sleep and turned toward the second bag like he was planning to embrace another body. "It's just me, baby boy," I said, and he turned away. The dirt was hard and cold under my body before I slept.

I woke up to the groan of a zipper. Waking up without hangovers felt very raw. I was alert to everything. The morning air was close and salty. The ocean made hushing sounds like it was trying to catch its breath: *Heshh, heshh, heshh,* wet sand stuck in its throat. Abe unzipped the flap to show a doorway full of sky, and then he peered inside. "So can you see it?" he said. "The ocean?"

"I see your face."

"Oh," he said. "Sorry."

Then he was gone, and the water was right there: a rustling blue strip under the bleached sky. The surface was busy with waves and little boats.

"Holy shit!" said Abe. "Goddamn *holy* shit."

"What?"

He said: "It's a dolphin."

I got up and stuck my neck out the flap. I peered at the water.

"No," he said. "On the shore."

He pointed at a gray shape on the sand. It looked like a stain.

"I think it's dead," he said. "I think it's a baby."

We walked down to see it. The body was curled like a comma on the cold beach, rubbery gray skin with its fin crusted in blood. Something had been at it in the night. There was a chunk of face eaten clean around one eye. "Jesus Christ," said Abe. "Let's go."

But I didn't want to go back. That felt like leaving it alone to die, even though it was already dead. Abe pulled out a plastic bottle of orange juice and a crinkly package of powdered dough-nuts, six puffy rings in a row. "Vending-machine breakfast," he said. "But now my appetite's shot."

My stomach closed like a fist. I took a doughnut anyway. It had been a nice idea.

We sat beside our tent and finished the juice at least. He reached into the backpack and pulled out a notebook. It was like the ones he'd had when he was young. I'd sent him special school supplies covered with motorcycles and cartoon characters, the brightest ones I could find, but in the summer he always brought simple notebooks in marbled black-and-white. He was all business right from the start.

Now he wanted to get me started with a five-year plan. It was a way, he said, of thinking small and big at once. You had goals for the next day, the next week, the next year, and so on. "Let's start large," he said. "Let's daydream."

I closed my eyes. "Okay."

"If you could do anything with your life," Abe said, "what would it be?"

"I'd like a little place of my own, I guess." Which wasn't even true. My favorite part of this new life was living with Abe.

"But what do you want to *make* from your life? That's the question."

"I don't want to make it into anything. I just want to get through it."

"Hmm," he said. "I see."

We talked about possible careers. He suggested professional housecleaning. He said I already had a résumé in this, from what I'd done in Nevada, and people would be impressed by a steady temp record at the bank. Maybe someday I could even run my own service. "Let's work from there," he said. "From an ideal outcome."

How would I get there? Abe had it figured out. If I started with one client, just one, and did solid work, she'd recommend me. Before I knew it, voilà. It could start like that.

"A simple flowchart," he said. "Make sense?"

The truth was, it was only showing me how another life could have gone, a life under my name, if I hadn't been the one living it. But I told him, "Now I've got a sense of where to start."

"Cheers to that," he said, raising the empty carton of orange juice. He handed me the plans, neatly folded. He said I'd want to keep them somewhere safe.

I made breakfast for Stella on my first day of work. I would've liked to make some for Abe, just that once, but he left early, like he always did. I was ready to use the metal thermos he had given me. "You'll want to bring your coffee from outside the office," he said. "Trust me." Stella gave me a sturdy pair of white sneakers for my daily commute and a little shoe bag to hold my pumps while I walked. I'd gotten a new set of blouses and pantsuits. *Sherry, egg-shell, celery, chartreuse.* These were colors I'd learned from catalogs.

I screwed up the coffee and it tasted like sludge. Stella told me it was thick like pudding and good, which was nice of her to lie about.

I walked to the bank towers in my new white sneakers. There was a courtyard full of stone benches where I stopped to change into my heels. I knew I was working in the shorter building. Abe had given me a contact name, Sylvia Rodriguez, and a floor (thirty-eight), and nothing else.

Sylvia was a short, busty woman from Colombia. Her accent made her sound amused at every moment. She met me in the lobby and took me upstairs, swiping her card through a maze of turnstiles and locked doors along the way. We stopped at a huge sweep of cubicles glowing sickly under bright fluorescent lights.

"Welcome to North America," she said. "This is your division."

"Okay," I said. "Sounds good."

"Now I will show you to the ropes." She handed me a piece of paper full of boxes: *Name of client. Name of account. Relevant persons. Level of risk.* The biggest one said: *Resolution?*

My job was basically running a computer program to make sure all the rich guys who had money in our bank weren't criminals. I typed their names into a database and then filled out a form if anybody came up as a hit. "It's very simple," said Sylvia. "But sometimes you get a mystery."

A man in a steel-gray suit and purple silk shirt introduced himself. This was Stan. He worked in the cubicle next to mine. "I'm a soprano fag," he said, right off the bat. He'd been one of the performers at the Excalibur casino, musical numbers and knight fights, but he'd gotten too old or too tired and he'd stayed unemployed for too long, running up credit-card debt. Now he was trying to get himself out of the hole.

"A lot of us owe money," he said, sweeping his arm to show the whole dim room. I imagined the scene like a musical number in an old movie: everyone turning to look at me all at once, nodding sadly in the same rhythm. "What's your story?"

"Just trying to get my life on track," I said. "That's all."

"Good for you," he said. He had a loud voice, but there was something quiet about him, too. He knew when to stop asking questions.

I ran names all morning, but no one came up hot. I knocked a jar of paper clips onto the floor and felt like a fool, crouching on the scratchy rug to pick them up, glancing over my shoulder to see if anyone was watching. I liked having my own file drawers, a space for the work I'd done, and the laminated security pass that Sylvia dropped on my desk. "Your clearance," she said, like we were spies.

By twelve-thirty, the place had emptied out. This was lunch. Everybody walked past with determined expressions. Where were they going? I called Abe on his office number. From my desk, I only had to dial an extension. I pulled out a small stack of menus from my top drawer, a few local restaurants I'd passed.

He picked up after one ring. "What's wrong?"

"Nothing," I said. "I was wondering if you wanted to get lunch."

"Oh," he said. "I don't really take lunch breaks."

"Why did you think something was wrong?"

"I just—I hoped everything was okay."

"It is."

"Good."

"How are you?"

"I'm fine, Tilly. But I should probably go."

He didn't call me *Mom,* never had, but there was a sting every time I heard him say something else. Which was silly. I'd called my mother Lucy since I left home, but I'd always wished—for my own sake, for hers—that it would feel more unnatural than it did.

I went out and bought a sandwich wrapped in plastic, brought it back to my desk, and kept working through the afternoon.

Abe came by before I left. "How was it?"

"I think it's gonna work out."

"Good," he said. "I'm glad."

I thought maybe he'd stay for a while, sit down and chat, but he made one jerky lunge forward, a kind of bow, and walked back to the elevators. He worked ten floors up. I tried to picture his view. Down here, in North America, we didn't even have windows.

In total, there were five temps working under Sylvia. Stan had been there longest. "Debt doesn't go away by itself," he said. "Plus, I keep making more of it." But I sensed he had an exciting life outside the office. He showed me photos from the Castro parade. In one of them, he wore a big paper hat that had empty beer bottles glued onto the rim. They pointed outward and made him look like the Statue of Liberty. "Come one, cum all," he said. "Isn't that the idea?"

There were two other men in our division: Omar, who was sending money back to his wife and daughter in Nicaragua; and Ted, an actor who'd been on several television programs. He was quick to share. "I guested on two seasons of *Law and Order: Pacific,*" he said. "You might remember me as the piñata bomber's estranged son?"

I'd never seen the show or even heard of it. I said, "I don't think I saw that episode."

"Episodes," he said. "Plural."

I let him keep going.

"It was a recurring role," he said, rapping his fingers on the desk. "What's your story, anyway?"

"I just wanted a decent job, that's all."

"Well, this isn't that." He laughed. "I hope you know."

The only other woman was named April. She had short hair like a pixie, and from the back, you could mistake her for a very young boy. She moved across the carpet without seeming to touch it, gliding past cubicles toward the communal bathroom. She often wore shoes that looked like ballet slippers, like Stella's. One time I asked her, "Are you a dancer?"

"Ha!" she said. "Wait till my therapist hears about that!"

She came from a teensy little town in the center of California, which made me feel like we had something in common. I'd been living away from cities for so long. "Goddamn buildings around here!" she said. "You can't see the sky anywhere." She was a woman who cussed in the office. You wouldn't guess from looking at her, her velvet skirts and gossamer scarves, but other people noticed, and I could tell it bothered some of them.

I was trying to improve my own talk a little. I wanted to sound respectable. I could see how hard Sylvia worked on how she spoke. I actually felt a little shy around her. She was the boss, after all, though Abe laughed at me once when I called her that.

"She's not *the* boss," he said. "She's got bosses and bosses and bosses above that. She was probably a temp a couple years ago."

"You said temps could move up."

"Not all the way. It's the difference between—"

"I get it," I said. "You don't have to explain."

"I didn't mean anything bad. I was only saying you shouldn't feel scared to talk to her."

I wasn't scared, exactly; it was just that when I thought about talking to her, I couldn't think of a single thing to say. Which I felt about a lot of people besides her.

One time she brought us bags of chewy coconut cookies. "These are treats from my country," she said. "I hope you enjoy them."

"Thank you."

There was a pause.

"Okay," she said. "Good luck with your morning."

At our group meeting, Stan whispered to me, "Honey, you've got crumbs." I saw he was right. Bits of cookie filled my shirt creases like dandruff. I brushed them off. I looked up and noticed April staring.

Eventually, I learned what to do with names that matched up to crimes or criminals on our database. "When the name is medium," Sylvia explained. "It's our bread and butter."

This was the language of our program. "Medium" was the tag that appeared when the client's name matched a criminal. Usually, it meant that some rich boy in Connecticut had the same name as a tax evader in Ireland or a drug dealer in the Bronx.

"What does 'medium' mean?" I asked Stan. "Why that word?"

He rolled his eyes. I knew he wasn't rolling them at me. He

was bored to death in his cubicle, and his face seemed to say; *You must be, too.*

"It means 'medium risk,'" he said. "Like they could be serious trouble, but thousand to one they aren't."

"Does it ever come back high?"

"Osama bin Laden comes back high. And maybe Saddam Hussein back in the day. But that's about it."

I wasn't sure if he was kidding.

"I wouldn't try searching them, though. The office doesn't like funny business."

I smiled. That was a phrase my mother used when me and Dora played our tricks: dropping flaming paper bags of dog shit on people's porches and ringing their doorbells. Dora only did it for a year before she started telling on me. *Funny business.* It was odd to have the same words show up in different parts of your life. It felt like going to sleep in your bed and waking up somewhere else.

Every day I made a little stack of stapled reports, one for each medium file, and turned them in to Sylvia. I'd never had a job that involved so much paperwork. When I packed my papers in Nevada, I barely had enough to fill a box. I liked the clean heat of pages from the printer, the smell of marker when I highlighted relevant names and dates. I was careful to let each page dry before I piled another page on top.

Sylvia was committed to every part of the job—the vocabulary and color-coded graphs, the cheerful smiling. One day I walked into her office and found her standing between two men. Their faces were red, their voices raised, their ties loosened. "Where do you *think* electricity comes from?" one said. Sylvia caught my eye and made a slicing gesture across her throat. *Come back later,* she mouthed. I closed the door without making a sound.

Stella was interested in my job. *Your work,* she was always saying. I always said: *My job.* She was never asking about the things I wanted to talk about. My strongest impressions were of the strange hospital smell of the place, the small satisfaction of keeping my white sneakers and my bag lunch in two separate file drawers. I had four drawers in total. These were the things I appreciated, but they never felt like the right answers to Stella's questions.

She asked, "Is it fulfilling?"

"How do you mean?"

"Does it feel stimulating? Challenging?"

"It's not like making a painting or finding the cure for a disease," I said. "But it's not bad. People treat me with respect."

I'd been thinking of it like this: I started at the same time every day and I knew when I was going to finish. I knew I was going to put a certain amount of money in my checking account at Wells Fargo Bank. These were satisfactions. I'd tacked two photographs onto the flimsy wall above my desk: one of Abe when he was young, holding Smoke in his tiny freckled hands; and a postcard of a spiky-sided cactus against a background of big puff clouds. The photo was from Arizona, not Nevada, but it gave me a feeling I liked. I tried to explain to Stella: I missed the West.

"You're *in* the West," she said. "This is as far west as you get."

I knew she was right, but it didn't feel that way to me.

"But what do you *do* all day?" Stella asked. "I mean, minute by minute?"

Abe was there, listening.

"A little of this, a little of that. Making sure the reports have all their pieces."

"But basically, you just run the same program over and over again?"

"Come on, Stella," said Abe. "What's your point?"

She gave him a look—of surprise and also hurt—that gave me a rush of pleasure. It was a victory I couldn't explain.

Abe asked better questions. He actually knew the place. "Do you have those free packets of oatmeal in your kitchen?" he asked.

"They're good snacks." Once he asked about my low hour—when did I get really bored? His theory was that everyone had one. His was five to six, when other people started going home.

"But you're liking it alright?" he asked.

I nodded. "To be perfectly frank, though, I miss the sun."

I asked him why we didn't have any windows. He said it had to do with the Miami branch. Someone jumped off the nineteenth floor and so they made a policy.

I kept the restaurant menus in my second drawer but never used them. They seemed to belong to another life: a life of power lunches and event, a life in the movies, or thirty years in the past, before I'd turned into myself. Downtown lunches were expensive, even just a cup of deli soup, so I started packing my own. I didn't see the point in spending so much money just to eat alone. I packed mine in brown paper bags like a schoolkid: yogurts and apples; sandwiches with fatty cuts of ham, like Lucy made, and lots of mayonnaise.

There was a homeless woman who sat with me on the benches. It was hard to say why it felt like she was sitting with me because she never sat particularly close. We never spoke. It had something to do with the way she carried herself, very stiff and proper, and sent respectful glances in my direction. She wore an old gray suit, a man's suit, with a black stain all over the chest pocket like her heart had leaked dark blood. Her sleeves were worn through in patches and you could see her elbows. She was a black woman but her hair was white, mostly covered by a broad straw hat. She didn't ask for money or say anything, just sat down as soon as I did and left when I got up, nodding slightly before she walked away.

After a few days I asked if there was something in particular she liked about the bench. She tipped her hat with one finger. "Just the company."

The next day I brought an extra sweatshirt tucked into my purse, wrapped around my lunch bag. Before we got up to leave, I tapped her on the shoulder. "I could sew the elbows of your jacket. I'd bring it back tomorrow."

"I'm much obliged," she said. "But I'd be a little chilly without it."

"We could trade." I pulled out the sweatshirt. *My Heart's Locked Up in Lovelock*. More than it reminded me of Fiona, it reminded me of her leaving.

The woman shook her head. "I can't."

"I'm not half bad at this stuff," I said. "Patching up and all that."

She gave me her jacket in the end. She took the sweatshirt, clutching it stiffly like a stranger's baby. Before she left, she told me her name was Toledo. She'd named herself, she said. Her mouth sparkled with gold fillings when she spoke.

I used red corduroy patches because I didn't have anything else around. Now she'd look like a professor. The jacket stank like rotten lettuce. It didn't smell like a woman. I washed it in my sink with a few squirts of dish soap. This was how I'd done laundry when I didn't have much cash.

The next day she brought the jacket close to her face. "Smells good," she said. "I woulda washed it too." She pulled a piece of paper from her pocket and unfolded it, a take-out menu from a Chinese place called Peking Palace. The other side showed the charcoal sketch of an old man's face. I took the paper and stared at the lines—strong and black, fluid like water.

"I saw that guy on the street yesterday," she explained. "Just sitting there and staring at his hands."

She closed my fingers over the paper and I understood: She wanted me to have something in return.

I started bringing her food. I never packed a separate lunch because I thought it might make her feel embarrassed. Instead I brought extras of whatever I'd brought for myself: another tuna sandwich, a couple muffins from Stella's work. One time I asked her why she'd named herself Toledo but she shook her head and kept silent. I didn't ask again.

I liked what she drew: long human faces with their wrinkles jagged like branches. Never anything imagined, only things she'd seen. She told me she used to do this for money all the time—"like that guy in L.A," she said, "the guy with all the poems"—but stopped because it felt like she was giving away too much. "Once you give it to another person, you can't keep it for yourself."

"I don't think that's necessarily true," I told her. "I hope it's not." The sound of my own voice surprised me. The word "hope" was like a splinter I'd choked on. Now I was trying to spit it up.

April often stopped by my cubicle on her way to the coffee lounge. It got to be a routine. She was nicer than she looked, told me things about being a small-town kid. *I used to count my rabbit's heartbeats. My mother made me drink vinegar every time I used a bad word.* She seemed surprised that I was interested. "You actually give a fuck about this crap, don't you?" She made me realize how ugly the words really were—fuck, shit, shitfucker, asshole—though I couldn't imagine her using any words but those. Her mother's vinegar wasn't anywhere in sight. I liked how these words contorted her face into definite expressions. I didn't see that very much from anyone. People were always hidden behind their faces. I knew I never was.

Stella suggested we use our weekends to explore the city. One time she got tickets to an art exhibit full of petroleum-jelly sculptures. A wall had gotten torn down, she said, to make room for the statues. She seemed pleased about this.

"I should warn you," I told her. "I'm not really an art person."

175

But we went. The exhibit even had a movie. It played in a dark room that smelled like suede. All the action happened on a whaling ship. There was a storm. Two lovers sliced each other with knives. Body parts floated away from other body parts. There weren't any words.

"What's it about?" I whispered.

"About?" Stella shook her head. "It's not that kind of movie."

She could be this way, impatient.

The upstairs was full of massive white molds that looked like somebody had bleached a bunch of gelatin salads. Lucy used to make fruit molds for PTA meetings no matter what time of day they happened. "It's always nice to bring something," she'd said. "It shows you care."

The statue I liked best was a fallen concrete pillar stuck all over with husks of shrimp and drizzled with glaze. Stella whispered in my ear, "Looks like a doughnut."

"More like a cruller," I said. "Those are the long ones."

It was hard to tell if the material was brittle or soft, jammy or dried. It looked like hardened jelly. Would it smear against our fingers? The sign said: DO NOT TOUCH. Maybe they'd broken walls for this one. It looked big enough.

That piece had a kind of power over me. I wanted to feel the shape with my fingers. I was tired of just looking. I had to clench my hands into fists. I kept thinking about touching it. There were times I needed, more than anything, to bring the thing *inside* me, to bring it close.

"What is it?" Stella whispered. "Are you upset?"

I could barely breathe. I ran downstairs and into the sunlight.

Stella found me in a park across the street. "What happened in there?" she said. "You okay?"

I was quiet for a moment. I took big breaths that felt cold behind my ribs.

We were only a few blocks from the office. I thought of Abe, somewhere close, typing spreadsheets. He worked most Saturdays.

Stella sat on the grass and patted the dirt next to her. She waited for me to speak, pulling up tufts and rubbing them back into the ground. I could tell she was trying not to say anything. The sound of her keeping quiet got to seem like a question on its own. We watched a woman farther down the hill, twirling with her arms high in the air.

"One time I saw a bird trapped in a house," I said finally. "A very *small* house. My house."

She nodded. I kept going.

"I didn't want to kill it. I just wanted to touch it. I stood there and clutched my one hand with the other until it got to feel so bad—like hurting or busting open."

"Did you catch it?"

I lied. I said, "It flew out a window."

At the bottom of the hill, the twirling woman started walking toward us. She looked a little like Toledo but she was walking funny, like she had a limp, and Toledo walked just fine. The figure got closer, kept getting bigger, and in a minute I could see: It *was* her. She was strung out on something, I didn't know what. She jerked her head back and forth. Her white sneakers were covered with little red lights that glowed with every stride.

It didn't seem like she recognized me. She pulled a square of newspaper from her pocket and unfolded it. It was covered with hard blisters of gum—white, green, yellow—and I could see a headline about the war. It could have been from days ago, or years. She kept pulling items from her pocket and laying them on the grass in front of us: a crushed milk carton, a shard of brown glass, a severed doll leg, a syringe tucked inside a plastic bag. She said, "I'm collecting everything I've ever stepped on."

"I'm sorry," Stella said. "But I don't have any money."

"I didn't *ask* for your goddamn money," Toledo said. She kicked the ground with her sneaker.

Stella glanced at me. She was afraid but trying to hide it.

"Toledo," I said, "do you recognize me?"

"You know her?" Stella whispered.

Toledo's eyes were roving. She shifted her weight from one foot to the other in a kind of dance.

Stella grabbed my arm. "You know her?"

I knew Toledo had a regular shelter, but they didn't let you in if you were drunk or high. "This shit is all over the place," she said, then picked up her objects and dropped them on the grass again: the doll's leg, the poster board of gum. "Right now you don't even know what they're doing to kids in other cities."

"What's going on?" I asked her. "What's all this about?"

She sucked in her breath sharply, and then she spat on the top of my head. I felt it through my hair. I looked up. Her eyes were like slits showing a nest of shiny black ants. I'd never seen a look like that on her face, or anyone's.

"My name's Toledo," she said. Like we'd never met. "It's where my dad was killed."

I could feel the spit on my face, but I didn't wipe it off. I said, "You need some rest."

"You don't even know the *first* thing."

Stella whispered, "We should really go."

I let her lead me away. We walked across the park. Stella was breathing hard. "Jesus," she said. "She *spat* on you." She pulled a tissue from her bag, made a cone of one corner, and started wiping my hair.

"Let me." I took the tissue. "Thanks."

I put two fingers against Stella's neck to feel her pulse. Her heart was going like mad. *I didn't want to kill it. I just wanted to touch it.* She flinched. She didn't want the spit on her skin too.

* * *

Dora waited a few months until she came. I'd known she would. She knew I turned everything rotten—sooner or later, it was all she'd ever seen me do—and she wanted to see her own daughter. What had I done to her?

Stella asked if I was willing to see her. I wanted to know, was she willing to see me?

Dora would be busy with work, was the answer, but she was willing to meet if I was. I was willing to meet if she was. Going in these circles hurt my head. There was an evening chosen.

Dora explained to Stella that she'd taken the asylum case of six Chinese women in San Jose. That was why she was coming. The women had been trafficked into prostitution, living with their pimp.

I knew Dora had reasons for coming that didn't have anything to do with these women or how to save them.

"These women were living in an *attic*," Stella said. "All six of them together." They needed her mother's help. There was a note of pride in her voice I hadn't heard before.

I remembered the bride in the photograph on Angel Island. Her eyes looked like something that could reach out and grab you. She'd been afraid, too.

Dora was only staying a few days. Stella and I agreed to meet her at a Chinese restaurant on Stockton. The owner had offered to let these women stay during the proceedings, so it had become Dora's unofficial base of operations.

I saw her sitting like a shrine—perfectly still, so elegant—in a room full of drunken Chinese businessmen. Her body had such clean edges, just like I remembered, as if she'd been perfectly carved. She stood when she saw us.

"Matilda," she said. "Tilly."

I saw myself as she must have seen me: ridiculous, with a run in my panty hose and a pair of sweaty palms, so nervous to be standing in front of her. I didn't speak. What did she want me to say?

She hugged me stiffly. "Well," she said, "here we are." I nodded. We sat. Dora turned to me. "I don't want this to be hard between us. I really don't."

I nodded again.

"Please *say* something. Just say anything."

"Mom," said Stella. "Lay off."

There was a pause. Dora looked at me. Stella looked at me.

"It's already hard," I said. "It's hard for me."

Dora sighed. "The restaurant wants to bring us some of their lychee wine," she said. "On the house."

The walls were draped in red fabric. In the corners of my vision, they gave the impression of bleeding.

"Oh," said Stella quickly. "None for me."

Dora smiled. Her terrible smile, as if nothing you could possibly say would ever ruffle her. "They're happy to bring you anything you want. Green tea, Peking duck. Frog legs, if you're up for it."

"Just tea," said Stella.

I smiled politely. "The same for me."

A girl came to the table and stood quietly with her hands tucked behind her back. She was wearing black pants and a red silk shirt, her hair pulled into a bun so tight it must have hurt her face. One ear looked wrong, flattened across the top. She didn't look old or young. She looked small. Dora wasn't much bigger, but she seemed bigger, and the girl slouched under my sister's loud voice like it was something heavy.

Was she one of the six? I pictured the pimp making her kneel, grabbing her hands behind her back, and drawing a knife down her back to split the silk blouse into open curtains. What had he done to her ear? She leaned close to Dora without moving her hands and said something quickly in Chinese.

Dora asked us. "Dumplings?"

I shook my head. Stella said, "It's fine. We ate at home."

Dora turned to the woman. "Shi," she said, then something that sounded like: "shay shay." She told us. "She's bringing some."

Stella started: "We said we didn't—."

"She wanted to bring them," Dora said. "So I let her."

"You speak Chinese?" I asked.

"I know the word for *dumpling*. And the word for *yes*."

"Is she one of—"

"One of my clients? No." Dora drummed her fingers against the table, anxious. She said, "I would never, *never* let a client wait on me like that."

"Oh," I said. "I didn't know."

Now I had to play back everything I'd pictured, like putting a film on rewind: tied hands, knife across the ear, slashed silk. It seemed like I'd hurt that girl myself, just thinking of these wrong things being done to her.

We sat there, quiet. Finally Stella broke the silence. She wanted to know what we remembered from our youth. Had there been games? Secret codes? Anything?

"Well," Dora said, "there was the tree village."

She explained how we'd planned a secret civilization. The most important thing about our plan was tree houses, everybody got one, and the second most important thing was justice: equal everything for everyone. We'd had pulley buckets for water and fallen fruits. We had sketches. The justice part was hazier, never sketched or planned, mainly a conceptual dimension, Dora said, sounding like the lawyer she'd become. I remembered waterslides made possible by gravity and rope ladders. We spoke nervously, me and Dora, afraid to let this go. But at least we were together in this fear. What would we talk about next?

It was harder to talk about our lives now. Dora didn't bring up mine, which was fine with me, or what had happened in the years between our lives splitting apart. I wouldn't have told much even if she'd asked. She wouldn't have understood. She said she'd been to Peru recently. Another business trip.

"Did you get much time to explore?" I asked. "After your work?"

"How do you mean?"

"Were you just working? Or did you have some time for yourself?"

"I put quite a bit of myself in my work."

"Come on," Stella said. "You know what she means. Did you take any side trips? See any sights?"

"Oh," she said. "Sightseeing. I went up to Machu Picchu."

"How was it?" I asked.

"It was great," she said. "A lot of fog. A lot of llamas."

"That sounds nice," I said. "I've never left the country."

Dora laughed softly. "You were always good at that."

"At what?" Stella asked.

"She makes me feel terrible about everything I've accomplished. She did it when she was young, too."

"Mom," said Stella. "Jesus."

"It's okay," I said. "She's probably right."

The Chinese girl came back and poured tea that smelled like moss. In my mind, even, I shouldn't have been thinking: *girl*. Dora was very careful about calling them women.

"One of these women," she said. "You won't believe what happened to her today."

"What's that?" I asked. I wanted to show Stella, wanted to show both of them, that I could do this. I could be fair. I could try.

"She was supposed to pick up some chickens from the butcher," Dora said. "A couple extras for the lunch rush. She got them live in wooden crates, but when she hopped a bus, the driver said live animals weren't allowed, so she snapped their heads—right there."

"I thought you said the girls weren't working for the restaurant," Stella said. "The women, I mean. I thought you said they were just staying here?"

"She was doing them a favor, that's all. You need to understand what they're running away from. It's complicated."

"It sounds terrible." I said.

"I mean, they had everything, absolutely *everything* taken."

"They're still here, aren't they?" I asked.

"You wouldn't—" Dora paused. "I think it's hard for any of us to imagine what it would be like to get sold."

We sat quietly, pouring tiny cups of tea, until the girl brought the dumplings. Dora ate one whole, popped it right in her mouth. I bit one in half and a brown soup spilled all over my chin. Dora handed me a pack of tissues from her purse.

I said: "I can imagine."

"How do you mean?" Dora asked.

"I was a prostitute," I said. "For twenty years I was. I know it's different, I mean, it's so absolutely . . . But I just mean, it's not the end of—"

"I didn't know," said Dora.

"You're not surprised."

"Oh, Tilly," she said. "I am."

I could see the shame in her eyes, just a blink. Even if I never saw it again, I would know the shame was there, like maggots under her skin. It would keep her asking: *How? When? Why?*, her wondering like worms growing into the old wound.

"I'm so sorry," she said. "So terribly sorry to hear that."

"Well, that's that," I said. "Now you know." I picked my purse up off the floor and pushed back my chair. It scraped awkwardly and almost tipped, like it does when I'm drunk, but I wasn't drunk. I wanted that to count for more.

"Don't go," said Dora. "Not again."

"She's right," Stella said. "You should stay."

I sat down. I kept my purse in my lap. I looked Dora straight in the eyes. "Did you think about me, even?"

She looked surprised. "When?"

"After I got kicked out, for starters, and all the years after."

"Did I *think* about you? Of course I did."

"You have this way of—you make everything I say sound like a stupid question."

"You were there and then you weren't. That's all. I wish there were another way of putting it."

I stood again. This time the chair moved easily. Stella bit her lip. "I'll see you at home," I said. She didn't say anything.

The restaurant door was locked, and I had to wait for a little girl, eight or nine, to fetch the key. She was shy. She barely met my eyes. I thought Stella might follow me but she didn't. The little girl bowed as I left.

For two hours I waited. I waited without drinking anything, on the couch, with the television on mute, then turned up loud, then mute again. When was Stella coming back? I imagined how she'd explain me to Dora. *She's sensitive,* maybe. *Her life is in pieces.*

There was a program about jellyfish, waving their glowing tentacles. But I was tired of the feeling that came from watching beautiful things. I got shock-eyed, still-bodied and admiring. I shut off the TV. I went to the fridge. I found a bottle of chardonnay—a screw-top, cheap. I opened it. I hadn't drunk wine in years, but I liked its roundness. It smoothed the edges off moments. For years it hadn't been strong enough. I'd needed something, always, to take me deep under—something that wouldn't leave anything behind, that would leave me saying *Fuck this, fuck it all,* let the whole world roll off my body like water.

The first taste was warm. It wasn't gin, not the flame-throwing, throat-stung burn of liquor. It took me gently. I poured a glass.

Maybe this could be it, only this one, like undoing the top button of your jeans to ease the fit. I could feel my whole body rising to meet the taste. It was taking me low, so sweetly and carefully. I poured a little more.

I thought about this feeling every day. But I hadn't remembered how good it was, how little it asked. It would take me to the old dark place—the deep sleep, the rest.

Stella was waiting the next morning. She'd made eggs, sunny side up. "They got cold," she said. "You're late for work."

She was washing the frying pan in the sink and I could hear the sound of the scrubbing pad, the metal sponge against metal. The grating rubbed behind my eyes and sliced my nerves down their shiny centers. The sound touched parts of me that hadn't ever been touched. I had a terrible headache.

"I'm sorry I'm late," I said to her back. "You didn't have to make this."

"I wanted to," she said. She turned from the sink. "I wish last night had gone differently."

It was in her voice, clear as day: She thought it was my fault. I said, "You think it was my fault."

She looked at me sharply. "You didn't give her a chance to respond to what you said." she said.

I took one forkful of eggs but they made my stomach flip. My mouth tasted dry, like it was full of crushed wads of paper. My scalp ached around every hair.

"Was everything okay last night?" she asked. "After you got back?"

I knew the look in her eyes. I knew what it meant. I hated that she was right.

"It's always been this way," I said. "With your mother, I mean. Even when we were young. It was like she *knew* me—not just who

I was but who I'd be in ten years, thirty. She always thought I was a slut."

Stella shook her head. "That's not a word she uses."

"She used it once," I said. "With me."

"She's not perfect. You know I . . . God knows I talk about it. But with *this,* with how you've been or what you've done, I don't think she judges it."

"I don't think," I said. "I know."

"You don't know. You just assume."

"You hear yourself?" I shook my head. "Suddenly you're her biggest fan?"

"She's not all bad."

"You talk about her like she's pretty bad."

"She's my mother. You've got to understand that. My *mother.*"

I stood up and scraped my eggs into the trash. "I'm late, like you said," I told her. "I should get to work."

Work was getting worse each day. Everyone else came into the office and sat down and got up, sat down and got up, and it seemed like it wasn't any trouble for them. But I was restless. I must have looked like a fool, always rustling my papers, uncrossing my legs and then crossing them the other way. I caught myself staring into space. Not space, really. The wall of my cubicle, my stupid photo of the desert. When I heard the word *desert,* I'd think about that postcard instead of the actual place. I took it down and threw it away. All day I was typing reports that no one ever read. My fingers felt like they had individual stomachaches. My knuckles got creaky. I'd been avoiding Toledo since we'd seen her in the park. She still sat outside the office during lunches, glancing in my direction, but I hadn't done anything to fix the shame I saw in her eyes.

Everyone else had a real life somewhere else. Ted had his television shows. Stan had parades of flapping flags and lovers. Omar had a beaming wife much taller than he was, at least in photos. His daughter had a lace dress as white as milk. She had a fondness, he said, for these swarms of flies that came off Lago Nicaragua. *Diablos pequeños,* he called them. Little devils. Hated by everyone but her. He missed her very much. *I miss a lot,* was what he said, and he meant things in particular: two of her birthdays, kitchens full of folks eating fried *platanos* and beans, and her first Communion, when she told the priest the wafer tasted like a brick. *I miss a lot.*

I asked if he had any plans for Thanksgiving, which was coming up in a week. He shook his head.

I didn't have plans either, but I invited him to Harrison Street anyway. And then, in a snap, I didn't just have plans, I'd made them for someone else too. I knew the holiday couldn't mean much to him. All our country had done was fuck his country over. At least that's the sense I got. But I thought it might be a nice chance to show some kindness. *I will accept,* he said, which meant he already had.

I hadn't asked Abe and Stella, but I felt like doing something like this—without their knowing or their help—my own plan for all of us. *You didn't give her a chance,* she'd said. But the times me and Stella fought were good ones, in their way. Like she took me seriously. This was what happened when lives got close and tangled.

Stan leaned over from the next cubicle. "You doing a stray-dog meal?" It turned out he wanted to come too.

Sylvia had plans, but April didn't, and Ted surprised me by accepting my invitation, barely muttered. "Count me in for now," he said. "I'll let you know if something else comes up."

One moment there was nothing, and then there was something: a plan, the thought of people laughing in a room, all together, because of something I'd made. I sat in the corner of the handicapped bathroom and cried like a little girl. I'd heard people using the word *family* and now, this one time, they were talking about mine. Kids cry when they get happy too. It's like you need to let the feeling break you into little pieces before you can collect them again.

It was my first time cooking turkey. All afternoon I kept peering into the oven window. Oil blistered the skin. The bird looked like it was folding its wings to make a nest between the racks. I stuck the thermometer into its thigh to check its roasting muscles.

When we pulled it out, Stella thought it looked too crisp. I thought it looked just right. I'd wanted to make it like Lucy's. Year after year she cooked the bird too long because she was afraid she hadn't cooked it long enough. The meat was so dry it sucked the spit out of your mouth. But I missed the feel of it.

Figured that I'd get the turkey right and let the soy turkey burn. "Holidays are meant for eating all God's creatures," said Stella, but April was vegetarian so I'd gone to the trouble. Then I'd lost track of the tofurkey in the rush of torching marshmallows over the sweet potatoes, until Stella smelled it—*like someone scorched a bowl of miso soup,* she said—and I pulled it out. It was a mound of blackened strips like fabric.

"Shit," I said. "God never meant for this."

"Just take off the skin," Stella suggested. "Or the soy peel. Whatever it's called."

I took a knife and cut away slabs. What remained looked pale and helpless, like it had just been born. I wrapped it with tinfoil to keep the heat from getting away.

The table looked like something from a fairy tale, all our food steaming: slices of turkey fanned like the pages of a book, roasted vegetables that were dark and crinkled at their edges, the charred ends of broccoli florets, black-striped carrots; a swamp of stuffing with squares of bread poking through the gravy like they were struggling for air.

Abe hovered behind Stella, flapping an extra heat glove as she pulled our sweet potatoes from the oven. "Watch that!" he said. "It's hot!" He touched her with care, as he had done with me.

Omar arrived first, holding a bottle of dark rum. "It's a favorite where I come from," he said. "If you have some Coca-Cola?"

We didn't.

"Ah!" Omar grabbed a glass from the table. He poured half an inch of rum and drank it straight. "Just plain, then. This is another local custom."

Every Friday afternoon, Omar sent an e-mail to my work account that said, *Many good wishes for your weekend.* He showed me how to respond in Spanish: *Para ti también.* It felt like we were writing song lyrics.

He handed Abe the bottle. Abe handed it back. "Not for me," he said.

"You should take some," I told him. "It won't . . . you know. If you want it."

"It's fine," Abe said. He seemed impatient.

April arrived in a denim skirt and cowboy boots with a scarf around her throat, pale rose and gauzy, and a bottle of wine in each hand. "One's for the table," she said. "The other one's for me."

I could taste the wine from looking at it, like one of those time-lapse television programs that shows an acorn becoming an oak tree, the stages quick as finger snaps: the opening pang against my tongue, the warm wash of draining the first glass, the phlegm in my throat after another, the dark thick feeling of my whole body swaying.

I took both of her bottles and then I guided her toward the couch, where Omar was speaking to Abe in gunfire Spanish. I heard something *loco,* and then I heard *super-grande,* the first syllable made to sound like soup. Abe's legs were crossed and his arm was draped over the back of the couch, *our* couch, the one that made me think of Haitian children, and his beard looked like a sweatshirt his skin was wearing. His fingers were pale. When he gestured, you could see the wires of his joints doing work under his skin.

"April," I said. "This is my son, Abe."

"Hey, Abe," she said. "Nice place."

"You work with Tilly?" he asked.

"We share a cave downtown," she said. "If that's what you mean."

"Is that so?" He smiled.

"Yep," she said. "Doing legwork for men without souls."

"Abe works there, too," I said. I'd told her before, I was sure.

He said: "My mom tells me you're a wonderful person to work with."

We waited for her to respond. She didn't.

"I didn't know you spoke Spanish," I said to Abe. "That you understand it."

"Only when Omar speaks to me like a child. All I got was: *El presidente tiene una cabeza que es grande* . . . and it was pretty much a wash from there."

"The president is a dick?" said April. "That's the general gist?"

"Ella comprende mucho," Omar said.

I went back to the kitchen and set April's bottles on the counter. Then I took the corkscrew and ducked into the bathroom with one of ours. I opened it, tipped it back—felt the wine, its deep red river—swallowed hard, and tipped it back again. I stashed it under the sink, right next to the toilet paper.

Stan brought a six-pack of home-brewed beer. "Recipe from an ex," he explained. "The head is better than his was."

Stella laughed. She said, "We're going to get along."

Ted brought a pan of brownies. "Everyone brings booze to dinner parties," he said. "But I'm not everyone."

"They look delicious," I said. I wrapped my arm around

Stella's waist. I spoke away from her face so she wouldn't smell my breath. "This is Stella," I told him. "You remember I talked about her?"

"You're very striking," he said. He kissed her hand. "And there's so much of you."

"Excuse me?" She frowned.

"It's a line from a movie," he said. "I forget which one."

"Oh."

"It is," he said. "I swear."

She picked up his brownies. "I'll put these in the kitchen," she said. "With all the desserts we already have."

We peeled the foil off our dishes and tested them with our fingers. We put them in the microwave. The bread swamp bubbled. The marshmallows puffed into sweet golf balls and then sank into popped balloons of dark sugar. We walked around the table with our plates, every man for himself, and settled into eating without anyone waiting for anyone. I went to the bathroom, crouched down, came back, joined the others. Abe tucked his napkin into his collared shirt. We talked about what it might have been like to discover the New World—the strange berries, the testosterone, the typhoid. Stan asked Abe what he remembered best about our summers in Nevada and he said, *Heat, mainly,* and everybody laughed. Abe looked at me with a question in his eyes, to make sure it was alright that they were laughing. I went to the bathroom and ate quickly when I got back to cover the smell on my breath. The stuffing tasted like a big mushroom sponge and the charred marshmallows ached against my cavities and chewing the turkey made my jaw sore because I really had cooked it too long and it really was too dry. Everyone was wet. They were drinking April's wine, then our wine, then April's wine again. Stan drank his own beer. He offered me a bottle. I said no.

We left battlefields on our plates: corpses of drumsticks, collapsed potato dams where the gravy made rivers. I stood up and clapped my hands and said: "Dishes by the sink. Nobody touches the soap but me."

Nobody touches the soap was Lucy's phrase. I'd been waiting for a chance to say it all my life, could still remember Dora mocking, *I'll touch whatever I like,* during one of her moods, though she'd always been happy to let our mother clean up everything.

I liked the warm water against my arms and the sound of voices from the next room. It was easy to fall into a kind of trance. The wine smell on my breath made a woozy bandage around my face. I rubbed my hands to make bubbles under the steady water.

I tucked another bottle under the bathroom sink—I'd finished the first one—and then I joined the others. I had to focus on both sides of the kitchen doorway to make sure I didn't bump my shoulders. I drifted left when I was drunk. It had to do with balance, maybe handedness.

Everyone had broken into clusters. Abe and Omar hunched over one corner of the table. Omar's sleeves were rolled, and he raised his clenched fist to knock it once, twice, three times in the air—like he was raging against the dark night beyond our skylight. Abe grinned. I heard him say, "Kay La *Styma?*" and Omar put his head in his hands, his whole body shaking with laughter. He raised his head and said, "Qué *lá*-stima!" This was a phrase he'd already taught me. They were talking about everything going wrong.

Ted was flirting with Stella on the couch and she was letting him. He pointed at his mouth and then the bottom of his foot. I heard him say, "For absolutely fucking *real,*" and then she laughed so loudly that I knew she'd forced it. I saw Abe turn to look at her. Stan and April sat at the other end of the table. Stan was holding his belly and April was taking small forkfuls of turkey and stuffing from his plate. So she was that kind of vegetarian. I watched without anyone watching me.

Ted got up from his seat and started to impersonate a mechanical bull he'd once ridden. "Patrick Swayze was there," he said. "Cheering me on like crazy." Stella sat with her legs crossed and a smirk on her face.

April took Omar's rum back to the couch and set it down in front of Ted. "Looks like you might need this," she said.

"I need it," said Stella, reaching.

They took a round of shots, and then Ted said he would show us a magic trick. He fetched his pan of brownies and set them on the coffee table. I sat down slowly, careful not to lose my balance or show how hard I was trying not to lose it.

"For this particular trick," Ted said, "I will need an assistant."

"Oh, Lord," said Stella. "Anybody want a smoke?"

"What's that?" he said. "You want the job?"

"Stella's playing assistant?" Abe said. "I wouldn't mind seeing this."

"Oh, fuck you," Stella said. "Pour me another shot."

"I'll also need some kind of cape," Ted said. "Or any kind of fabric."

I leaned over to whisper in Abe's ear: "I knew a woman who made capes." I covered my mouth with my hand, but he smelled it. I could see his face fall. His eyes went wide. "You're drunk," he said.

"Don't worry," I said, shaking my head. "You shouldn't worry."

He touched my wrist, but I didn't look up. I kept shaking my head. I kept my face down. I could feel my eyes getting wet, and I didn't want him to see. I didn't want to see him.

"Hey," he said. His voice was hard. "Look at me."

I looked at him.

"This is a problem."

"Please don't make a scene," I said. "Don't ruin this."

"I'm not the one—" He bit his lip. "I'm not ruining anything." He got up and walked into the kitchen. I sat perfectly still. I wasn't sure what to do.

Ted cleared his throat and unfastened his top button. "If there's not a cape lying around, I suppose I could use my own shirt."

"Keep your shirt on," said Stella. "I'll get a dish towel."

"My lovely assistant," he said, gesturing in her direction.

"Can I eat one of this cake?" said Omar.

"Amen to that," said Stan. "Where's the knife?"

"The brownies are part of the trick!" said Ted. "Leave them alone."

Stella came back with a pale red dish towel. She dangled it in front of Ted's face and said: "All we need is a bull."

Ted said: "Hold it right in front of the tray."

She held it like a curtain. His hands fiddled behind it.

"First we had brownies," said Ted. "Now we have . . ."

Stella lifted the towel.

"Brownies on fire!"

A meager blue flame licked the crust of the brownies. The tips of fire were the shade of nectarines. They died as soon as they flared. "Okay," said Stella. "So now they're burned." She tossed the towel onto the table. The corner landed in the tray and caught fire immediately, bursting into a sudden rush of orange.

"Jesus *Christ*!" Abe cried. He fumbled in his briefcase and pulled out a bottle of water, ran across the room and poured it on the cloth. The flame hissed out. "Sorry about your brownies," he told Ted. They were soaked. He glanced at Stella, and she burst out laughing.

"I'm really, really sorry," she told Ted. "I'm a little drunk."

Ted held up the rum. "I didn't use it all," he said, and poured another shot for everyone. They toasted being temporary—*to getting out*, they said—and then they toasted being drunk. I went to the kitchen sink.

"Let's play a game," April said. She suggested charades. Everyone clapped or groaned. These were ways of saying yes. Stan rolled up his sleeves and Abe took off his shoes, and that was when I knew it would get serious. The wine made me feel transparent— like all of my thoughts were coming through my skin like sweat, leaking thin trails of hope and worry. I was wet with need and weakness, dripping everywhere, ruining everything.

We wrote the names of famous people on slips of paper and stuck them in Abe's baseball cap. Then we drew for roles. I begged off going first. I was afraid to look a fool. Stella was terrible at Ronald Reagan, pretending to ride a horse then sitting ramrod straight at an invisible desk, smiling so hard she must have hurt her jaw. I got dizzy watching. My head felt heavy. The edges of my vision were fidgeting like the whole room was a child who wouldn't keep still.

Ted did Madonna and April got it in two seconds flat. Abe requested help on Jack the Ripper and killed Stella from behind while she made sexy eyes at Stan. I laughed along with the others.

April stood up next. She twisted her skirt to one side so the zipper made a line from her belly button. She mussed up her hair and sat at the coffee table. She scattered napkins all over the floor and bent forward, ass in the air, to pick them up. She crossed her legs and then uncrossed them, did it ten times fast like an old silent comedy. Ted guessed Charlie Chaplin but he was wrong. Abe guessed Bozo the Clown and everyone laughed.

"Is that even an actual person?" Stella asked. People shrugged.

April took a sip of rum and then tipped her shot glass onto her own shirt, pawing at the stain with her delicate hands. It was a nice shirt. "Well, fuck it, guys," she said. "Wasn't it obvious?"

Nobody said anything.

She smiled. "I was Tilly at the office."

Ted laughed loudly, then stopped himself. Everyone looked at me.

"It's true," I said. "I'm pretty clumsy."

Everything had broken. Everyone was watching. I wanted to stand, but I was afraid I wouldn't be able. I wanted to leave. I wanted the others to leave. I didn't want anyone else to see this hurt, I just wanted to make it go away—the bathroom cabinet, the warm sour rush, the only way I knew how.

"Who wrote that one?" Abe asked. "I want to know who wrote it."

"It wasn't on a slip," April said. "I just thought it would be good."

I stood up carefully, using one hand to balance on the coffee table. I couldn't stumble now. I couldn't. I took April by the arm. "What made you want to?" I could hear my own words slurring: *Wha madju wanna?*

"Whoa," she said. She pulled her arm away.

"That's how I really look?" I heard my own voice coming back into my ears a second later, everything shifted sideways: *Thasow I look?* Her eyes were large and frightened. It made me angrier, seeing her scared like that. It was how Stella looked at Toledo in the park.

"Jesus," she said. "You're drunk."

Stella stood up. She looked horrified.

I felt Abe behind me. I kind of fell into his body and he took my weight without stumbling, held me for a second so I could get my footing again. "Come on," he whispered. "I'll take you downstairs."

Stella stayed behind. I couldn't imagine what she was saying: *She's been under a lot of stress. This is something she's been working on. She hasn't been herself, not really, since she was twenty years old.* Abe got me sitting on the bed, tilting a little, and set a glass of water on my nightstand. "I assume you can get yourself to sleep," he said stiffly. I realized he was blushing.

"I couldn't," I said. "This isn't what I wanted."

My words weren't arranged. They wanted to get from my throat to his eyes, to change the way he was looking. "I'm sorry that—"

He held up his hand, the red of his palm. "Whatever it is, don't bother."

This came as a relief. I wasn't sure I had anything to say.

I woke up early. My heart was beating in my skull. My stomach felt hard and dry as bones. I couldn't tell if I was still drunk or just remembering being drunk. Hangovers made my head feel like the inside of a car on a hot afternoon. I didn't know if I'd vomited the night before. I couldn't smell it.

I cupped my hands under the bathroom faucet and drank so much tap water I could feel the weight in my stomach. Water helped but it stood like a dirty pond inside. The apartment was quiet. Abe was at work, even though it was a holiday, and Stella was sleeping.

I took out a couple hundred from a Wells Fargo ATM, my account still fat with my midmonth deposit, and got myself a motel room. It had curtains the color of pepper and sheets the color of mustard, a coffee table covered in cigarette burns like black acne. It rented by the hour, a room for hookers or poor men cheating on their wives. I booked it for three nights. It was only a five-minute walk from the apartment. I thought about Abe or Stella walking below and never knowing I was up there.

I got three liters of gin and a carton of orange juice. I bought five frozen burritos and put them in my minifridge. It had a brown stain up its side, like the floor had vomited upward. I locked the door and chained the lock.

There were storms all weekend. I lay back and let the mustard bed give way underneath my body. I took the gin straight once the juice had run out and tried to change the patter, the *tick tick tick* of rain, just by tapping my fingers. The rain kept falling just the same. *Tick tick tick:* nails against the motel window, my mother's well-trimmed hands. I took long sips that burned my throat, felt like they were peeling my skin right off, until I'd taken so many they didn't feel like anything. I let them fill every part of my body. I let my fingers go limp. I let the rain fall.

I went back to the bank on Monday, but I didn't go inside. I waited on the bench. The air got chilly. I watched workers leave the building. There was a rush at five, another at six—Abe's low, *when everyone goes*—and only a trickle afterward. I thought I saw Abe, walking quickly with his head down, but then I realized it was someone else, another big man moving like a spy. Sylvia came through the revolving doors with a pair of pumps in her hand, wearing running shoes, and ducked into the BART station.

It was dark before Toledo got there. She sat down without saying anything. Every day she watched the blue sky going black. This was her life. Where would she sleep? Would it be cold there?

I said, "Haven't seen you for a while."

"I didn't treat you with respect," she said. So she remembered. "You've always treated me with respect, and I didn't treat you with respect."

"How are you now?"

She held up one hand. I could see a stub of charcoal between her fingers. "I like sketching when it's dark out. You can't see what you're making." She glanced up at the sky. "I don't have enough paper."

It looked like she'd been drawing on her single sheet for hours. It was a mess of marks. She moved closer on the bench. Her elbow patches were still firm and bright. I liked feeling her close, sitting there, saying nothing.

"Was that your daughter that day in the park?" she said. "The other lady?"

"Kind of."

"She looked scared."

"She was," I said. "A little."

I picked up the paper. Across the top she'd written: *Big Tears*. I wondered if she meant rips or crying. I got up to buy us two hamburgers. She ate hers in pieces: buns separately, then the meat, the wilted lettuce last, damp with ketchup. She asked for another.

"Do you have a place to spend the night?" I asked.

"There's a place I go."

"The shelter?"

"No." She shook her head. "Not anymore."

"But you've got somewhere?"

"Yeah," she said. "I do."

"I'd like to go with you," I said. I paused. "I know it sounds crazy."

She shrugged. "I've heard crazier."

She took me to an old convenience store with boarded-up windows. The awning was ripped to shreds but a flapping plastic sign still showed the words *Deli Liquor Snacks Cigarettes*. We entered from the alley. She twisted one of the plywood boards, turned it like a clock hand to two o'clock, and we climbed in the gap of window behind. "Careful," she said. "There's a little glass left."

Inside the ceiling had been stripped for parts and pieces. You could see through the building's rotten wooden levels, sandwiched like layer cake between stripes of ragged cotton-candy insulation. "This place doesn't get cops," she said. "Or dealers."

The shelves were mostly bare. There were a few cans of dog food and a bag of candy on the floor, tucked under one of the empty fridges. I could still remember the first time Nick entered my body. I'd focused on two cereal boxes—*Happy Trails Granola, Sweet Harvest Flakes*—while he was busy coming.

Toledo pulled out a sleeping bag and a few old rags, a dirty tin box, that she'd stashed under the counter. There was a cash register but it was junked. Half the buttons had been pried off and the paper was unspooled like a loose spring coil.

"You keep your things here?" I asked her. "They're safe?"

"They're not safe anywhere." She tossed her rolled bag, cinched tight with knotted rope, into the air. "I just don't like the extra weight."

She untied the bag and laid it across the central aisle, then unzipped it and spread the whole thing to make the surface wide enough for both of us. "I cleaned the floor last week," she said. "So don't worry about that."

I lay on the bag, on my back, and she lay next to me. We were perfectly straight and parallel, like two kids picking out constellations in the sky. I'd done that once with Dora: *Don't you see the stars of his knife? They're right there, three in a row, falling off the belt. Don't you see?* She got frustrated when I couldn't. *Is there supposed to be a turtle?* I'd asked. *No,* she said. *There isn't.*

"I was strung out, but I wasn't lying," Toledo whispered.

"What?"

"My father," she said. "He really died in Toledo." Her words sounded husky and strange, as if she had an entirely new voice that only existed near the floor. *You always treated me with respect*, she'd said, meaning it.

That night I slept inside a world that she'd built from nothing. I dreamed about her body dreaming next to mine. She woke me while it was still dark and said we had to leave. We did. We climbed out the window just before dawn.

STELLA

be had large hands that he didn't know how to handle and a beard that made him look like a lumberjack. His eyes were quick and scared like live brown creatures trapped under the glass of his pupils. *That's every one of us,* I thought. *Trapped.* For those first weeks he lumbered through his own rooms with shy surprise, nervous and uncertain, blinking at us like strangers. He apologized for his place, how it wasn't very nice. *Personal* was what he said. It wasn't very personal.

In truth, it was empty. His voice had a skittering quality, like it was running away from the huge shadow of his body.

The first day Tilly couldn't stop touching his marble counters. "You've got a pretty place," she said. "I knew you would."

We brought home noodles for dinner, but he was late. The noodles got cold. We watched the clock. We didn't eat for two hours, and then we finally did. We had to reheat the food. Brown gravy splattered the inside of the microwave, and Tilly spent ten minutes scrubbing it clean. She nearly cried from too much hot sauce. Her gaze was pained and restless, moving to the door and back again, flicking to her wrist to check the pass of hours, minutes, the ticking hand of single seconds.

"Maybe he's not coming," I said. "He could be spending the night somewhere else."

"He's shy with women," she said. "I've never heard about anyone." She hesitated. "He said he was coming home."

I know he did come home eventually, though I don't know when. I didn't see much of him for a few weeks. He was gone early and home late. I saw his cereal bowls in the sink. He walked to work at dawn.

"Cereal in the dark!" Tilly said. "Unbelievable."

The first thing she did every morning was wash his bowl and put it on the rack to dry. But it was clear he made her proud. "He turned out like his dad," she said. "Never stops to take a breath." She knew it wasn't the money that kept him going. It was something else. "He had a lot of shame growing up," she said. "That can make a person, if it's strong enough."

I got a job at a bed-and-breakfast called the Seven Sisters Inn. I found an advertisement in the local paper. The job title was *"Innkeeper (Assistant)."*

My shift ended at midnight, but the inn was pretty quiet after the end of our twilight wine and cheese. Mainly I answered the phone, booking rooms and helping people figure out what they wanted: a view of the bridge, a view of the bay, a canopy bed, or a Jacuzzi. "We need king-size," one woman told me firmly. "We can't do any smaller."

Louis had always gotten rooms with king-size beds. I couldn't touch him without rolling over entirely. I'd seen my parents' California king—played in it, even—without realizing how much space it left between their bodies every night. They'd always known what they needed, their bed a compromise and declaration. It took me years to find that distance, to stretch my hand into its darkness, seeking the hard rise of a man's back, and find only rumpled sheets, already cool.

I'd cried at that, feeling his body out of reach, and then I felt ashamed for crying. He stroked my back and said, "Please don't." I'd seen the fear in his eyes, and I thought he was afraid of feeling close to a woman. Looking back, this seemed foolish. He'd been afraid of a woman feeling close to him. *I didn't miss you. But I'm glad to be with you now.* He'd never promised me anything. The disappointment had been of my making entirely. There were times I saw his face flushed red with regret.

One night at the inn I got a late call from New York, well past midnight for them. The man said brusquely, "I need to speak with the assistant."

"You mean the manager?"

"I mean the assistant."

"Tom?" I said.

It *was* him. He wanted to know what the job was like. "So you finally got one?" he said, as if I'd been unemployed for years. I told him it was very diverse, a word I wouldn't have used with anyone else. I said I was designing a new publicity campaign for the owners. I maybe exaggerated a little.

Tom's teasing made it easier to talk about what was hard—the strange hills of this other city, the way fog settled over everything. We argued about our towns. New York had better street music, he said. I said yes, it did, but it was also dirtier. It was back and forth. New York had better subways but more pigeons. "You haven't said any good things about your city," Tom said. "Only bad things about mine."

"Our pigeons aren't just fewer," I said. "They're better, swear to God. They're brave. A lot of them are crippled. They're survivors."

"When you put it like that," he said, "it sounds fantastic."

We spoke night after night. We'd never spoken with such ease. The distance had done it, maybe, the fact of needing someone far away from where we were.

"They must keep you pretty busy at work," he said. "If you've got all this time for me."

The next night, five minutes into our conversation, I made a point of pretending I had another call. I did the same thing the next night, then the next. "Fine," he said, laughing. "I get the point. You're very busy."

It wasn't until later that I thought: *What about him?* Every day after work he was alone at home, calling to ask why I wasn't busier.

After every shift I drove home through the Tenderloin and parked in a private lot at Fourth and Bryant, two blocks from the apartment. The neighborhood was thick with car theft. Windows were broken for a few cents' change. Usually, I had to open the lot's fence with a key, but one night it wasn't locked. I saw a small crowd gathered around a steel drum fire. One guy leaned against the side of a dark Jeep, or maybe it was a woman, tipping a bottle of something into his mouth, or hers—I couldn't catch the shape, wine or a forty, but I saw firelight glinting on the glass.

I got nervous. I circled the block once, thinking, *Should I stop? Am I crazy?* and finally drove in. There were four of them—now I could see each figure clearly. One was leaning down toward a car window, and I wondered if that meant there was someone inside, a fifth, napping or fiddling with the car stereo. I could hear faint music, something electronic and jagged like a seismograph, moving one of those men like a puppet. He raised his arms and writhed like a shaman under the streetlight.

It didn't have to be complicated. I'd park and then I'd open my door and then I'd close it behind me. I'd walk to the street. I wouldn't lob my fear at them—the way you can, the way I'd done—casting glances over hunched shoulders. I'd walk away.

Three of them turned to face my car and clinked bottles. The shaman kept dancing, still glimmering under his yellow spotlight. The one against the Jeep wasn't a woman, I could tell. I pulled up the emergency brake and unbuckled my seat belt. I didn't want to be afraid.

They didn't come any closer, but two of them walked toward the open section of fence, two large swinging panels, and pulled them shut. I felt my throat and my stomach go knotted. I took a deep breath, and it hurt. My eyes steamed with tears. Maybe imagining the worst thing would mean the worst thing couldn't come true.

I checked the rearview mirror. The dancing man wasn't dancing anymore. The other guys were standing by the fence they'd closed. I pulled out my phone. I needed to bring another voice inside the fence. I needed that voice to tell me what to do.

"Stella?" Tom's voice was gruff with sleep.

"I'm in the middle of something," I said. "I'm a little scared."

I was almost crying. I knew the second I opened my mouth it would be out there, the salt sting and ache of it, my throat clamped with fear. Just wishing I was anywhere, *anywhere*, else.

"What's going on?" he said. Now he was wide awake.

"I'm in this parking lot, and there are these men," I said. "They're not *doing* anything, I mean, but they closed—"

"What guys? What are they doing?"

"They're just—it's this closed lot . . ."

"Are you—Do you think they might hurt you?"

"I think they want to scare me," I said. "I think they might want that."

I didn't say the words "homeless" or "black," though I could see they were both. This wasn't about that. This was about women and men together in the dark, what might happen.

"I need to go," I said.

"Call me back, alright? To let me know you're okay?"

I hung up. I called Abe. He picked up on the fourth ring.

"I'm sorry," I said. My voice was shaking. "I know it's late. It's Stella."

"You sound strange."

"I'm at the parking lot on Bryant. There are some guys. I need you to come."

"I'm—Jesus Christ. Yeah. I'm coming. Are you—I mean—are you hurt? Did someone hurt you?"

"Just come," I said. "Please?"

I hung up the phone but kept it close to my ear. I called my own answering machine so it would look like I was talking to someone. I kept checking the rearview mirror. The guys had wandered a little farther from the fence, but it was still closed. They hadn't wandered far. One of them climbed onto a small blue sedan and started jumping on the hood.

This is Alice calling your Connecticut cave . . . This is your mother and I think you're on the road . . . This is Tilly, I think the beep already happened, I think you're coming home at three . . .

I hung up. I checked the mirror again. Now the man was cross-legged on the roof. He hurled his bottle at the window of a nearby car. There was the high, fragile crackle of glass breaking, then the frantic thrumming of the music once more. I checked the sidewalk both ways. I closed my eyes. I'd count to twenty and then I'd open them. There had to be a way to make the moments pass faster. To get through them, any way I could, that was all.

I heard tapping. I put my fist into my mouth to stop the sound in my throat. I was an animal, my stomach rising raw and fast. I wasn't making choices, just listening to the fear.

It was Abe. I could see his big white pupils, one hand pushing his glasses up his nose. I opened the passenger door and he slid in. I leaned across and grabbed whatever parts of him I could—his cold hand, his solid thigh—I pulled his shoulders close and gripped hard. Now I was really crying, throat heaving into something like hiccups. "Thank you."

"Hey," he said. "Sorry I scared you."

"You didn't scare me."

"Looks a little sketchy down here," he said. "Kind of a bonfire situation."

I laughed and rubbed my hand across my face. The skin was slick and wet from tears, all over my flushed cheeks and my mouth.

"I didn't see you coming," I said. "I was watching."

"I came in off Bryant. Looks like the other fence is closed."

"I know," I said. "They closed it."

I checked the rearview mirror, and sure enough, there it was, where he'd come from: the other gate swinging out. It had been open the whole time.

"They're strung out," he said. "They're bums. They don't know what they're doing."

"They were trying to fuck with my head. It's what they can do, make people afraid. It's all they've got. It's fucking *absurd*—"

"Hey," he said. "It's alright to be scared."

I stepped onto the concrete. I could hear the music louder now, the machine of its buzz, traveling through the tar like an underground river and humming against my shoes. It was feedback off an underground microphone. There were pulses of crackling. I saw the dancer man lying in a pool of light. He had his arms and legs spread like a snow angel's. The man sitting on the car was watching us leave. "Hey!" he said. "Lady, hey!"

Abe put his arm around my shoulders. "Good night, man!" he called out. His voice didn't have any kind of question in it.

"Lady don't like my look? Is that the trouble?"

"There's no trouble," said Abe. "We're just heading home."

"Your lady thought there was trouble." The man turned to me. "Didn't you?" He raised his fingers and snapped them right in my face. "You're scared of it," *snap*, "scared of it," *snap*, "scared of it . . ." He grinned. "Until you want it. Just like that."

He was close now. He smelled like cigarettes and burnt garlic.

"Want what? What do I want?"

Abe tightened his grip. "We're just heading home. No trouble at all."

"No trouble, right," the man said. "You got your lady and all that."

"What do I want?" I said again. "Why don't you tell me?"

"Don't you know?"

"I don't know."

Abe whispered in my ear, "We should go."

"I really don't know," I said. "You should tell me."

"You want *me,*" he said. "Looking at *you.*"

The next morning I found three messages from Tom. *Guess you forgot.* And then: *Fuck you for forgetting.* And then: *Call me back or else I'm flying out.*

I called him back.

"You had me worried," he said. "You get that?"

Abe's loft was in the middle of an area south of Market that yuppies were beginning to claim—lot by lot, loft by loft—from the prowling bums and drug addicts, the mechanics who crouched in shadowed auto shops. It had a name like Manhattan, SoMa, only here the sun set close over the water, behind the stadium.

Good-looking men and women strolled the dirty streets in polo shirts and ethnic skirts. They smiled at the homeless folks they passed but didn't give them money or else gave money without smiling. The sidewalk was lined with entrance areas in cages, where people kept their welcome mats. Each one, it seemed, was home to a small pair of running shoes.

All the buildings had multiple locks—outer locks, lobby locks, courtyard locks—and no doubt more locks, locks we couldn't see deeper inside. Lofts were glass holes tucked inside sheer cliffs of stucco. Artists lived in this part of town, big thinkers and independently wealthy dreamers. Big windows showed elaborate tracks of industrial lighting, white canopy beds on open hardwood floors, a leaning canvas studded with dolls' heads.

I was learning the city and our own small corner inside it. Tilly and I went to breakfast during those first weeks, as a way of exploring. But it seemed like she got tired of this, tired of talking, tired of *my* talking, so I started exploring alone.

I kept coming back to the Tenderloin, farther north, where whores chose corners and stood on them all night. It was a strange pleasure, watching those women, like slowing for a wreck. Their legs were skinny as twigs and just as crooked. They leaned against boarded doors in their black tights and cheap pumps: ketchup red, faded teal, the bright orange of processed cheese. I wondered if Tilly ever saw them. She was always in the apartment by sundown, tucked into her basement. Most days she was in the apartment all day long.

Abe started to meet me in the parking lot every night. I liked seeing the calm that hinged his parts together on those dark streets, where any sudden clatter made me clench my jaw. I never turned. I only flinched against turning. *It's alright to be scared.* His words wriggled into me like fingers. They wanted to make a feeling inside me, of gladness or gratitude, and then claim it as their own.

I liked how he walked: shoulders squared back, hands in his pockets. I liked the size of his body. Women weren't supposed to want these things—men saving us, dwarfing us, protecting us— but I did. I wanted to be dwarfed. His arms were solid and they gave off heat in the fog.

If I was nervous about the streets, Abe was nervous about everything else. "Are there enough towels at home?" he asked. "How's the shower?" In his living room, boxes still stood in crooked stacks. "It's not a real home yet," he said. "I know."

At home he was one person, insecure and eager to please, but once you put him up against the world, his voice sounded like a cold, bracing liquid had seeped into it, running glossy through his veins. *I've always known how to be in public,* he told me. *In private I'm never sure.*

"Are you happy?" he asked me one night. "Out here, I mean, with us."

I hesitated.

"I never really knew why you came in the first place."

"I like it here," I said carefully. "I thought it might help Tilly. I'd hoped it would."

I could have asked him the same thing: *What made you want us here?* It could have been for Tilly's sake, and probably it was, but she was right that there was a loneliness in him. I didn't want to face it directly. I was afraid of his candor. I thought it might come too fast.

He always offered to cook for me when we got back from our walks, milkshakes or grilled cheese sandwiches, but he never made these things for himself. He talked about food in a vague way, as if he knew it was part of other people's lives but it was still strange to him, an idea he was always forgetting and then remembering again.

At first I said no. Lots of ways I said it. *No, no thanks, not tonight.* I wanted to keep the woman—the one he'd seen that first night, tears and snot all over my face, cowering in my car—separate from the rest of me. He'd seen the parts of myself I liked least.

Tom and I still spoke, but less frequently. We kept shoving our cities together like action figures in a pretend war. But every time I thought of New York, I could only think about Louis. It was nearly impossible to picture him as a father, which was part of why I spent so much time picturing it. He'd take his little girl to the woods of Vermont and show her a carpet of leaves in the fall, a clear cold sky, a fireplace full of flames; he'd keep her from touching their hot shifting tongues. He'd keep her safe.

I thought of how he'd raise her in the city. There were so many things to show: *Look at the shadows on the Brooklyn Bridge. Look how they made the poets speak.* She would be, more than any lover, the possibility of himself replicated in flesh. He could teach her to love what he loved. *There's this deli on Ludlow,* he'd say, *their lox will turn your tongue to seawater.* He'd watch her chew the pink sleeves of salmon between her baby teeth. *So?* he'd say. *Tastes like the ocean, right?* She might not know what to say. She might not finish her bagel. Maybe she'd grow up with a tight fist in her throat: What did he want to hear? When all was said and done, she'd have his sharp words filling her youth like glass in the mouth, gleaming and triumphant. Or maybe it was only me who'd remember him like that, his cruelty moving me like a hand puppet. Maybe this daughter would know a different man, a better man entirely.

After a week of hearing *no,* Abe pulled out a skillet one night and started heating some butter. "I'm fixing a grilled cheese," he said. "You're welcome to join me."

I joined him. He made the sandwich with so much cheese it spilled over. It tasted great. I ate mine in large bites that greased my lips. We sat in silence.

"Sometimes it's nice," I said. "Just staying quiet. Not having to say anything."

"Good God!" he said. "I think so, too."

His cell phone buzzed. "You'll have to . . ." He pointed at it. "I have to." He smoothed his shirt and tightened his tie before he picked up. "Don," he said. "What the fuck is rolling in Pittsburgh?"

This voice was like none I'd heard from him, loud and jangly, like a large sack of coins shaken onto a table. He was grinning. *What was rolling in Pittsburgh?* Now he knew.

He made a spiral around his temple with his finger, indicating *crazy*. Did this mean him or the other guy? I didn't care. I liked seeing him summoned into this strange world and imagining the way he was important there, the way he shook off his own stuttering questions and spoke clear and forceful words, never apologized to anyone.

Tilly obsessed herself with turning his bare loft into a home. She arranged and then she rearranged, asked me what I thought of her new arrangements. One blue ceramic vase migrated across bookshelves, nightstands, perched briefly on a little table near the door. "This table is for mail," Abe said. "I thought that's what it was for."

Tilly moved the vase back to its first shelf.

It was hard to see her life right up to its edges. I knew she didn't have anything else. I worked night shifts but started taking afternoons as well, to get away from the constant scraping sounds of her effort—chairs dragged across floors, the rustle of fabrics, the dust of books she'd unearthed from boxes. I knew that part of it was a way to keep busy, to say: *Today I will not drink. I will dust.* Her life was a series of substitutions. But I couldn't look at her without feeling I could see right through her.

The bed-and-breakfast was in an old Victorian on Hyde. Getting the job had been easy. "We like your look," the owner said. She was Gail, a meaty middle-aged matron. When she said "we," she meant herself and her partner, an elfin woman named Bea who looked like she could fit inside her lover's armpit. They didn't ask where I'd gone to school or what I'd studied. They only asked if I knew how to bake, and they didn't seem to care when I said no.

I took pleasure in setting tables and sweeping crumbs. I felt the entire house as a set of nerve endings. I got uneasy at the sight of an object out of place—a dirty mug on the fireplace or an old tea bag hardening in a mug—and drew a keen satisfaction from its restoration, like the sensation of clasping a necklace. I enjoyed using my hands. I hosed the dishes with hot water and lathered them with lemon soap, scrubbed blisters of jam from the grainy wood. I surveyed the breakfast tables once I'd set them for the next morning: each cup and saucer neatly stacked on glass that gave off the scent of firm, soapy polish.

Tilly didn't like to see me leave for work. "Leaving already?" she'd ask, even though I left at the same time each day. After a month she got a job of her own. This gave me some relief. Now things were moving forward; I could help.

I offered to give her typing lessons. I'd learned methods, tricks and shortcuts, in a special fifth-grade elective course. I could still remember Ms. Murcatino, a woman who didn't do anything at our school except teach touch-typing. Even the gloss of her life sounded like one of our practice sentences: *Who is the teacher who will teach our touch-typing course this term?* Laura Spencer and I made fun of her bright manicures and her hard curls of yellow hair. One day she caught us whispering and tapped me on the shoulder with one red-lacquered nail. I giggled harder. "You might be laughing now," she said. "But you'll regret this moment later. You'll remember it."

We used typewriters in her classroom, to hear more clearly the sound of our fingers hitting the keys, and copied sentences that focused on clustered sections of the keyboard. *A sad fad fast. Jill, kill Lolo.* Our fingers ached. One day we typed with paper bags over our heads to keep us from cheating, and then we wore them for a second day because we'd been so goddamn slow the first time. *Goddamn!* Ms. Murcatino wasn't a woman afraid of using all the words. "Just don't call me Mrs.," she told us. "I've been there and back."

Tilly never got the hang of typing by touch. She kept hunting and pecking right up to the end. Abe said her job mainly had to do with spreadsheets anyway. "There's not a whole lot of text," he said. "I think she'll be alright."

I suggested that he clear out his liquor cabinet. From the looks of it, he didn't drink much anyway. His full bottles, still sealed, had gathered fine silts of dust.

"You don't think it'll offend her?" he asked. "I mean—if she's serious about this, she's serious about it, right?"

"She's serious," I said. "But that doesn't mean we can't help."

We boxed the bottles and drove them to his office. They clanked around in the backseat of his car. "Great," he said. "Now I'll look like the one with the problem."

Tilly showed us her new business wardrobe. It was just five new pieces, but they made six outfits, seven if you counted her catalog pantsuit with its cotton-candy polyester. We saw every combination. I was aware of Abe's body next to mine on the couch, a thin magnetic wire running between us. I could feel the curve of his large rib cage sitting close, and the heat of him like an oven. He sweated more than most men. His forehead often shone.

Tilly appeared in a light green blouse, the one she called celery. "How do I look?" she said. "You think it'll work?"

Months later, she told me about a bird getting trapped in her trailer, and that's exactly what she looked like in her ridiculous clothes, an animal crashing into windows, something you might watch with pity and disdain at once: Why couldn't it tell the difference between glass and sky?

I caught Abe staring at my breasts under my turtleneck. But I didn't mind. He glanced back quickly to Tilly in her green blouse, chartreuse if not celery, or celeriac or anemic or something, one of those corporate names. It was like a comfortable humidity in the

air, Abe's desire, a way of getting around the split fork of our family, desert on one side and ocean on the other, the memory of my
grandmother, *his* grandmother, with her skin bleeding all over the
rug. But this was something new we made: His eyes on my body,
my body not turning away.

I liked the strange glow of our secret hours after midnight,
both of us knowing they were turning into something we wouldn't
have words for. Which made the other words come easier.

He asked me if Tilly liked the apartment. Could I tell? Did
she tell me? And how did she feel about the city, the idea of a job,
the bank itself. It was always: *the apartment, the bank.* He never
said "my." He rarely talked about his work. He stored his briefcase behind the couch so he wouldn't have to look at it. "Don't
let me talk about all that jazz," he said. He used phrases like an
old man might. They came from early days spent with his father
and no one else. He permitted me to ask *how was your day?* just
once each night, and he gave a thumbs-up, or a middling tilt of
the palm, or a playful tug of his hair to show that it was driving
him crazy.

Sometimes we drove around the city in the dark. The streets
were empty enough to take the hills fast. I felt my stomach flutter
at the peak of each rise before we barreled down the other side.
Usually Abe was quiet, but on the roads he was sly and unpredict-
able.

He taught me how to play road bingo. We made messy grids
on coffee-stained napkins. It was slim pickings: *drunk driver, speed-
ing lover, accidental high beams.* Mostly items about headlights.
Pediddle was what you called a car that only had one. He said Tilly
had taught him that. She'd taught him road bingo, too, but they'd
mainly played from buses.

We played a version of this game with all-night restaurants,
staring through diner windows and seeking human sights from
lists we'd already imagined: *a couple falling in love, a couple get-*

ting divorced, a runaway teenager, a lonely artist. Sometimes we disagreed. One time we saw two women in fancy dresses eating sushi. Their faces suggested different kinds of birds, pigeon and humming. They held small trees of broccoli in front of their talking mouths. He thought sisters; I thought lovers.

Another night we found a green sedan marked ZONE DIET and followed it from house to house. It was dropping healthy meals at doorsteps. We imagined the people inside, their heavy bodies and spinach-spackled teeth, their toothpick-limbed dreams.

Sometimes we went to a doughnut shop at the corner of Fifth and Harrison, where Korean hipsters convened until dawn. They compared their cars, heavy with spoilers and rims, sleek and fishgilled. They stroked their hoods and felt for dents or grit. "Just look at them," said Abe, awed. "Petting away."

Abe never finished his doughnuts. I always finished mine. He said he got too caught up in our conversations. I was flattered. But I was also jealous. I could never forget my body, my mouth, that constant pull and tug: *more, stop, more.* Living with Tilly made me feel the fixation more sharply, the sight of her body moving through space—taking up energy and setting it free again, every nervous glance at Abe, all that longing practically weeping from her pores. She sweated heavily, like her son, and this also seemed like a signal of the energy chewing her up inside.

Abe asked me if I thought her sobriety was successful. After a moment, he added: "So far, I mean."

"She's not drinking," I said. "I think that successful sobriety is just, you know . . . staying sober."

"So she's doing okay?"

"You could ask her."

"She's like a stranger most of the time. It's hard to explain."

"It's not that hard, is it? I mean—you were estranged."

"We weren't estranged. I just lived with my dad."

I said nothing. I didn't want to intrude.

"When she was taking the checks, I felt like I was really doing something. But then—I don't know, I realized how bad things had gotten. I felt like a fool."

His face wasn't bitter. His voice was clean and quivering as peeled fruit. It was full of evaporated feelings clustered like moisture on the roof of his mouth. "I hope it's different out here," he said. "She's starting from square one, I guess, nothing to remind her of the old stuff."

I asked about his past. I pictured Vegas etched entirely in neon. What was it like to come of age under the strip, hot letters buzzing like insects and swallowing his voice-cracked prayers? I wanted to know if the city dimmed its constellations. *Of course it did,* he said. *It's got the single brightest light on Earth.* I wanted to hear the raw memories of a child: ice knocking against ice, tumblers leaving moisture stains on green velvet tables, the pitter-patter of his footsteps on plush hotel carpeting; the chorus of men cursing themselves, their luck, as their withered hands pitched the dice.

"It's a terrible city for making a life," he said. "But it made me."

Wouldn't that kind of place seem wondrous to a boy if he didn't have to see the aching underneath? If he could grip his father's hand, red like meat but perfectly cool, not sweaty at all, and know it was possible to pull the secret strings that made everything dance? Abe told me that his father had taken him to all the big stakes in town. "He told me to look at the faces of the losers, not the winners," he said. "He said that was how I'd learn."

Sometimes I asked about his here and now. I couldn't stop myself: "What do you *do*?" I knew that precise words mattered: mergers and acquisitions. Tom felt strongly about both parts. "Do you buy companies? Write reports?"

Abe shook his head.

"Write reports about the guys who buy companies?"

"I write reports about the guys who write reports about the guys who buy companies."

"Sounds tricky."

"It's pretty simple, actually. That's what we don't tell anyone."

"Why do you do it?"

"I usually say money," he said. "Or I'll talk about my dad and his genes, how I'm programmed for the big bucks."

"But?"

"But what?"

"You said 'I usually say.' Like you were about to say something else."

He shrugged. "The truth is I'm not sure."

"But it's your life."

"It's not my life. It doesn't feel like my life."

"What does?"

"Right now?" he said. "Maybe this."

I wanted to put my hand on his and say, *You can't need this.* We hadn't made anything. What we shared was the sense of fleeing something else.

"I like the city at night," he said. "Like I can claim it."

"And in the day?"

"Just the opposite. I feel like I've been claimed."

He kept a beard even though the company had a policy against it. "Not exactly a policy. Just strong discouragement."

He pointed out its colors: Rust. Pepper. Silver.

"It helps to keep it," he said. "Otherwise I'm just wearing a costume."

His costumes were pin-striped suits and undershirts, a closet full of matching jackets and a hamper full of dirty cotton. I snuck into his room when he was gone, brought his button-downs close to my face and smelled them: coffee and Clorox. They'd traveled to the distant country of his office, where he was a different person, and I wanted to know that version of him, too. I felt his dirty undershirts, the yellow apple halves of their sweat stains. I liked feeling close to him this way. Not everything turned into words we had to shuffle back and forth.

I didn't just smell his clothes. I washed them. Or at least I washed the washables, with detergent that smelled like swimming pools. His suits were usually crumpled in the corner, but I let them be. He had a dry-cleaning woman on Stockton. *Yucy Please,* he called her. She pointed out stains like she was angry: "You see, please! You see, please."

Tilly saw me washing clothes one day and took a pair of his boxers from the hamper. "You don't have to wash his things," she said. "I could do them."

"I don't mind."

"What am I doing all day anyway?" she said sharply. "I'd rather do them myself."

From then on, I let her.

I wasn't picking up many of Tom's calls, but I listened to his messages right before I went to sleep. They often stretched across recordings: *Midtown gets so quiet at night. Except for the guy playing his sax at Fifty-ninth and Lex, but he's not any good. There's another guy who tried to sell me a jar of salt from the inside pocket of his leather jacket. He seemed crazy and he smelled like glue. He told me his name was Scooter and then a minute later he told me his name was Bolt. Where did you go out in this town, anyway? I'm thinking I should take up going out. The guys from work are big on titty bars—more than you want to know, probably—but that's never been my thing. I don't even feel like drinking, just maybe going out, mainly because I'm sick of thinking about other people going out. Some nights, I swear, there is a smell like a campfire all over this city.*

He said he wanted to make me miss New York, but his messages only made me miss him, and it was a strange kind of missing. Not the kind of missing that came from losing an actual closeness but the missing of having glimpsed him—only briefly, for moments—and never gotten more. He made me remember how lonely the city had been. *The rain feels like somebody pissing but now . . . now I think it might be stopping, it's stopping; it just stopped—now everything is dripping—it happened so fast, for no good reason, piss-hard until it wasn't, and now things are wet and everybody is holding their breath, every goddamn one of us, and what do we even think we're waiting for?*

The first day of Tilly's job, I woke up confused. My sheets were flung across the bed, sticky under my scissored legs. My body turned violent when I slept alone. I'd been dreaming—something to do with a house made of birds.

Tilly cracked the door and peered in. "Awake?"

"It's yours," I murmured. "It's not mine."

"What's that?" she said.

I tried to catch the dream before it left completely. The birds were wingless and paralyzed, as if bound by invisible twine, and there was a boy with dusty skin. I was building him a throne with their warm rustling bodies.

"Breakfast?"

"What?" I propped myself up. Tilly looked taller than usual. My body felt thick with fatigue. The night before, Abe and I had driven the city for hours.

I never ate in the morning. But here she was, asking. I pulled my limbs from sleep.

I found her standing over the kitchen sink, pouring coffee from the pot while she used a spoon to strain. "The grounds got in," she said. "I don't know how."

She wore a gray skirt threaded with stitches of yellow, her thick legs jammed into black pumps. Her hair was blow-dried into the puffy, swollen shape that comes from applying heat without skill. It was positively triangular.

"How do I look?" she said. "Is it too much?"

I glanced up and down. Her panty hose were bunched into the pockets below her knees, their thick seams curled like keloids around her calves. The yellow stitching of her suit created something—a general impression, a pattern—that reminded me of vomit.

"No," I said. "It's just right."

She frowned, bent down, and twisted her panty hose. "Funny thing, right? No matter which way you turn the seam, someone's gonna be looking at it."

We split the *New York Times* that Abe had left on the table. I took the Style section. *This would have disappointed me,* I told myself each time—about gallery openings, new downtown gastro-pubs and the roof farms where they got their local produce.

"Anything good in there?" she asked.

I shook my head. There was a lightness to her that morning—something bumbling and earnest, gestures of *here, take this,* a kind of trying. It gave me vertigo to see it.

She cut her toast into pieces with a knife and fork. She had very particular ideas about being civilized. I glanced down at my mud bowl of coffee and small animal hide of blackened bread. She'd tried so hard.

She picked up a stack of papers from beneath her plate and kept shuffling them, licking her index finger and flipping their corners. She told me they were menus for restaurants near the bank. Places she and Abe might try, she said, during their lunch breaks.

I couldn't imagine this happening, but it was an important part of her—believing that it might. Inside her words there was a small and perfect hope, something all those years had left untouched.

* * *

The first time Abe kissed me, I wasn't surprised. I guess I should have been.

"I've wondered what it would feel like," he said. "But that was even stranger. Better."

I ran my finger under the wiry underbelly of his beard, tipped his chin back, forced his eyes to look at mine. "Good," I said. "I'm glad."

Then we were in it, impossible to say the steps or stages, who slid tongue against tongue, along teeth, sucked lip hard enough to leave it chapped, sucked skin hard enough to leave a welt. We were both of us, everything. Who did what first? The facts were fossils lodged deep and invisible inside the rock of our bodies intertwined.

I felt the sandpaper of his checks—*rust,* I thought, *pepper, silver*—and the pressure of his lips, the half-hums murmuring out. Usually kissing felt like dissolving. This felt like curiosity. It took me a minute to realize the difference. My eyes were open.

He took off his pants but not his shirt. I tried to unbutton the top few buttons with my teeth but ended up using my fingers instead. I bit his nipples and pulled strands of his chest hair just to hear his breath catch. My shirt stayed on but my pants were down, underwear stretched around my ankles, tight enough to snap.

Elsewhere he was timid but now he didn't ask: *Is this alright? Does this feel okay?* He didn't give me a choice. I wanted him to come so much it was almost like coming. I was outside myself, saying: *There. There it is.* At one point I said, "Harder," but it came out sounding like a question. My voice cracked to show there was something in me that was almost broken. He could break it if he tried.

I felt him come and then I started crying. I watched my bed from above, its pathetic squalor, his big body heaving with all the loneliness he'd known. This was what I'd always wanted: the expansive, amniotic feel of some sadness larger than myself. I'd made so many comments about pain I'd almost forgotten how it felt. I could not explain why I was this way, so alone.

"It's amazing to see you cry," he whispered into my scalp. "It really is."

His words quivered strands of my hair. I felt his breath like he was humming. We were curled up and our limbs were touching. Touching but not holding.

"I'd like to teach you a game," he said; he didn't say which one. I was glad for words, any words, that weren't the usual ones. *You were nice that was nice what are you thinking about now?*

"Your body is perfect," he said. "You know that?"

I rolled out of his grip. I thought of Lucy's body, how her skin rippled whenever I stirred the bathwater with my fingers. Abe hadn't watched her die.

I asked him, "Have you ever seen a woman get old?"

"I wish I'd known her," he said. He'd known who I'd meant. I watched his face as he spoke—kind and careful, offering me these parts of his regret.

We slept on a bare mattress, sheets bunched at our feet, and I liked the sight of his body—the up-and-down of his breathing— but felt restless at the slight susurrus of his snoring, and the heat of his breath, and the probing of his hands, worrying my shirt like he wanted to rustle some part of me loose.

The next morning, still sleeping, he was a stranger again. He looked like a giant from a picture book, huge and slain. His beard was complicated-looking, like a thicket, and cool to the touch. I fixed his bowl of cereal and brought it back to bed. It was the first day I'd seen him sleep past dawn. This thrilled and disappointed me. I wanted him to break every rule of his life just for me, but I also wanted him to be a man who didn't break himself for anyone.

I put the bowl right next to his sleeping face and straddled him, gripping his wrists together. I knew he was naked under the blanket. He was naked and now beginning to eat—like a girl, it would seem, the spoon delicate between his fingers. He said, "You look serious."

"Abe," I said. "I have something to tell you."

"What's that?"

I said, very solemn: "We have committed incest."

He laughed. "I guess we have," he said. "It would appear that we are cousins, and we just made love."

Made love. He wasn't much for *fucked*.

Abe took me to a Middle Eastern coffee shop where old men sat in bright silk shirts and lifted hookah tubes to their mouths. They stared me up and down. They drank spiced tea full of floating nuts, almonds, and cashews. They played checkers and backgammon. "These guys keep going all night long," Abe said. "I love that."

He put his hand on my back, the blue fabric of my cotton dress, and I let him. My hair was neatly washed, my skin clean and smelling of coconut. The last time he'd seen me, I'd smelled like the inside of my own body.

At our mosaic table, he flipped open a small velvet box with a snap clasp. It was full of domino tiles the color of rice. "This is the game I meant," he said, and handed me a tile that was warm from his palm, like a small hard loaf of bread. "My father was the one who taught me," he explained. "It was training wheels for poker."

The air was sweet with smoke. Hookah water bubbled fiercely in glass pots all around us. We sat under a heat lamp. A man with a striped vest and a long braid came to take our order. His braid was dark and solid at the bottom, like a pigtail some little girl had sucked to soothe her nerves. Abe ordered Turkish coffee for both of us without asking what I wanted, which was exactly how I wanted him to do it.

He taught me how to play each tile off the next, how to turn doubles against the flow. "It's all about fives," he said. "That was the first thing Dad told me."

He showed me how to build roads across the board and how to dead-end them once other people tried to follow. He told me about drawing from the pile when you ran out of options. "We call it the boneyard," he said, and there it was: tiles askew under the lantern. He told me we'd always leave a few turned over so we'd never know each other's hands completely. "That's a personal rule of mine," he said. "I thought you'd appreciate it." He showed me his lucky combinations and some of his tells, the way he rubbed his chin under duress.

I told him, "I don't want to know your giveaways."

He said those days were over. Now he wore a beard over his skin. "You've got to play with just your fingers," he explained. "Not your whole body."

The vested man returned to pour our coffee from a beaten silver ladle. It reminded me of a mouth, how soup might dribble from the creased corners of an old woman's lips.

I wasn't a quick learner. I'd always been okay at counting—I had fingers like the other kids—but always a little disappointed by arithmetic itself. I thought multiplying would mean more than adding over and over again.

I kept missing doubles and drawing from the boneyard when I didn't need to. Abe was patient. He only smiled. "You'll get the hang of it."

I got frustrated. "Why aren't you more impatient?"

"My father was an asshole when he taught me. I thought I could do better."

I wanted him to be more like his dad, the bigger Abe I'd never met. I kept meeting the gaze of an elderly man playing chess at the next table. He cornered his opponent's king with humble pawns—moving his papery hands like a magician—and then, at checkmate, he grinned straight at me and invited me into the moment.

My forehead bristled under the red coils of the heat lamp. My organs felt sweaty inside, lungs and stomach too close together. I wanted Abe to hurry up and win. "Be mean," I said. "Come on."

"You make me meaner than I used to be," he said. "Trust me." He took my hand and squeezed, like he'd made a joke. But it hadn't been a joke, and we both knew this. I was always squinting at the world, turning it into a flat line of wit or judgment, and this wasn't his language, but he'd learned it because it was the one I spoke. He still had my hand but only because he hadn't figured out how to give it back.

I went to bed reeking of coffee and sweet hookah, my breath and skin, and knew I'd wake up to the smell of myself. I had my period and I could feel that I was leaking onto his sheets. I hated leaving stains shaped like continents all over the beds of men. I knew it wasn't my fault, this bleeding, but it was something my body had made. I brought a washcloth from the bathroom. I crouched to scrub the sheets. "Stella," Abe said. "You don't have to do that."

He thought I was doing it for him.

"I don't want it there."

He reached for me. "I still want to taste you, even now."

I pushed his hand away. "It's not—"

"I don't see you like some *body*," he said quickly. "You're not just something that made my sheets dirty."

I tried to explain. I told him about the years I'd starved myself dry, stopped my leaking body from bleeding over everything, and how it still felt like a failure to return, to bleed from fullness—as if I'd given up.

I thought he would say, as others had said—my therapist, my mother—that this way of thinking didn't make much sense. Instead, he said, "Sounds like a way of holding on to the disease."

I'd thought this was what I'd always wanted, some man analyzing my life, so fascinated that he wanted to make sense of it, but now I wanted to keep my history hidden from sight. His attention made me feel expansive, as if the old wounds were staining everything, bloodying his tongue between my legs and staining his smile as he bent—*No, no, my pleasure*—to clean everything up.

I turned my back to him. I didn't want him all around me. "Don't take this the wrong way," I whispered. It wasn't about him. It was the only way I could sleep.

Tilly was curious about the inn: what it looked like, what I did there. *Sounds nice,* she said, and it seemed like a rebuke. *Just trudging through* was how she described her own work. There were days we barely saw each other. I found relief in this, but I also felt swindled, as if she'd slipped from my grasp. I'd come here for her, and now our lives had become these parallel lines. We were getting through the days but I couldn't tell if this counted as progress. I was fucking the man she'd given birth to. It wasn't a betrayal, exactly, but it felt like one.

Tilly wanted to come for one of my shifts. I said I wouldn't be able to entertain her. She said she didn't need to be entertained. She just needed to be distracted, especially around dusk. *Sundowning.* Those twilight hours summoned our truest selves—like threads pulled from sweaters, leaving us unraveled—and her self was always thirsty, always aching for the old familiar numb.

We picked a day and I set aside one of the guest suites so she could use it while I worked—take a bath, enjoy the bed, watch a movie. I gave her the key when we arrived.

She wanted to watch me in the kitchen instead. I spent my evenings baking breakfast for the next morning. I made puffy scones studded with the open wounds of wet-baked cranberries, sugar-dusted lemon bars, fruit pies whose dark syrupy bellies swallowed their skeletons of latticed pastry. I filled the whole place with the hot breath of sweet dough rising. Tilly helped. She tasted with a fork, gently and invisibly inserted around the edges of things, under their crusts. She cleaned up the wreckage of dirty dishes and countertops: bits of cooked fruit dangling like loose fibers, crumbs dusted over everything. It looked like pies had been slaughtered rather than baked.

I remembered her curled on that motel bed. *Something is wrong in there.* She hadn't experienced her body as a set of operations she could control, but here she was—trying. I could see something I'd never seen in her, a physical grace that eluded her everywhere else.

I tried to convince her to take the upstairs suite. I pressed the key into her hand. "The room is your oyster," I said. "Please?"

She smiled, sighing, but agreed. She even seemed pleased.

The inn was nearly empty. There was an elderly man in an immaculate suit who sat on the porch all night in the cold, waiting to meet a daughter who never showed up.

Tilly still hadn't come down by the end of my shift. I found her sleeping on the big canopy bed, legs spread over the sheets like she'd been trying to walk somewhere in her dreams. I tapped her on the shoulder and said, "I have to close up the room."

She sat up and rubbed her eyes. "Sorry," she said. "I got the pillows wet." She'd washed her hair. The sheets were creased, pulled nearly off the mattress. She'd been having nightmares again.

"I'll just be a second," I said. "You can wait downstairs."

I replaced the wet pillowcase with a fresh one and refolded the sheets until the corners were tight. I left the room like she'd never been inside it.

I found her waiting in the car. She was sitting very straight with her hands tucked in her lap. She said, "You had to clean up after me, didn't you?"

"I didn't mind. I wanted you to have a couple hours' peace."

"Well," she said, "it's gonna take more than that."

"Did you enjoy it, at least?"

"You should have told me you were gonna have to clean it up," she said. "Now I feel like a burden."

"I didn't really clean up. It's my job."

This wasn't true, exactly; there were maids. But it didn't look like she cared. She was staring straight ahead. She didn't turn to look at me.

"It's not a big deal," I said.

She said, "It's a big deal to me."

In high school we read a book about a girl who offers her breast milk to an old man to save him from starving. During class, the boys traded sketches of stick-figure men with big lips latched onto half-moon tits. The girls smiled and crossed their arms over their chests. Colin Travers called out, "Old man suckling!" and I knew that for the rest of my life, after that moment, I would never forget his name. The girl in the book did it because the old man was so hungry. He was going to die no matter what she did. But she did it anyway.

What about Louis's wife, a woman I'd only seen in photographs? When she nursed their baby, did she sit rigid or curl over like cursive? I pictured the infant at her breast, then Louis himself, leaning in to her chest with his cracked lips. *You're so curious about the world,* he'd told me once, meaning it.

But I was sick of myself, sick of my fascinations. There were moments when the simple fact of living inside a body was so hard and unforgiving it could take your breath away. The girl who fed the old man with her milk was going hungry, too. She'd been whittled into a sharp point of desire jutting through the story.

That was what made us cross our arms over our breasts. There was a difference between imagining pain and getting your fingers dirty with it.

Tilly told me once about the experience of giving birth. She said she screamed louder than she'd known was possible. "It was the first time I really heard my own voice," she said. "I wanted it to keep on hurting forever."

On Thanksgiving, strangers walked into our home, and I could see it as they must have: boxes still stacked, bare patches of floor where furniture might have been, the table arranged with desperate plenitude, like we'd been expecting royalty.

I looked at Tilly, really *looked* at her, and there she was, a woman with feet too small for her large legs, the seam of her hose still darkly splitting her calves, the wide shelf of her hips and skirt making a cone of her thighs. Her silver hair ran like fluid from her scalp. The ghostly line of foundation across her neck made a mask of her whole face.

I felt like a fool. I'd been living with her all this time, believing she could get better, believing it could be so easy: three days in a seedy motel, sweating it out, and then she'd never go back. I caught the look in her eyes and thought, *My God. How did I think I could change this?*

She stayed away for five days. I don't know where she went, only that she came back. Abe and I spent those nights in a haze of worry and frustration, snapping at each other, picking separate rooms for the long hours of waiting. He slept more than I'd ever seen him sleep. I asked him how. Wasn't he anxious? He said he'd learned it from Tilly, how to sleep away a sense of fear or pain. *Nights are the worst time,* she'd told him. *You get them done with, and maybe the other side's better.*

The other side wasn't better. Tilly came home with a face as pale as dough. We could tell there was poison running through her veins.

"I'm sorry for Thursday," she said. "It was a terrible night."

"Don't apologize for that," I said. "Apologize for skipping out. You just left, you know? What were we supposed to think?"

She sat on the couch and unlaced her sneakers. "I'm sorry for that, too."

"You want something to eat? I could make you something."

"No," she said. "But thank you."

"Where did you go?" I asked. "Tell me that, at least?"

"I was safe," she said. She bent to kiss me on the forehead. Her lips were dry as paper. "I tried the best I could," she said. "I know it doesn't seem that way."

Her life grew quiet in a way that made me angry. What would happen next? I needed to know. She took long walks but I wasn't sure where she went. For long stretches of time, she was simply in her room. I knew she was drinking, but she wasn't drinking in front of me.

I kept going to work. Abe kept going to work. We didn't know what else to do.

She kept washing Abe's dirty cereal bowl every morning. He kept leaving it. She washed her dishes and made them dirty again. She stood over the sink and sighed. "It doesn't end, does it? The mess we make."

One night I overheard Abe on the phone. "But the temp job was working out just fine!" he said in a louder voice than usual. Then, more quietly: "I guess you're right."

He told me he had a two-week business trip that he hadn't been able to shunt onto anybody else. I wasn't sure I believed him.

The house felt lonely and overfull at once. It felt hard to breathe. I didn't blame him for wanting out.

He was going to Detroit. His was the kind of business that happened in huge, forgotten places—cities you'd never go to unless you were buying or selling something there, unless you'd grown up there or loved someone who did. I wondered if he was doing this for me, if he thought I wanted this—for him to get up from the bed where he was always lying, waiting. And maybe I did want this, and he knew it better or earlier than I did, that I needed the vast winter of Detroit between us.

He left the keys to his car, a green sedan that hummed like an insect, and Tilly started driving down the coast. *For kicks,* she said, but her voice deflated when she said it. She came back with little trinkets from seaside towns: lighthouses made from shells, wind chimes with clacking resin dolphins, a macramé planter with beads like shiny brown nuts. She never invited me to go with her. At least she was leaving the house. She said she was driving faster without fear. "I like it shuddery," she said. "That way you can really feel the ride." I made her promise she wouldn't drive when she'd been drinking, but this made me feel as if I'd implied that all the other drinking was fine.

She started planning a garden for the communal courtyard. "I'll let the raspberries grow wild like pubes," she said, but never bought any seeds.

She watched even more television than before. "I don't watch all the time," she said. "Just when I get lonely."

But it was always on. Sometimes I joined her. I wanted this to feel like I was giving her some company, at least, like I was helping, but mainly I felt like part of a story about giving up.

She still liked shows about nature and the workings of our planet. One day it was a show about deep-sea creatures coping

with impossible situations, thermal vents so hot we couldn't measure them. Squids got trapped in the heat and worms came for their corpses, feeding off sheaths of bacteria they shed like snakeskin. "Hell for one beast is heaven for another," a low voice told us. Blue eels swarmed around the geyser vents, ruffled like fabric, and the world was named for them: Eel City. Tilly tapped my arm like a child. "Abe and I saw a dead one," she said. "A dolphin. A baby." Her voice cracked in the middle like a twig. She'd been crying right beside me, and I hadn't even noticed.

There was wonder left inside her. I could see it. It ran through our blood. *You're so curious about the world.*

Tilly had the ocean like her son had the sky. *A space fiend,* he called himself, and Tilly loved this about him. It was something she'd seen from the beginning. Now she could claim another world as well, its tender monsters shimmering across the flatscreen. "I love those whales," she said. "Running on their songs like fuel."

Later, I found her crouched in the darkness of the living room, barely visible, perfectly silent, like a feral creature waiting for safety.

"Tilly?" I said. "What's happening?"

"I'm fine."

"You're not," I said. "You're drunk."

"I'm fine."

Her breath smelled bad when I bent close. Not only drunk but souring. I helped her stand and kept her steady while we took the stairs—slowly, each one precisely balanced—down to her room. I felt sure of myself for once, my pale arms like liquid moving through the dimmer liquid of the darkness, gin ribboning through tonic, as I helped her undress. I saw a bruise on her leg, violet and shadowy, from falling God knows where, God knows when. I told myself it looked larger than the hurt felt. I hoped. I caught sight of myself in her mirror—bending over awkwardly in this posture, trying to help.

She drifted in and out of sleep, murmuring about her first days as a runaway: a house with roaches and melting light, veggie stir-fries, vivid hallucinations that plucked her mind like it was made of guitar chords, music in the dark. She told me about the man who'd watched her making love. *That fucker,* she said. *He ruined lives.*

"You were so young," I said. "You must have been lonely."

"I was."

How ridiculous the phrase seemed, *her problem*, as if she needed the same stupid words I'd used about myself or my hipster friends, their own finest spin doctors, who went to rehab to make the stories of their lives more interesting. Tilly was a drunk. But she was also a woman I saw every morning. She liked TV programs about the ocean. These were ordinary things. She wasn't doing well. She took four or five baths a day.

How had Lucy put it? *My whole body itches.* The water left her more shriveled than she'd been before. Like prunes, people said, but she said something else: There were little fires all around her edges, and the water put them out.

I thought back to my nights drinking at Lucy's, that solace, to understand why Tilly needed it so much. I'd been blanketing my mind with small dark points of forgetting, moving from point to point like hopscotch, black to black, afraid of getting trapped inside some moment of memory. I practiced this sport without calling it by any name.

Tilly told me she and Grandma Lucy had gotten drunk together, just once, years before. They hadn't meant to. Her mother had pleaded, *Let's get out of the house, please, just for an afternoon*, and wore a strand of pearls to brunch at the prettiest hotel in town, the pink one where the movie stars went. They ordered mimosas and French toast and they really, really tried. They talked about the newest woman in Lucy's bridge group—from somewhere in

France, always bidding too high, always trusting her trumps. They talked about a kind of casserole that had bananas you couldn't taste, used for secret texture. They kept ordering mimosas like royalty. *The thing about drinking,* she said, *is we were still ourselves, only more so.*

Tilly spilled her third drink and everyone looked, actors and agents, and they watched orange juice run through the cobble-stone gutters and Lucy spoke in a hushed voice, *Mop it up,* and Tilly said, *What's that?* And Lucy said, *You heard just fine.* And Tilly admitted she was probably speaking pretty loudly: *Speak up,* probably yelling, *if you've got something to say to me,* and tipped the other glass all over her mother's lap. *You should fucking say it, why don't you? Just say it.*

"When I hear the story how I'm telling it," Tilly said, "it sounds like everything was my fault."

Abe said Detroit was beautiful. This was a secret the middle of the country was keeping. After snow, the whole city looked like it was covered with frosting. Abe woke up and watched smokestacks spread their steam over the cold dawn sky.

He asked about Tilly. I gave him pieces. She was using his car for excursions to Inverness and Half Moon Bay. There was a day she'd planned a garden and that was a good day, one of her best. He wanted the bigger picture. He wanted to know if she was okay. I told him I didn't know. He kept asking. He wanted *that,* not *if*— wanted to know *that* she was okay, *that* I was okay, wanted these things blooming in the faraway middle of his smoke-breathing Detroit.

It wasn't lying, exactly. Sometimes Tilly did seem okay. One night we played music in the living room and plugged in a plastic disco ball she'd brought from her trailer. It turned around and around, scattering jewels across the walls. We danced to songs so fast we couldn't tell if they were supposed to be angry or happy. We collapsed on the couch. Tilly kept looking at the door like she was waiting for it to open.

Hours later, I woke up to the sound of my cell phone. It was her. She said, "I'm calling from the living room floor."

I found her curled on the hardwood. She had an empty bottle in one hand and another one broken near her hip, leaking cheap red something.

I knelt next to her. "You okay?"

"No," she said. "Not really."

Her hands opened and closed like claws, grasping out. She said, "I'm sorry."

I drove her to the emergency room while she dozed against the window of my car. "Don't think I haven't seen it," she mumbled. "Lord knows I've seen it."

What did she mean? I didn't know.

"What's that?" I said loudly. "What are you saying?"

I had no idea what she was talking about, but I wanted to keep her talking. She had to stay awake. I remembered: reindeer, bubble bath. It had almost been a year. I turned up the radio to fill the car with sound. It picked up a Hispanic station. A man sang with the voice of a boy: *"Mi profesora en el amor, y en tus clases de amor . . ."*

At the hospital, she gripped the nurse's slim wrist and said, "No catheter. No catheter." She tried to tell me she wanted her stomach pumped. She gripped her belly and grimaced. "Right now," she said. *"Jesus,* now."

The nurse shook her head. "Whatever pain you've got, this won't feel much better."

She led Tilly into another room. I pictured her behind the swinging doors: gripping the paper-covered table while they threaded tubes through her nose and pulled out the poison in a salted trickle. Suppose she hadn't called? Suppose I'd found her an hour later? What then? Suppose her brain had already gone dark from the liquor? Suppose we got home from the hospital and she couldn't remember the word for "apple"? Or "door"?

Suppose suppose suppose. The heart rails like an animal inside.

A young doctor came out and found me. He was frowning. He had dreadlocks and a long scar running down his cheek that made his skin look like hardened lava. He said her blood alcohol was .41. This was a number that meant you could die. He explained about running the liquid charcoal inside. He mentioned a vitamin drip.

"Was she fine?" I asked. "With the procedure and everything?"

"Oh, she knew the drill. She knew it better than I did." He paused. "She needs to be taken care of. You get that? If she keeps this up, she'll kill herself."

I found her sleeping. I searched under the covers for her cold-sweated hand, but I was careful to hold her palm from beneath. She had an IV tube slid into her skin. It looked like a long vein that had been pulled, clear and gleaming, from her body. It was connected to a hanging bag of yellow fluid.

"The nurse calls it my banana bag," Tilly whispered. So she was awake.

"How was it?"

"The doctor told me I had rollers. He meant my veins."

Apparently, they kept rolling away from his needles.

"But they finally got one," she said. "What they needed, I guess."

Outside, dawn was lightening the sky. The shades were made of thin fabric, and they looked a bit sick themselves. "Do you want me to raise them?" I asked.

"No," she said. "Keep them down."

* * *

I called Abe and got his voice mail. I called again and again, probably ten times, until he picked up. I knew he never switched off his phone.

"I work, you know," he said, but his tone was easy. "Or maybe you forgot?"

I told him where we'd been. "She spent the night," I said. "We both did."

"You said she was doing better," he said, voice hurt. He said he'd catch the soonest flight he could manage.

She told both of us: It wouldn't happen again. She'd seen how bad it could get. She showed me where she'd been keeping her liquor—a few handles under the bed, beside the toilet, behind her slippers in the closet—and we took everything outside in big black garbage bags.

I told Tilly there were programs that could help, but she told me there wasn't a program for what she had. She'd tried a meeting once, but it only made her feel worse. Abe had gone with her, but then he'd ducked out early, upset. Someone had stopped her afterward, a perfect stranger: "Your son won't stay ashamed forever," she said. "Trust me."

There was one thing Tilly wanted. She said she needed a liquor nanny. *I wanna trust myself,* she said. *But I can't.* Could she sleep with me? In my room?

We pumped up an air mattress and put it under the window. She took my bed. I liked seeing the stars and the blood glow of an old Coca-Cola billboard. There were noises I heard all night: the sounds of bums' shopping carts creaking along the rutted ground, the keening sobs of squeaky wheels.

The inflatable mattress had a leak. I'd wake up on the hardwood floor, lying on a sleeve of rubber. One night I turned on the pump to reinflate, but it groaned so loudly and so long that

Tilly woke up like a spook—*snap!* just like that, her body stiff as a board—and said, "I didn't take it!" I knew I'd cut right through to her dreams. Her eyes were open wide, but she was still asleep, you could tell, the whites were blank as bones.

The home Abe left was different from the one he returned to. We still made love, but it was more tentative now—we were careful with each other's body, careful to keep quiet. *Why can't she stick with something?* he said. *I've always stuck with everything.* I let him hold me for minutes, sometimes hours, and then I pulled away. I let him sleep. I slept with Tilly.

I missed waking up with him, both of us drugged with the muscle memory of sex, the stick and pith of half-remembered dreams. It felt indulgent to mingle so much of ourselves, to lose track of our edges. But there was something even better about shivering against the wood, waking up with my sore spine and knowing, *knowing,* that I'd shared the night with a woman who would have been alone. We filled that room with our breathing, night after night, and didn't mess it up with all our talk. She woke up sober every morning and we opened the window, leaned out in our nightgowns, maybe smoked a cigarette or maybe didn't, and thought, *We have no idea what today will be.* And believed it.

One night Abe asked me to stay in his bed. "Maybe we should tell Tilly," he said. "About us." Maybe she deserved that. She needed to get better, I said. We needed to tend her closely, let her heal.

He was sick of secrets. He wanted to live like lovers in the open. I was tired of negotiations. I pushed him back and tugged down my underwear. I asked him not to treat my body like he cared for it. His shirt sent up the scent of soap. He pushed my legs open and stuck his finger inside. The sudden pang made my whole body shiver. It hurt like the first time all over again. My first lover had

had trouble arranging my legs. The pain, finally searing, felt like victory. He'd arrived. A part of him remained for all the others.

My own voice shamed me coming back, full of pride and wounds, full of its own sound, sharing my history with Tilly: *He was so old, so stupid, so cruel; he was so goddamn young but I loved the lies he told me in the darkness . . .* I'd thought up names for what it might have been, what summoned them, some holy loathing of self or sex or need, some unholy greed. They'd come into me and then I'd let something suck them out again. Just once there had been another word for what cleaned me dry, the cannula, with its numb and steady whirring.

Abe pulled off my underwear and my lips were in the dip of his shoulder—kissing him once, twice, tasting the slight salt—and I could hear the crinkle of the wrapper, and then I felt the rubber, smelled it. I dug my fingers into his neck, his back, thinking about the bruised paper of a nectarine's skin, how I could break the crust of him with my nail and find flesh like fruit. I wanted to draw his blood. I wanted to taste it. He wrapped his arms around my waist, and there I was, a thin reed quivering, my teeth against his teeth, our foreheads knocking.

"Take it off," I said. "Come in me. Without anything."

He pulled out and there was a coolness, air breezing my inner organs, and then he pushed back in again harder, and then he came, that sudden warmth, and I did too, a sweeping heat. It bloomed like ink in water, spreading darker, wider, and then shuddered into closing beats—one, two, three—of sparked charge. The muscles pulsed like a second heartbeat.

I was perfectly still, breathing. I was a live wire singing with electric light.

They lasted through spring, these nights of putting my body next to his and then sleeping next to hers, waking to the solid hours of another day. There were weeks. We had weeks. It seemed impossible that they'd last, and impossible that they wouldn't, and in the meantime I kept waking up and fixing coffee, asking her, *"How are you doing? What did you dream?"* and clinging eagerly to every word, wary of seeing that hard glass of drunken stupor cloud her eyes and give away the secret of her hurt. So we had weeks, each one stronger than the last, all of them built on the possibility, the mounting bodies, of all the weeks that came before.

I found her that Tuesday because I'd run out of toilet paper. Her bathroom door was closed. I knocked. I heard the sound of small splashes, then silence.

"Could you bring me a towel?" she called.

I heard it in her voice. I said, "You okay?"

"Just drop it outside the door."

"What's going on?"

There was a pause.

"Tilly?"

Then her voice again, slow and cautious, trying to hide its slurring. "Don't worry about it."

I opened the door. She was lying in the bathtub, her body white as plaster under the water. Her arms were draped over the edges, fists clenched, and her face was dirty, red around her lips like an infection. There was a paper bag on the floor, and I could smell the afterstench of hamburger meat gone grease-cold and charred. There was a bottle perched on the faucet, balanced between the knobs. She wrapped her arms around her chest, under the water, to cover her body. Her long hair floated in a webbed collar around her neck. "Just go away?" she said. "Please?"

"You have to let me help," I said. I walked closer. "You can't—"

She tried to stand but slipped. Her knee cracked against the porcelain. Her low-slung breasts showed the impact, shuddering. Her thighs buckled.

"God, Tilly . . ." I offered my hand.

"Get the fuck away from me!" she said. She nearly screamed it.

"Okay," I said. I stepped back. "Okay, I will."

I called Abe at work and told him we should get out of town for a few nights. I was sick of her, sick of wanting to help, sick of never helping enough. *Get the fuck away from me.* So I would. I hadn't ever listened properly. I hadn't even listened to Tom, especially Tom, asking what was I thinking? Where would I keep my crucifix?

They were true, the doctor's words. She'd die if she kept living like this.

I didn't tell Abe anything about her. I knew he'd be willing to do anything I asked. And he was. He left the office like a teenager ditching homeroom. I didn't tell him how I'd found her. I told him I wanted to drive to Vegas. He'd told me once that I needed to see that town to believe it. I was ready. We drove over the Bay Bridge around noon and followed the ribbon of the highway past bleached hills and windmills, cow lots that stank of shit. Mile signs flashed by and gave a sense of our velocity. I thought of Tilly's whales. Her television programs numbed her life, sure, but they brought her up against the wonder of the world: huge shadows moving through the deep on the speed of their songs.

We stayed on the second floor of the highest skyscraper in town. Abe explained his trouble with heights, which didn't surprise me. *It's alright to be scared.* I knew he believed it. We watched the city below our windows. It was too warm, strange for the season, as if something had gone wrong with the world or the sky. I thought, *He's thinking about her*. I was thinking about her. I knelt on our balcony and kissed his ankles, the backs of his knees, the rise of his stomach. I wanted to swallow how he tasted. *He is a good man,* I thought. *A good man.*

Tilly was alright, back there. She had to be.

We ate dinner at a fancy restaurant. I picked at foie gras, spooned small bites of fig reduction. Abe wanted to know why we'd come all this way. I asked: Could he just trust me? I couldn't tell him what she'd looked like, her naked body sweating in a dingy motel or rising from a cold bath—drunk beyond speech, beyond knowing me or even herself, those gin liters marking the map of her thirst, tepid water holding the wreck of her body. I wanted him to trust me.

We split a chocolate-kumquat tart and didn't say a single word. This silence felt different than our silences had felt before. It was simply between us, inevitable, without a sense of possibility or liberation.

We slept on a strange plush bed. I missed the hard floor. I missed the chatter of lonely folks on the streets, whispering up through the windows. Here everything was beeping, ringing, shrilling with strangers' cries of glory and surrender.

That night I dreamed about kicking my mother's body with the toe of my boot. We were back in the desert. Dark lines of sunset streaked over the horizon like blood springing up, bright and sudden, to fill the line of a fresh cut. I smoothed back my mother's hair, felt her scalp beneath a mess of blood-sodden strings. I kneaded her wounds and they softened beneath my fingertips like something I was sculpting from clay. "I'm making it better," I told her. "In this place I can."

Wounded women. Blood. My dreams turned me into such

simple lines of meaning. Single sentences, punctuation. An exclamation point!

Abe woke me up in the middle of the night and whispered, "Did Tilly ever talk to you about getting hurt? I think there was a time she was beaten."

"Go to sleep," I said. "Nobody's beating anyone."

"I'm not talking about now," he said. "I'm talking about then."

His words were like insects under netting: *Did Tilly ever . . . Was there a time? I think maybe there was a time.* I couldn't get back to sleep. I reached across the bed to touch his shoulder. "Abe," I whispered. "It's getting bad again. She is."

He sat up abruptly. "What happened? What did you see?"

I spoke into my pillow. "I don't know."

I felt him behind me, his knees fitted into the back hollows of my own, his arms around my stomach, his voice hot in my ear: "You have to tell me what you saw."

But I kept silent. *I'm talking about then. Maybe there was a time.* Maybe there had been hundreds of times, of bruises. I braced myself for sleep. I knew those bruises. I knew they wouldn't let our dreams alone.

I woke to find him already dressed. His suit looked perfectly crisp. We had to leave, he said. He couldn't believe we'd come at all. She needed us, he said. I was still waking up. She needed more than us, I said. She needed real help.

"Well," he said. "She doesn't need us skipping town to fuck."

He'd always been a *made-love* man. And now here we were: fuckers.

"How bad was it?" he asked. "Whatever you saw. Just tell me."

I wasn't protecting him anymore, only myself—what would he say, could he say, if he knew what I'd fled?

*   *   *

The drive felt longer than the sum of its hours. The tar wind gusted through our open windows and lifted my hair into tumbleweeds around my ears. We were returning, like criminals, to the place we called home.

"I thought you *got* it," he said. "Better than I did."

"Got what?"

"How bad she was, how far she'd gone."

"I was . . . I don't know, Abe. I was trying."

"You were so sorry, right? For everything your mother did, your whole family. You wanted to be some kind of hero. But you didn't, really, or else you would have stayed."

Here he was, a harder Abe than I'd seen, showing me my own life as I'd been living it—picking up a woman like a paper doll, tattered in the middle of a desert. I'd found this new city where I could tell myself stories about my mother and how I wasn't becoming her: Stella the tenderhearted, the patient, the redeemer. I believed them until I crumpled them into paper balls and wrote new ones: Stella the lover, the make-lover, the earnest listener and spooned-up sleeper. But they were just that, only stories, turned ridiculous by the full sight of Tilly's ruined body.

Maybe we couldn't keep this up, I told him. Maybe we were done. He said maybe I was right.

I felt the opened seam of myself, gleaming. With love, I kept learning the same thing: I could hurt so much without anyone having done wrong. I wanted his ache like a stone polished from handling, to hold in my palm. But he wouldn't bleed. He turned away his aquarium eyes and left me to the terrible privacy of his silence.

*   *   *

When we got home, Tilly's door was closed. Abe knocked hard enough to wake her and called out, "Tilly!"—more than once—and then "Mom!," a word I'd never heard him use. He tried the handle. It was open.

She was sitting in bed, painting her fingernails. She turned her head away to cough, and I saw the back of her hair, matted like you'd find in a shower drain. But her eyes were clear. She looked sober. The room was immaculate. Her desk was clear: no cats in coats or snowdrifts, no dolls made of Popsicle sticks. There was a suitcase on the floor.

Abe walked to her bed and bent to kiss her cheek. She cupped her palm around the smooth curve of his jaw. He'd shaved in a gas station. I knew what she'd be feeling: the holes of all those fresh pores, a coolness like his skin was breathing. Afterward, the underside of her palm would smell faintly like forest.

Abe sat on the edge of her bed and cleared his throat. He said he was sorry we hadn't told her—about us, about all of it.

She wasn't angry about our loving each other, she said, or whatever we'd done, only the secret. She wished we hadn't kept it. She turned to me. She only wanted to hear about her son. What had he been to me?

There were true things I could think to say. He'd been kind and honest with a body I'd hurt so many times, for reasons I couldn't quite explain—reasons that, after a while, were nothing more than the residue of reasons that had come before.

I looked at him. He chewed his lip, remembering, and gripped the bed with one big red hand. I said, "He took care of me."

She reached for him, clasped his head in her hands and kissed the top of his hair. She whispered something into his scalp. It could have been: *You learned it.* Or maybe: *You were it.* She told us she was leaving.

I said, "You can't."

"I can."

I said, "Where will you go?"
She didn't know. She'd find a place.
"I don't know what to do," I said. "Tell me what to do."
She shook her head. "Nothing at all."

I went to bed alone and lay awake to the sounds of Harrison Street: the liquid hush-hush of the freeway, the Velcro meow of our neighbor's cat, moans catching in her throat, and two bums arguing outside. I couldn't sleep. I got up and dressed. I walked to my car. It was the middle of the night. It was strange to walk without the cloak of his huge streetlit shadow. I couldn't have predicted it, but there it was: I was going south. I wanted to see my mother.

Years ago she and I had gone to see an exhibit of glass flowers. They were finely structured and proportional, tiger lilies and daffodils. Their blossoms reflected the sun like a professor's spectacles. I marveled at their natural geometry. I sounded out their scientific names. My mother didn't understand what all the fuss was about. The room was cold. Most rooms, to me, back then, were cold.

This was in the middle of my sickness. We knew the problem, I wasn't eating, but my mom wanted to know *the problem behind the problem*—a favorite phrase of hers. It meant: *cut the bullshit*. The problem behind this problem was I wanted to be sick.

When she'd first seen me, she bit her lip in surprise. This was one of the things that gave me power, seeing myself reflected in other people's eyes—my body shocking, its form unthinkable. "Oh my God," she'd whispered. "How did we get here?"

We, she said. But the truth was I'd gone somewhere alone. My body was the way I told people I'd gotten there.

And so: *Acanthus spinosus.* Bear's breeches. *Penstemon barbatus.* Bearded tongue. We'd had lunch before we came, an arduous trek across the Charles for dim sum. She believed in the power of activity, in doing things to keep the hours at bay. I could feel the food settling in my stomach, multiplying, a petri dish gone patchy with mold, gray fuzz creeping across the gelatin like windblown ash.

Gypsophila paniculata. Baby's breath. I craved the pure sounds of their names without any concessions to the body hearing them—this body that was so much heavier than all their brittle petals and fragile syllables. *Bearded tongue.* My insides were mossy with everything I'd consumed.

My mother stared at me without touching me. "You look like glass," she said. "The light comes through your cheeks."

Her voice held the admission that she never could have done this thing that I was doing. This was part of why I'd done it. She had forgotten her body so absolutely that she'd almost dissolved it. She could crackle like pure energy against the cold room, as if composed entirely of its naked, furious light.

"I just keep looking at you," she said. "I can't stop."

I was a mystery to her for once. I'd summoned the full force of her gaze.

Now it was four in the morning and I was arriving at her house. The office light was on, which meant that she was working or else she'd fallen asleep working. As she'd grown older, she'd started to need more rest. She hated this. *So I have to lose hours along with years?*

She came to the door quickly, ghostly, a stick figure in her white nightgown. Her hair was mussed and unnerving. Dye jobs were one of her only vanities, but now her hair looked like a striated cliff face, red rock beneath a band of gray. Her hand fluttered up to her scalp. "My roots," she said. "I know."

We hugged, careful with each other. I recognized the smell of her shampoo. When I was younger, I'd snuck into the bathroom after her showers to feel the humidity of the air, full of smells I associated with her skin.

I told her everything had gone to shit. With Tilly. I'd tried to make it better, but I'd only fucked it up worse. Now things were as bad as they'd ever been.

"She does that," my mom said. "She makes you blame yourself."

I shook my head. It wasn't like that. I'd done her wrong. I'd lied. Now I wanted to rest. "Here," I added. "I want to sleep here."

She offered the guest bed and said, "Or you could just share mine." I said: "Yes," I wanted that. I didn't bother taking off my jeans or sweater. I curled into her bed—still the old king, so large for a woman alone—and clutched one pillow to my chest like a lover. I stayed awake to hear the steady rhythm of her sleeping breath. I fell asleep with my hand on her shoulder, feeling the rise and fall of her chest, knowing it would last until morning.

$\mathcal{T}$ILLY

I took this room because the rent was cheap, but now I guess you could say I'm a den mother. This place has a reputation for helping women get their shit together. There's plenty of space and usually somebody to look after your kid if you need to work a shift. It's a junky blue clapboard that used to be pink. You can see the old color where the new paint's cracked. It's right off the interstate, first exit south of the penitentiary.

I forgot how cold the desert gets after the sun goes down. You tell yourself you remember every little thing about a place but really you forget most of it. The land goes on for miles and miles and there's nothing to swallow the cold or send it back where it came from. Sometimes I sit on the front porch for hours, watching other girls passing through the door and out again. Most of them work at the fast-food joints along the highway. They're coming and going all the time. Most of them have kids of their own. Some of them are trying to kick habits. Some of them are pulling tricks.

Winnie is the one who needs me most. She's six months pregnant and today she came back in pretty bad shape. She told me she hit a man's car with hers and she doesn't have to tell me that she doesn't have insurance. I bet she barely has a couple hundred in her bank account on a good day, and now she's got this baby on the way. She was crying like a baby herself. "I backed right into him," she said. "And then I sped off."

She was afraid he'd seen her plates. Maybe he would track her down? She was talking so fast, I could barely understand what she was saying.

Becca walked in from the TV room. "Jesus Christ!" she said. "Shut your cry hole!"

I gave her a look. I didn't need her interfering. I made Winnie sit down and drink a glass of water. "I'm fucking *hungry* too," she said. "Is that weird?"

I found some leftover Easter chocolate, old and white around the edges. Mostly, we keep our food to ourselves, but there are a few things that have been around so long they're pretty much up for grabs. Chewing didn't stop her crying, but it changed the sound a little.

"Did you hit him hard?" I asked.

"It felt hard."

"But you're okay?" I pointed at her belly.

"I think so," she said. "Nothing hurts. Something would hurt, right?"

"You'd know if something was wrong."

She looked at me, grateful. It's funny what people need. What's good enough. She was bawling her eyes out but all she wanted was somebody saying: *You'll be alright,* based on nothing, and she'd start feeling better.

Winnie has a history full of capital-letter problems, stories you could make into movies. The first night I met her she lifted up her shirt to show her scars, thick and swollen like fingers under the skin, crossed back and forth like they'd started going one direction until they got confused somewhere and turned around again. Her husband used to snap a belt across her back.

"He wasn't a good man," said Winnie. "But I loved him."

She started sentences like that: *He wasn't a good man but.* They had different endings: *But he made good money. But his momma raised him better. But he was a real good daddy.*

Turned out Winnie had a little girl who stayed when she left. "She knew I wasn't coming back. She wanted to stay anyway."

She said the scars itched like hell. They itched worse when she got anxious. Her hands kept sneaking back to scratch them.

I knew something that could help, a vitamin full of yellow sauce. I would've given her ginger if we had it, but we didn't. At least this would help the marks fade. The syrup oozed out like cooking oil and I rubbed it into her scars. Their raised edges guided me like roads. I told her the greasy part would help the scars dissolve entirely.

"Entirely?" she said. She sounded scared of losing them. She winced when I pressed.

"It's only nerves," I told her. "They're coming back to life."

"How does it get so goddamn cold out here, anyway?" she said. "I thought this was the desert."

I put more wood on the fire. It came from a broken play set on the back porch that someone took apart for pieces. Most nights we've got plenty of junk to burn.

I felt the knots of her muscles and kneaded them back into the folds of her shoulders. She said she could feel the little baby kick whenever I worked a knot back into the flesh. "He can feel it," she said, "how good it makes me feel."

She didn't know it was a boy but she had a strong suspicion. She hoped that living in her belly had taught him to be better than his father. This made me feel sick. What lessons had he learned in there? I had to ask. "He hit you while you were pregnant?"

He. Gregory. She'd told me his name but I didn't like using it.

"Not after he knew."

"But yeah?"

"Yeah, maybe. Once or twice."

"Lord," I said.

"You didn't guess?"

"I didn't know it was that bad."

"You think I'd leave a little girl behind for no good reason?"

"I knew you had a reason. I never thought—"

"It's hard to explain," she said. "But he wasn't all bad."

She said he was nifty with his hands, a man who made wooden carvings so delicate you had to squint to see all their tiny parts. He was a big man with a big dick. She wasn't afraid of that kind of talk and neither was I. I could tell this made her feel easy around me. He'd grown up in the dirty sticks of Tennessee and jumped on the first bus he could find, worked for a couple years as a lobster fisherman in Maine. He liked the water. Before that he'd only seen the center.

And he was good at telling stories. Sometimes too good. Winnie gave their little girl a stuffed rabbit one Christmas and she loved it to pieces. *Literally pieces,* Winnie said. She had to sew back the ears with bright red thread that made the animal look like something from a horror film. That was when her husband started making up adventures: *Horror Bunny Makes Breakfast, Horror Bunny Finds China, Horror Bunny Kills the Easter Bunny and Takes Over His Game.*

"I didn't like that last one," she said. "It had a mean spirit to it."

"You made up stories too?"

She shook her head. "I'm no good at that stuff. One day she was showing her friends: *Look at this bunny from my daddy.* Like he told so many stories that it belonged to him. But I gave it to her. It was me who got it. I sewed it up when it was broken."

I tried to picture a little girl, seven or eight, who loved things so hard she broke them. I imagined jam-sticky hands, breath that smelled like cheese crackers.

"You know," I said, "you never told me your daughter's name."

Winnie paused. She said, "Rita."

Her voice was messed up like something had gotten stuck in her throat. I could tell why she never told me before.

The wood moaned in the fireplace as the moisture smoked out, wheezing like it hurt from the heat, and the embers got so hot and brittle they sounded like broken glass when I poked them. She looked around for her jacket. This meant she had work. She knew how I felt about her job, stripping at a club south of town.

"The guys don't mind the belly," she explained. "Some of them even like it."

"It's not about them," I told her. "It's about you and your baby."

Her face got hard. She was mad and she had the right. What did I know about her life? It was hers. It was theirs, really, hers and her baby's.

At least she has a reason to go into the world and bring back money, even if it comes from the wrong places. *We're two of a kind, you and me,* she told me. *We both loved a lot, but we never did it right.* Maybe that's true but we ended up in different spots. She's looking out for another life besides her own and I'm not looking out for anybody but her, another stranger on the list of strangers I've looked out for. She has the baby living inside her, and when she does him wrong at least he can kick back and say, *What was that?* He can say, *I'm still here.*

Once Winnie has her baby, who knows how much help she'll need? I've got so much love to give her little boy. There isn't another person who could have so much.

One night I saw her dance. She forgot to bring her dinner to the club and asked if I could bring it. *Damned if I'm spending my rent check on their lousy burgers,* she said. I packed her a sandwich and some of the banana juice she's crazy for. She thinks it'll make her baby strong and keep him from catching cold. I don't think babies can catch colds inside your body but I've never told her that. What do I know, anyway? Lucy said I had the hiccups even before I was born. Maybe some things start early.

I drove by the Wal-Mart, where possums are always getting smashed. They scuttle across the highway toward the big Dumpsters. They get so bloody they sparkle. It's like a code message from the universe spelled out with their gut-strewn little bodies. You get the gist of it fast: *Fuck you fuck you fuck you.*

Her club didn't have any windows. The awning said *Live Girls Live Girls Live Girls.* Who were they? They'd come from one-road towns in the middle of the country. They'd grown up watching the sunset and thinking: *Maybe, someday.* They wanted the absolute West. They wanted an ocean to stop them. Now they were here.

The club was nearly empty. Music came from speakers tucked behind zebra-striped booths. The stage had a single spotlight cast like a bright pupil on the wood. Winnie was hooking her leg around the pole. She leaned back like she was fainting, slid toward the metal until her crotch was against it. She wore a lace tunic over her belly. She spread her legs into an open V and cupped her open palms over her breasts. They were huge, and they must have been sore. Her body was getting ready to feed another body. There was something happening that was almost beautiful but I couldn't name it: the heavy motion of her shadow, the thump of each foot hitting the stage with her whole weight and another weight that wasn't hers. I couldn't look away. I wanted to.

Afterward I gave her the juice and the sandwich, like she was a schoolgirl. "You shouldn't be doing this," I said. "It's just not right."

She tightened her dressing gown to cover her stomach. "I know you mean well," she said quietly. "But I'm the one it's gonna love."

I told her I was sorry. I understood. We both knew what she said was true.

* * *

These days I'm trying not to drink until it's dark. Which means that once sunset comes even later, in summer, I'll probably make a new rule or else get rid of rules for good. The empties stay under my coats, in the closet, with red-coated men on their labels. In the dim light, it looks like a whole line of them marching.

It wasn't quite dark when Winnie left for work, driving her Datsun—now dented—down the road, but I poured a finger anyway and drank it on the porch. I sat on one of those plastic cars that kids move around with their feet. The wheels are broken on this one, so they hold it up like a skirt while they walk around. There's an inflatable kiddie pool covered in turtles. It's got a hole that someone tried to patch with a piece of plastic tablecloth. The gin tastes good and makes the air feel like a cool leather jacket.

I like getting all warmed up with memories but some nights I get stuck with the wrong ones: Stella watching me puke or Abe's little fingers clutched tight around his dragon. You never know which ones will be the hardest, good or bad. The bad ones hurt for a moment, but the good ones get stuck behind my eyes and won't go away all night.

Abe sent me a box of things I'd left at Harrison Street: my old electric toothbrush, a gift from him, and a little soap-dish duck that I made with Stella. There's the pair of sneakers she gave me. Now I'm using the mailing box for empties. I keep the whole thing covered with garbage bags so they don't stink up my suits. I don't know why I brought those suits but I do know I don't want them smelling like my own drunk mouth.

I think about all those mornings spent dressing for work and now look at me here, spilling clear liquor all over a dirty rug, and I imagine April *laughing,* laughing like she laughed that night—and the whole time I'd been the only one, the *only* one, who hadn't seen myself playing the fool.

Abe packed the little drawing that Toledo gave me, the old man with his charcoal face. Abe was careful to tuck it inside a book, one of his alien soap operas, so it wouldn't get ripped. For all I knew, Toledo was dead by now. Maybe she finally took a trip to where her father died, or the impossible heaven he went to afterward. I just don't know. You do a good turn for somebody—buy her lunch, fix her up a little, try to make her feel like the whole world doesn't hate her—and it does a little good or else it doesn't, but either way it disappears. It's like it never happened in the first place. Abe sent a note along with my things: *You could still come back*.

He probably knows it too, I never could. All I do is tuck into a bottle every night. He knows I don't blame him for anything. One time he sent me a text message saying, *Saw dolphins in the bay!* And I thought my whole body would clench around that phone, I gripped it so tight. I didn't put it down for hours.

My second tumbler is usually the one that gets me sad, and then I come into the third and get warm. I get some peace and quiet. Everything after that just deepens the glow. Out here on the porch, I focus on my feet against the rough wood. If I blink fast enough, the empty lot across the way looks like a beach, disappearing into nothing. It gets me dizzy to think about all the people I've been, the hard groaning of my throat through all these years of talking, shushed once more by the gin heat rolling down its passage. I start blinking. The whole world looks frantic, like it's flailing, but the gin makes liquid patterns in the dark behind my eyelids and blooms like water where there isn't any for miles.

When I was young, our beach got flocks of crabs that only stayed a few days, like common colds, after the tide exhaled their hard scuttling bodies across the sand. They drilled dark points into the whole shore. These were the holes of their leaving. There was a stranger who came up and said: *They won't bite.* He said: *They only pinch and only if you hold them wrong.* He showed me how to squeeze their pincers just so. I shook my head. I didn't want to. *What does it feel like?* I asked him. *Just like a seashell, only squirming,* he said. *It won't hurt you.* He smiled his lips were salt-speckled his teeth were the color of burnt cookies. *Not what does it feel like for me,* I said. *What does it feel like for the crab?* He wasn't old or young. He came every summer. I knew he had a daughter but she wasn't my age. His red hair was so thin I couldn't see it on his arms, just glints of light. *Oh,* he said, *we can't know about that.*

My head shook faster, back and forth, ears full of seawater sloshing between them. *No.* His hair got thin around the top and his scalp was like a big shell too. He uncapped his hand next to my shoulder and let the crab go. It scuttled down my arm and then the rest of me, bony fingers tapping my skin. *Not so bad,* he said, *was it?*

Dora had promised she would come look for barnacles but then she hadn't. The beach was full of people and now it wasn't. *I think it wasn't so bad*, he said. *I think you're only pretending.* He stood behind and reached his hand around my thigh and dug his fingers under the elastic of my swimsuit. It was the one-piece with the green stripes. *Shhh.* I wasn't surprised. Why wasn't I surprised? I couldn't see his face but I could hear him breathing. His breath smelled like beer and sandwich meat gone sour. I felt his voice again: *Shhh,* hissing like waves.

Later Dora was waiting: *You find any good ones? Can I see them?* Stood there with hands on hips, expecting. *You didn't find any?* There were so many moments she felt like a stranger, but I think that was the first.

Sometimes Stella calls. I told her I didn't want to talk and she said we didn't have to. Now we sit in silence for minutes at a time, holding our mouths near the phones. I can hear her breathing and I know she can hear mine too.

"I see you talking on the porch," Winnie said. "Who's it with?"

"We're not talking," I said. "We're just quiet."

I told her it was my daughter. It was something I'd been wanting to say for a while. Not because it felt exactly right but because I wanted to try the shape and size of it. What would it feel like as the truth? In this place it can be.

Winnie comes back and I'm still on the porch. The bottle doesn't make her flinch or even look twice. It's nearly empty. She knows about my life, what it's become.

"I know the feeling," she said. "I'd drink if I could."

The truth is, I've seen her do it plenty of times, but she swears it off every couple of days. At least she has a reason. I've wanted so badly to be stopped, for so many years, but I look at her big round stomach and know there's not a damn thing stopping me now.

"You need something?" she says. "You want some help getting to bed?"

I'm quiet. I don't even raise my head.

"You okay?"

I press my temples with my dirty fingers. I start blinking. My eyes get blurry and so does the whole world.

"You want me to call your daughter?"

Maybe her little boy is really a girl. She'll love it anyway. She'll get to feel its breath right next to her face, all warm and milky. It'll break the silence with its crying. Her whole life is going to change. It's a promise she can't get away from. Even the other promise— her little girl with her broken bunny—she hasn't gotten away from her either. She knows that.

"Should I call her?" she said. "I think I should call her."

I'm not blinking anymore. I'm turning my head from side to side like I'm following a magician's finger with my eyes. This means no.

"What do you want? Just say *something*."

I turn to her. I want her to see the look in my eyes, I know it must be there: how much I want to love her and her little baby too. I want to kneel on all these rusty porch nails and put my cheek against her stomach and feel him kick. I can't think of a single other thing I want. I say, "I want a drink."

And here it is again: the steady glug and then the bittersweet. I want to be alone and this is something I can say to her without pause or shame, and I do say it, and she does leave, and now it's just me, filling my throat and blinking to make the beach once more. I can see her running down the sand, fearless Dora, long hair opened like a sail into the wind. I'm waiting behind, holding Lucy's hand, clutching. Lucy is pointing: *Look at that girl. Not a single thing stopping her.* Lucy is squeezing my fingers. *You're my girl too.* I see the dark spots of crab holes and then I see them melting back into the sand. Dora runs like her whole body wants it. She comes back with her shirt gathered into a satchel. *And where have you been?* Lucy asks. Dora's purple bathing suit is wet and shows her ribs. *Getting these.* She shows me her barnacles in splendid rows. *And you,* she says, *what do you have to show for yourself?*

Being pregnant gave me the steadiest sickness of my life but now I miss the bitch of it, the worst parts most: throwing up in the trailer living room, hair getting caught on my wet lips. The sight of Fiona struggling slowly up from her big chair, trying to help, making me feel even sadder, sad for both of us.

I miss Lucy in the deepest hours of the night. She always knew what I'd be scared of before I was scared of it. She took the books with the scariest pictures into the hallway before I went to bed.

I couldn't stand their drawn figures watching when I slept—witches and goblins, bad guys from fairy tales. Lucy was a lot of things but she was always my mother. I never had another one. I knew she would've had advice about being pregnant but I never got to hear it. *Don't mess this up,* she might have said. She would have told me all the good vitamins. She would have known the best positions for sleeping.

I thought those were the loneliest days, carrying the little sack of him when I didn't have anyone. But how could I have been lonely? Scared maybe, and broke, but I had the bulk of him wherever I went, the slippery clutch of his skull, shoulders, everything. It wasn't loneliness. I could feel our pulse with my fingertips whenever I wanted.

Now it's just one *tick-tock* muscle under my ribs. It gets so loud sometimes I can hear it in the quiet of the night, muttering like an old man trying to remember a tune: *ba-bum, ba-bum, ba-bum.* Just my one heart, only one I ever had. Still beating no matter what I do.

TELLA

We heard in the middle of the night. A woman called Abe and Abe called me. The woman's name was Winnie and she was very direct. She said, "Your mother killed herself."

Abe hung up without responding. He'd gotten a cramp in his foot, he told me, shooting all through his leg. He said it was the most painful experience of his entire life.

"Oh God, Abe. Of course it was."

"I don't mean like pain in your heart. I mean it *hurt*. My whole leg."

I waited for a moment. This was over the phone. I hadn't seen Abe in months. I said, "You shouldn't be alone."

"I told this woman we'd—There are things that have to get done, I guess. I need to go out and do them."

I heard him crying. It was a very liquid sound. I wasn't crying yet.

After a moment he said, "I'm going to hang up now."

"Please don't."

He didn't reply, but I could still hear him breathing, and then there was a click and I could tell he was gone.

* * *

He called back just after dawn. I was living across town, where the light seemed to burn clearer and earlier through the clouds, harsh on the bare floors of my single-chaired room.

"I'm going," he said. "I'd like you to come."

"That's what you want?"

"We can't leave her body out there."

"I'll do it however you want, Abe. I want to make it better. I don't want to make it harder."

"This isn't about me. It's her. You mattered to her."

When he picked me up, his body was hunched over the steering wheel, and he raised his hand gently and gave me a little wave. I got into the passenger seat, leaned over, and put my arms around him. His body didn't yield. I felt the gearshift digging into my side. We drove in silence across the bridge. We nearly had it to ourselves.

"Are you okay?" I said.

"I won't be able to give you too much talk. Not about this. Not yet."

"Don't be sorry," I told him. "You don't have to be sorry."

"I didn't apologize. I only said I couldn't." Pain had stripped him to his hardest nerves. He drove fast and reckless, swerving into lanes, but his face was rigid. His speed wasn't about pleasure, flying over the hills of the city at night. It was about getting rid of the distance.

In the middle of the desert we hit an animal on the highway. It could have been a dog or a raccoon. I didn't even see it crossing. Abe cried, "Oh, shit!" He jerked the wheel right and veered in front of a minivan. There was a honk that seemed to last a whole minute. Abe started laughing beside me.

"Holy shit!" he said. "Did you see it go *flying*?"

He was laughing harder now, shoulders shaking. "It was really . . . It was like some kind of fucking meteor."

"Jesus, Abe."

He clutched the wheel harder. "It was really . . ." His laughing hushed into a wheezing. "It was really something." ·

I put my hand on his, on the wheel, over his knuckles.

"I think I need to pull over," he said. "Just for a second."

He drove onto a narrow stretch of weedy dirt. We could feel the cars on our left, rattling our seats. I cupped my hands under his chin and pulled his face toward mine. I kissed his mouth. I kept my eyes open. I missed that.

He pulled away, shaking his head. "It's not . . ." he said. "It's not *yours*."

He rested his forehead on the steering wheel. The leather must have been sun-hot, but he didn't flinch. He was sobbing but he didn't make a sound. I saw it in his shoulders.

Her house was a dump. I don't know what I was expecting but I wasn't expecting its open mess: a splay of dirty plastic toys and junked furniture in the yard. There was a couch with all its springs showing. Abe didn't think it was the right address until I found the number scrawled in paint across the curb. "Yeah," he said. "I guess it's the one."

The woman who answered the door was wearing purple sweatpants and a sweatshirt that said *Kiss Me I'm Contagious.* She looked like she'd been asleep for years and only recently woken up to do some drugs. Her eyes had a sadness that looked like it was from nightmares.

"You must be her kids," she said. "You need to see for yourselves."

Kids? I frowned but said nothing.

She pointed up the stairs behind her.

"Upstairs?" Abe said. "She's still there?"

"We didn't know what to do," she said. "We didn't . . ." She shook her head. "You need to see it for yourself."

The stairs were covered with dust and littered with empty beer bottles. They made a trail like scattered bread crumbs in the forest. There was a syringe perched on the banister. The bathroom door was closed, and somebody had wedged a chair under the handle to show it shouldn't be opened. It looked like someone was being prevented from escaping. Abe kicked it out. The door swung.

She was naked in the tub. The water wasn't red. It was brown. Her head was tilted back against the wall like she was napping. Her eyes were closed. Her skin was ghost-pale and creased into folds: her chin, her belly. Every wrinkle was a stitch that had come unsewn. Her mouth hung open to show the edges of her teeth and the curved bluish belly of her tongue. One arm disappeared into the murky water and the other dangled over the side, wrist sliced deep enough to show white moments of bone under the skin. Her fingers dangled down against the floor. Ants crawled up her nails, along her palm.

I walked to the tub, dropped to my knees and heaved. My stomach rose against my lungs. I felt the warmth of vomit in my throat but not my mouth.

Abe stood behind me. He said, "She didn't do this."

I shook my head. I didn't say anything.

He said, "When did she do this?"

I was quiet. Still looking. Still wagging my head.

"She's just been lying here?" he said. "All night?"

I twisted around. "Abe," I said. "Oh, Abe."

"Abe what? What the *fuck*?" He grabbed my hair and pulled up my head so I was eye level with her body. "You have to look."

I looked at the arm, Tilly's arm: its streaks of brown blood, its wet show of slivered muscle and wishbone. I looked away. I felt the warmth again, of vomit rising. This time I could feel it in my mouth.

What happens to a body after it dies? This was something we had to figure out.

Tilly stayed in the Lovelock hospital morgue for three days. Her body did. Then she was moved to a funeral home and burned into ash. A man named Bobby helped with logistics. He called himself a death services consultant and wore a blue tie covered with tiny white terriers. His shoes were gleaming as if they'd just been polished. He seemed like a man who was trying to piece his life together after a great fall. I imagined him waking up each morning. *Little steps,* he'd tell himself. *Little steps toward happiness.*

We got a plain jar in a plain box. There I was, staring at rows of painted urns and taking her home in a cardboard box. Bobby put his hand on my shoulder. He understood. "It doesn't make sense to get one of the expensive ones if you're scattering the cremains."

Cremains. I couldn't even say the word. Jokes had been made about it, probably, paper shields against the dumb brute wordlessness of grief.

"Just bring a scoop," said Bobby. "Most people wouldn't think to do that."

The box was sized to hold a cake or pie. It was wrapped in newsprint with no news on it. I imagined an entire day of history erased, ink headlines dissolved off the page by rain or design: COLLEGE MASSACRE KILLS 33. JUSTICE BARRED FROM GUANTÁNAMO. The world was full of wrong things, but I could only feel this one.

We put the box in the car. I fastened one of the back seat belts and then tucked the box under the strap, snug, a tiny rectangular passenger. *I like it shuddery. That way you can really feel the ride.*

We brought the ashes into the house. It didn't seem safe to leave them in the car. The sun felt bright enough to burn anything, even ash.

Winnie was sitting at the kitchen table, breastfeeding her baby. *She's upstairs,* she'd said earlier, just like that, her voice not cold but curled into a tight space. I found the ugliness of her baby fascinating. All the soft features huddled in its face like they needed shelter.

"She doesn't like new folks," Winnie said. "She'll probably start crying." But the baby just kept quietly sucking on her mother's body.

I glanced at the sink, full of dirty dishes. There was a window behind that showed an empty lot, riddled with weeds, and the asphalt curve of the freeway beyond. The whole room smelled like a very hot wave had come and scorched everything, soaked all the grime, left the world bruised and steaming in its wake.

Abe set the box on a crate by the door. Winnie spoke to us from the table. She told us how much Tilly had cared about the baby. Too much, she said. There was one time Tilly had barged into the bedroom and knelt to push her ear against the swell of Winnie's belly. That was one bad night. There were other ones.

Abe said, "Why did she—" Then he stopped. We looked at him. He continued quietly, "Why do you think it happened?"

"We had a real hard night beforehand. She took the baby into her room, and she wouldn't . . . she wouldn't let me *in*. I kept pounding, and pounding and then she came out and started screaming her filth—I wasn't the right kind of mother, any kind of mother, and she grabbed my shoulders and I saw my baby stretched out on the bed behind her, screaming and screaming. You could hear it through the whole house. Her little heart was beating so fast when I got my hands on her. Your mother was just a *mother,* I guess, like an animal. She wouldn't let my baby go."

"It doesn't sound like her," said Abe. "Not any part of it."

I wasn't sure about that.

"She seemed like a very loving person." Winnie paused. "She seemed—"

"She was a loving person," I said.

Abe touched my arm. He wanted me to let her talk.

"I don't know what happened in your family," she said. "But there wasn't a day she wasn't thinking about you. *My son's in San Francisco,* she said it so many times I thought it was the lyric to a song." She turned to me. "She said nobody ever loved a daughter quite like she loved you."

It was true. I had not been loved, by her, quite like any daughter could have been.

Winnie wasn't the one who found her in the bathroom. Someone else did. "I guess she didn't leave a note or anything," Winnie said. "I guess that was just it."

I went over to the sink and started washing dishes. Here I was, cleaning, saying, *Let me do this one thing in the middle of your terrible life,* now that her life was done, a woman who might have left these shreds of tomato and hardened noodles crusted on a glass casserole dish, maybe the last meal she ever ate. Whatever I was giving, I wasn't giving it to anyone.

The sky was darker now, and I could see my own reflection in the window. The steam brought smells from the plates below, meat and sauce. This dense heat was hers, the smell of everything humid, everything gone to rot, sweating and swearing up at you.

Winnie walked upstairs with her baby. We could hear her voice singing, getting softer as she went.

I ran the water cold and filled two cups of water. Abe and I sat at the table. We brought the box over from the fruit crate. We wanted to keep it close.

He looked at his glass of water. I looked at my glass of water. Neither one of us was drinking. My lips were parched.

"We had things," he said. "We really did. Just me and her."

"Then tell me. If you're willing."

"There was one summer," he said. "It was the best summer. I don't know why. It just was. We made lemonade and tried to sell it. We ended up drinking most of it ourselves. That whole state—this whole state, I mean—was like a drying machine. She said, *You wear something nice and they'll lap up your sauce like dogs.* And she was right. I put on this little starched white shirt and started selling three pitchers a day."

He stopped. I looked at his face and then his fingers, white from clutching his glass. I drank the rest of my water in small, steady sips. There was some comfort in that. I couldn't say what it was, going through the early motions of afterward. Watching Abe drink his too.

We drove into the desert at dusk. We were the only ones for miles. We licked our lips against the wind. The sky was raw pink like chapped skin. There were mountains in the distance without range or names.

I didn't have anything prepared to say. There hadn't been any time before we left, only the dull stomachache of waking up too early and riding cold and hungry for miles, not knowing what we'd find—impossible to imagine exactly this moment.

"I wrote something down," Abe said. "I kept trying to get it right." He pulled a sheet of lined paper from his pocket, neatly folded in four. On the ground between us, the box rattled in the hard wind. He read like a schoolboy in a recital.

I was twelve years old, and she convinced me I wasn't going to die. I was staying at her trailer and I woke up in the middle of the night and I couldn't move my arms or my legs or any part of me. I thought I couldn't speak but then I could. I said, "Tilly." And then I said it louder: "Tilly." I never called her Mom. I tried to wriggle my toes and couldn't. I tried to roll my shoulder and I couldn't. I shouted, "Tilly! Tilly! Tilly!"

You have to understand, I was a kid who was pretty good at keeping quiet. I took care of stuff on my own. I didn't shout about what I needed. I did it for myself. But that night I really thought I was dying. I thought maybe somebody snipped something in my spine or my brain and now my body couldn't talk to itself anymore.

She came and sat on my bed. She said, "Baby boy, you've got to be patient." She stroked my hair and I said, "I can't move anything but my mouth," and she said, "God knows you've still got that left." She rubbed my whole body, starting with my feet. Her fingers were something I could feel. My parts were all deadweight on the bed, beyond my reach, but they weren't gone yet—I couldn't feel them but I could feel her palms on them.

She said, "It's okay to lie still in the dark and let another person take care of you." Then I asked it and I don't know why I did. I heard the question like it came from somewhere else, another body with all the parts moving, saying, "Is that love or something? Someone taking care of you in the dark?" She said, "It's not love. But I wish it could be."

He paused. "That's all I wrote."

"She would have loved that," I said.

"She loved everything about me." There was sadness in his voice, and pride. "Do you believe it? That one moment can stick around through all the other bullshit?"

"Actually," I said, "I do."

He used a pocketknife to slice the tape along the seams of the box. He had to keep his foot on the edge to hold it down as he pulled out the jar.

"Hold this?" He handed it to me. "It's heavier than it looks."

It was. And cold. I held it steady while Abe screwed the top off the jar and reached in with the scoop. He swung his arm in one long arc, throwing a gray trail into the pale sky toward the darker mountains. The breeze kicked up and blew the dust back onto his knuckles. It gathered in the wrinkles of his sleeves. "It's incredible," he said. "She used to be a woman."

It's only the body that goes, my mother had said. But the body is so much.

We left our jar on the cracked ground. It wasn't tall, but it was the tallest thing we could see. There were still some ashes left inside. We knew the wind would get them, too.

At the motel we ordered Chinese. I overate and then my stomach cramped. We'd gotten separate rooms but it felt too lonely to use them both. I was afraid of the quiet. I ate my fortune cookie without reading the slip. We turned on the TV and watched a show about dinosaurs. When we turned it off, the screen crackled with static before it went black. We could see our faces, side by side and tired. I wanted grief to fill every part of me but it didn't, only struck me dumb whenever I tried to turn away from it.

"You can sleep here if you want to," I told him. "I want you to."

He unbuckled his belt. "I can't sleep in my pants," he said. "But you already knew that."

Here was a man who wouldn't hurt me even when I'd practically begged him, over and over again. Now I could see inside his purest wound. He curled around my spine and cried. I'd never felt a man cry. I'd seen it, but I'd never felt it, not against my skin. He didn't touch me like a lover, only like a boy who'd lost his mother, though there was something else in the grip of his fingers, like we could take our terrible lives and find a stupid, saving symmetry. *It's okay to let another person take care of you in the dark.* Was that it? I wasn't trying to take it for myself, the stab in his heart. I wasn't even trying to make it better. I just wanted to lie next to his dreams. *Don't think I haven't seen it*, she'd said. *Lord knows I've seen it.* I could see it now too.

Acknowledgments

I'd like to offer deepest thanks to Andrew Wylie and Jin Auh, whose faith and work found this book a home, and I am lucky that this home was with Amber Qureshi, whose huge heart and hawkish eye made it better than I'd imagined it could be. She has been passionate about this novel from the beginning, exquisitely attentive to its language and its citizens, generous with her enthusiasm and her intellect.

Thanks to all my teachers—especially Charlie D'Ambrosio, who gave me courage and a true beginning. I am grateful to Brigid Hughes at *A Public Space* for publishing my first work.

I have been lucky in my friends: those who have shaped this book—Aria Sloss, Nam Le, Jake Rubin—and those who have simply shaped me: Abby Wild, Eve Peters, Amalia McGibbon, Charlotte Douglas, Harriet Clark, Miranda Featherstone, Kiki Petrosino, Nina Siegal, Julia Wong, Colleen Kinder, Louisa Thomas, Margot Kaminski, Meg Swertlow, Emily Matchar, Josh Gross, Micah Fitzerman-Blue, Ryan Carr, Nathalie Wolfram, and Jim Weatherall. Particular thanks to Katherine Marino, guide from the sanctum onward.

Thank you to Sam Cross—who knows, I hope, what he means to me.

Acknowledgments

I have been blessed in my family for all those infinite particular reasons that will never make their way to these pages, especially my aunts Kay and Kathleen. I thank Sabrina, a sister unlike any other, as well as my brothers, Julian and Eliot, for years of joy; and I wish wonder for the little ones, Yue Yue and Andrew "Che" Milton, whose joys have only just begun. I send love to my aunt Phyllis, wherever she might be.

To my parents, Dean Jamison and Joanne Leslie, I feel a sense of gratitude that is hard to hold in words. I thank my father for his faith and his generosity; and I thank my mother, quite plainly, for being the deepest source of love and support I've known.

Finally, to David: thank you. You are the one with whom I wake each day, the one with whom I dream this life.

About the Author

Leslie Jamison was born in Washington, D.C., and grew up in Los Angeles. A graduate of Harvard College and the Iowa Writers' Workshop, she has also spent time working as an innkeeper on the coast of California and as a school-teacher in Nicaragua. She is currently a Ph.D. candidate in American literature at Yale University. She is twenty-six years old.